Praise fo

"You are about to be carried away to a world more vivid and, in this case, a hell of a lot scarier, than the one you're living in."

—John Dufresne, Author of New York Times Notable Books of the Year—*Louisiana Power and Light* and *Love Warps the Mind A Little; Storyville; The Lie That Tells the Truth: A Guide to Writing Fiction*

"The pages flew by in a happy blur. What more can one ask for in a legal thriller? Even more amazing is that this well-crafted story is a debut novel. Mandy Miller is the real thing, a writer of consequence who I'm certain will have a long and distinguished career."

—James W. Hall, Edgar and Shamus Award Winning Author of the Thorn series

"Miller's debut, States of Grace, about a weary war veteran and lawyer working her way back to redemption, is a twisting, dark and gritty mystery set in South Florida that takes you on a harrowing ride until its final, shocking ending. You'll love Grace Locke and you'll love this book."

—Jamie Freveletti, internationally bestselling and award winning author of the Emma Caldridge series and *Robert Ludlum's The Janus Reprisal and The Geneva Strategy.*

"States of Grace is a powerful, compelling crime debut that captures the dark side of South Florida with verve and style. It pairs nicely with Grace, a three-dimensional and memorable protagonist. Miller paints a bleak, realistic picture that readers will not soon forget."

—Alex Segura, acclaimed author of *Star Wars Poe Dameron: Free Fall* and the three-time Anthony Award-nominated *Pete Fernandez Miami Mystery series*

"Miller's States of Grace takes us on a tense and wholly entertaining romp across the Florida landscape of pain clinics, jail innards, and snooty posh schools populated with a mélange of edgy characters from Vinnie, her former mobster landlord to her aptly-named tripod dog Miranda. Watch out, Iraq vet lawyer Grace Locke, a woman beaten but not broken, will win your heart as fast as she wins her court cases."

—Christine Kling author of the Seychelle Sullivan series

"A down on her luck former prosecutor, Grace Locke has been given a second chance—as a criminal defense attorney for a young woman who appears a slam dunk for a life sentence for murder. Mandy Miller's legal thriller, States of Grace, grabs you from the first page and doesn't let go until the last page. Full of twists and turns, this book sets a new bar for authors in the legal thriller genre. Well done!"

—Chris Goff, award-winning author of *Red Sky and Dark Waters*

Friday Night in The Glades

A Grace Locke Mystery

Mandy Miller

Literary Wanderlust | Denver, Colorado

Friday Night in the Glades is a work of fiction. Names, characters, places and incidents are either the product of the author's imagination or are used fictitiously, and any resemblance to actual persons, living or dead, business establishments, events or locales is entirely coincidental.

Published in the United States by Literary Wanderlust LLC, Denver, Colorado. www.LiteraryWanderlust.com

ISBN print: 978-1-956615-06-7
ISBN digital: 978-1-956615-07-4

Cover design: Pozu Mitsuma
Printed in the United States

Dedication

To my Dad who taught me that there is no better place to learn what lies in the hearts on men than on the field of play.

1

Tonight is a night for football. The second Friday in October. The Glades Bowl. The only day of the year dreams have a chance of coming true in Sugar Bay, a hellhole of a swamp town wedged between Lake Okeechobee and the Everglades, where mosquitoes grow as big as bats and football's the only thing folks have to look forward to.

Everyone except me, that is. Sugar Bay is the last place I want to be tonight. Being here means I have no choice but to lie to Hachi, my best friend—or at least, she was my best friend until I spent the last year dodging her calls. And maybe it's not a lie I'm telling, but simply a secret I'm not. For her own good, is what I tell myself, to save her the heartache. Hachi doesn't need any more of that. Neither do I. And neither does the one counting on me to keep my own counsel, and his.

I park my rental car between a rusted-out work truck and a neon green compact jacked-up like a praying mantis. Head down, I bull my way toward the gate marked VIP, past vendors hawking their fare under hand-lettered signs. None of the standard concession offerings, however—hot dogs, popcorn, pretzels. No, these are homemade delicacies—ribs sizzling in barrel smokers the size of tanker trucks, char-grilled gator kebabs, corn on the cob oozing butter, turkey legs like the limbs of prehistoric creatures. My empty stomach growls.

A beckoning hand sprouts from the crowd, cigarette between index and middle fingers, tip glowing like a firebug. Then Hachi's whiskey voice, a gravelly bass beyond her thirty-five years. "Grace! Hey! Over here, Grace!"

I sidestep a gaggle of teenagers thumbing phone screens, the bustling world around them reduced to key strokes and pixelated images, virtual reality preferable to their hardscrabble lives out here where cane is king and kings dress in two-thousand-dollar suits bought off the backs of workers dressed in rags.

Hachi drops the cigarette butt in the dirt and crushes it under the heel of a scarred cowboy boot. "Thanks for coming. Been too long."

Neither of us steps in for the hug that once would have been natural.

"Sorry I haven't come by lately, but the case, and I . . ." I abort my rambling, ill-conceived apology. It sounds like what it is—a chickenshit excuse. I'm not much of an actress, nor keeper of secrets for that matter. Not anymore.

She raises a hand. "Forget it. We all got our own lives to live," she says, swinging a foot back and forth, kicking up dust.

We both force tight smiles, silenced by the questions we're not asking, the answers we want but aren't going to get. Not tonight. Tonight is a night for football. Only football.

So, why am I here? Why have I've driven the sixty miles west from Fort Lauderdale, through swarms of bumper-coating lovebugs and buzzard-pecked roadkill? Because Hachi asked me, that's why. Without her, I'd have been on a slab in the morgue wearing a toe tag a long time ago. That and the fact that her beloved nephew, Sugar Bay's star running back, Ozz Gordon, is playing his last high school game tonight and I've run out of excuses for not coming to see for myself what Hachi's been bragging about for as long as I've known her.

She gives me a cagey sideways glance.

"What? What are you looking at?" I ask.

"How'd it go?"

"How'd what go?" I ask, trying to sound nonchalant, even though I'm more than a little paranoid. Maybe the game is a pretext to keep my mind occupied. Or maybe it's that other client of mine she wants to discuss. One I can't discuss. Not ever.

She catches me flicking my eyes to the exit. There was a time when booze and pills were responsible for making me twitchy, but now it's the truth.

She flings her hands in the air. "I read the papers. Come on, Grace, how'd it go?"

A sense of relief washes over me. "Oh, you mean the picker case?" I say, referring to my most important case, the case every lawyer in South Florida with a reputation to protect and cash in the bank recoiled from like spoiled milk, the case Hachi convinced me to take a couple of years ago.

She slaps my arm. "Damn straight that's what I mean. What did you think I meant?"

I force a smile. "For a moment there I thought you meant Manny."

Hachi's jaw tightens. "Yeah, I saw that too. You and Mr. Big Shot at some society gala."

"It was nothing. Just a night out for a good cause." I poke her in the ribs. "We're still good and divorced if that's what you're worried about."

"Right," she says with a roll of her eyes.

"We agreed you'd lay off my ex. I mean, he did save my life."

"Right," she replies with another eye roll. "Again. It's becoming a habit. Maybe that's how he thinks he'll win you back."

A smile flickers at the corners of her mouth when I stand mute. "Okay, okay. But just this once I'll keep my mouth shut.

Guy's still a jackass in my book."

"Let's get back to the pickers, why don't we?"

"Talk about jackasses," she replies. "Big Sugar is the biggest of them all."

"Now on that we can agree," I say, following her in the direction of the entrance, my back aching from three weeks of eight-hour days battling the corporate behemoth Sunshine Sugar Industries, also known as Big Sugar in these parts.

I should be grateful to Hachi for the work, and I am, but it's been two long years of fighting what she called "The Man" as if that might entice me to sign on. And, she was right. It did. Nothing pisses me off more than those with power screwing those without. In this case the screwer is Big Sugar, and the screwee a group of migrant sugar cane pickers.

"My future, and those of 'your people,' as you call them, is in the hands of one retired teacher, an exotic dancer, and four other citizens who either weren't smart enough to figure a way out of jury duty, or worse, wanted to give up three weeks of their lives huddled together in a windowless room with a bunch of blowhard lawyers and get paid forty bucks a day for their trouble."

She shakes her head. "Have some faith for once, why don't you?"

I let my gaze drift west across miles of cane fields, the last orange lashes of the sun peeking out above the horizon. "Faith is something I can't afford, H. Faith is a fantasy."

She hands our tickets to a brick-house of a woman wearing a black T-shirt proclaiming, "Sundays we pray. But Friday nights, by the grace of God, we play!" in gold letters.

Hachi jerks her head at the ticket-taker. "Now that's what I call faith."

We both laugh, which feels good, normal even.

The ticket-taker peers at us over sunglasses the size of dinner plates. "Section A, seats one and two. Nice! You girls are gonna be right up front for the ass whooping." She stuffs the ticket stubs into Hachi's hand and points us in the direction of our seats with a talon of a fingernail emblazoned in gold with the initials SBH, Sugar Bay High.

"From what I read in the papers," Hachi says, pausing, letting linger the fact that she'd been keeping up on the case not from me but from a third party, "you did justice by my people."

"I hope. I really need this one to go my way."

She cocks an eyebrow. "And they need it too, Grace. Even more than you."

I look away. "I know, H, I know," I reply, trying to soften my tone, which has the habit of taking on a rapier edge when I'm stressed.

I shiver despite the balmy evening air. The memory of the courtroom earlier as the jury trooped out to deliberate, the gallery filled with three dozen cane pickers for whom home means one-room shacks with propane burners and dirt floors, is more real to me in this moment than the pandemonium all around. All of their futures, my future, rest now on whatever powers of persuasion I was able to unleash against Big Sugar. Lose and I'll still be living in a no-tell motel, and my pickers will have to move on up I-75 to pick some other crop for some other overlord with the same nasty habit of not paying their laborers' wages. Win, and who knows? People might even want to know my name again.

Hachi links her arm through mine. "Come on, girl. Let's go watch Ozz whoop up on them Red Devils, just like his namesake, the great Osceola, chased you Yankees back up north."

I shake off her arm.

She jerks back and eyes me. "What, you lost your sense of humor right along with that leg?"

Any other time I would have laughed at the maudlin taunt. Hachi's way of dealing with loss and sadness is much like that of my Army buddies, at least the ones lucky to have survived, lucky enough to have war wounds to nurse. But right now, my heart's thumping in my chest, faster and faster the deeper she pulls me into the crowd. I hate crowds.

"Hey, H, maybe instead I should . . ."

She yanks me by the sleeve. "Should nothing, woman! You should hurry the hell up, that's what you should do. Game's about to start."

I take deep breaths as she drags me along like a willful child. She's been raving about the Glades Bowl, the high school version of the Super Bowl, since I met her at my first NA meeting, rhapsodizing about how caravans of big-time college scouts make the pilgrimage every year. How this one game can change a boy's life. Get him noticed. Get him out of Sugar Bay, which is exactly what Ozz Gordon needs, even more than Hachi knows.

We emerge from the tunnel into the floodlit stadium, a roiling sea of raised fists punching the sky. Manic chants of "Su-ga-bay! Su-ga-bay!" echo through the night.

Hachi's now several yards ahead of me, pointing at a row of seats behind the Sugar Bay Panthers' bench. I grab onto a railing to steady myself, all the while suppressing the compulsion to turn and run.

"Are you ready?" booms the announcer. "I can't hear you. Are you ready for some football?"

The reaction from the crowd is volcanic. Everyone's on their feet, arms skyward, dancing, screaming, freed from the bonds of their lives, for now, at least until the final whistle blows.

Holding my breath, I make my way toward her, passing row after row of fans, some holding banners, others cheering, all with eyes glued to the emerald field as if they were watching God. These are not people who left the office early to mill around lacrosse fields, craft beers in hand, swapping stories of how the stock market is doing, or whether granite or marble would be better for the new kitchen counter. These people mean business, and football is their business tonight. These are people who wear third-hand rags from the church thrift store so their kids can wear Nike cleats. Play well at the Glades Bowl and their sons will leave behind paying for groceries with food stamps and get a college education, then millions in the NFL. That's why these people are here.

I reach my seat and press my hands over my ears.

"Think of it as friendly fire," she says, patting my arm, which does nothing to quiet the frenzied drumbeat in my head. "This is one place in Florida you can experience an earthquake."

Point of pride or not, the fever-pitch intensity is unnerving. I suck in the deepest breath I can manage, unclench my jaw, and pan around the jam-packed stadium, a concrete and steel facility worthy of a top-tier college team.

"This is quite the place," I say.

She leans in close. "Panthers never forget where they come from. They give back big. Rest of the school—hell, the rest of the town's falling into the Glades, but this here . . ." She casts an arm out like a docent exhibiting a masterpiece. "This is where the magic happens." She leaps onto her seat and joins in the chant. "This year, right here! This year, right here!"

I glance down at my tailored suit and manicured nails. The last football game I went to was the Harvard–Yale game more than a decade ago, a battle of geeks for the dubious title of Ivy League Champion. This game, the Glades Bowl, is not that. This game is war dressed up as sport.

"I said are you ready?" the announcer says again, drawing out the length of the word "ready," to whip up the crowd. "Please welcome your Sugar Bay Panthers!" he roars, and a phalanx of young men bursts from the tunnel in a cloud of smoke, modern-day gladiators primed to play for their one-in-a-million chance. Unlike them, I've had plenty of first, second, even third chances. I pull my jacket tight around me.

Hachi's up on her seat, dancing, like the carefree girl I never knew her to be. Or perhaps that she never was. Her cinnamon skin glows under the lights. Her mahogany, almond-shaped eyes clear, it's easy to forget the trouble she's seen, the troubles people still endure out in this forgotten Florida, far from the glitz and glamour of South Beach, far from azure seas and sand as soft as dredged flour.

She reaches down for me. Tentative, I grip her hand with one hand, and with the other guide Oscar, the prosthetic hidden under my pants' leg, into place.

"There he is. There's Ozz!" Hachi stabs her finger at an Adonis of a kid with skin the color of burnished bronze, the fortuitous product of Seminole, African American, Caucasian, and whatever other kind of roots his ancestors mixed and matched in this swampland.

But I don't need her to tell me which kid Ozz is.

"He's a big boy," is all I say.

"Sadie and me, we went hungry so that boy could grow up big and strong. Gonna be the first person in our family to go to college."

I compose a stiff smile. "And where is Sadie?"

Hachi shrugs like one who expects few favors in life. "Working a double shift at the prison."

"Tough gig."

She shrugs. "At least it's work. You know how it is out here? You either gotta pick it or guard it."

"Ladies and gentlemen, please remove your hats and stand for our national anthem." The announcer's voice, low and sincere, quiets the crowd to the point that I can hear Hachi breathing.

The teams retire to their respective sides of the field and stand at attention, while a teenage girl in her Sunday best belts out the Star-Spangled Banner as the crowd stands, hands over hearts and hats in hand, facing the flag.

I bite my lip hard at the "bombs bursting in air" part.

Anthem complete, the announcer introduces the home team's players first. When his name is called—"Team Captain Ozz Gordon, number ten, running back"—Ozz jogs past a line of teammates, high-fiving. His squared shoulders and confident lope say, "I've got everything under control. Just leave this to me." But I know better.

Next, Palmetto Grove's team, the Red Devils, clad in crimson and silver, takes the field to a tidal wave of cheers from its supporters. Only eight miles north, Palmetto Grove may be Sugar Bay's archrival on game day, but its fans work side by side with Panther fans in the fields, which makes them allies every other day of the year.

Hachi's eyes lose focus, as if, in her mind's eye, she's seeing Ozz suited up as a Patriot, or a Bear, on any given Sunday, in a city far from Sugar Bay. I'm not sure about how any of that might come to pass now, but standing here, surrounded by swaying cane as far as the eye can see, the pulsating energy, the determined "take no prisoners" look in the eyes of the players, the intensity with which the coaches pace the sidelines, what I am certain of is that there is no more perfect crucible for forging football players than the Glades.

"Where did Ozz decide to go to college?" I ask, as if I don't already know.

"The University of Southern California," she replies, smiling ear to ear. "'Bout as far from Sugar Bay as you can get. He had scholarship offers from the University of Miami, Florida, Florida State, Alabama, and USC, but our Glades boy is goin' Hollywood."

"Impressive," I say and mean it.

But what is more impressive is how many bullets, literal and figurative, the kid has dodged to get this far. If he can hold on for a little longer, he'll leave Sugar Bay in the rear view and his past buried forever. "Bet his Mom's going to miss having him around."

A dark shadow passes over her face. "We'll all miss him."

"The Trojans, right? USC's a great program," I say with purposeful enthusiasm.

"It's only right that a good boy like Ozz ends up in the City of Angels." Hachi pulls herself up to her full height, a good six inches fewer than my five feet nine. "But he's not just about football, you know? He's got straight A's. Wants to be a doctor."

To avoid any further discussion, I join in the cheers. "This year, right here! This year, right here!" At least until Oscar slips out from under me.

I stumble sideways into Hachi. As I start to fall, she grabs me around the waist. "Hey, be careful. You're gonna hurt yourself."

Her eyes soften with concern, yet a familiar spark of anger rises in my chest, and I have no choice but to let her help me down.

"Tomorrow's the day, huh?" she asks, an obvious attempt to fill the void.

I puff out my cheeks.

"Thank you, Grace. For helping when no one else would." She grabs my hand and squeezes. "Everything's going to work out. I can feel it, here." She lays a fist on her heart.

I drop my eyes. I hope to hell she's right, but things can turn to shit real fast with a jury no matter what you feel, what you did, what the truth is.

"You okay?"

I snort out a laugh. "That's why I like criminal clients. They don't keep me up nights. Give me a plain old ax murderer who did it any day."

She jabs me in the arm. "Yeah, that and the fact that most of them've done something, even if it ain't what they're charged with. Isn't that what you used to say, Miss Assistant State's Attorney Grace Kelly Locke?"

I turn my palms up. "Roger that."

Speaking into a shoulder-mounted microphone, the referee calls the team captains together for the coin toss. Ozz sets his helmet down on the Panther bench and jogs to the fifty-yard line to face Palmetto Grove's captain, its quarterback, a daddy long-legs of a kid with arms to his knees.

"Home team gets to call it," the referee says into the microphone, and turns to Ozz for his response. "Heads it is."

There's a collective intake of breath as the referee flips the coin. As if in slow motion, the coin levitates, twirling and twisting in midair, before plopping onto the grass.

"Sugar Bay has won the coin toss and has elected to receive," the referee proclaims.

Amid deafening chants from the crowd, Palmetto's quarterback returns to his bench. But Ozz remains at center field. He glances back to the VIP section. To us? To *me?* I could swear he's looking in my direction. He wouldn't, would he? We've never met, is what I told him to say if anyone asked. Unless it's the cops.

He turns away, drops to his knees, and tilts his head up as if taking communion. His image, angelic, eyes closed, face expressionless, looms down from the gigantic electronic scoreboard.

"What the heck is he . . ."

But before Hachi can finish the thought, Ozz pulls a pistol from under his jersey, rests the barrel against his chest, and pulls the trigger.

2

Three Months Earlier

Coach Elijah Wynne pointed to the tailgate of his piece-of-shit pickup, and then at Ozz and Antoine White in turn, looking each boy in the eye.

"You boys, sit your sorry asses down right there," Coach said, his voice low and slow, but with the look in his eye he got when he meant business, which today meant the business of winning football games, the one thing in his life more serious than his faith in his Lord and Savior Jesus Christ.

Ozz's stomach turned queasy. He reminded himself that this was the last time he'd have to do this. Soon enough, he'd be long gone.

Coach gnawed on a toothpick. "I'm sure I don't need to tell you knuckleheads the rules. But just in case you forgot since last year this time when we was out here, I will repeat, so listen up." He widened his stance. "It's simple. The one of you two who bags the most rabbits starts the first game of the season. That's it. You got that?"

"Yes sir, Coach," Ozz muttered. And he did know. Ozz knew the rules as well as his own name. Coach's rules were his ticket out. That and guile.

Ozz surveyed the desiccated cane field, the smoldering stalks like the detritus of some hellish apocalypse.

He shook his head. Focus! Just this one last time. One last sprint to the finish line, the starting line for the rest of his life. For four years of high school, he'd started every season chasing damn rabbits, a Glades football tradition, one born of the need for speed and the need for food. Late summer, before the harvest, the farmers burned the cane, flushing the rabbits out into the open, squirting through the muck, running for their lives from the inferno. And, as it turned out, chasing those same rabbits was the perfect training for football. To avoid sinking in the muck and catch a rabbit, a runner had to be quick, know how to cut and turn on a dime, to reverse field, zig this way, zag that. Chasing rabbits was the reason "Them boys from the Glades got speed," as the big-time scouts said.

Coach extracted the toothpick, spat out a wad of phlegm, and returned the soggy twig to the corner of his mouth. "You boys must not have heard me. I said, do you got that?" His face had turned puce, the protruding veins on his bulbous nose a road map for a lifetime of hard hits and cheap hooch.

Ozz and Whitey nodded in unison, but with enough nonchalance to make it seem like they didn't care. But Ozz cared. Whitey too. Ozz knew all too well that Whitey cared at least as much as he did, maybe more, given Ozz had beaten Whitey's ass in the cane for three years in a row to keep his job as the starting running back for the Sugar Bay Panthers, the Florida state high school champions. And Whitey knew better than anyone that second stringers don't get college scholarships, that they have no choice but to abandon any hope of playing in the pros, of a better life, and to resign themselves to a short life of hard labor and broken dreams.

Yes sir, Ozz cared more about what was about to happen than

he could ever imagine caring about anything ever again. This was it. Senior year. Do or die time, and Ozz had no intention of dying. He was going to bag as many rabbits as it took. Then, he would flatten as many defenders as it took to leave this shithole of a town in his dust. His straight-A average would have gotten him into college if his high school had been in a suburb with cookie-cutter houses and teachers who gave a crap, but Ozz went to Sugar Bay High, a failing school in the Everglades where football was the only ticket out, other than a pine box.

Coach motioned for them to stand. "And I don't think you need remindin' that the loser'll be warming his happy ass on the bench come Friday night, thinking about what coulda been." He paused, his gaze drifting out over the smoking cane. "And take my word for it, boys. Regret is a lot harder to deal with than physical pain."

Ozz stole a sideways glance at his competition—Whitey, the last person standing between him and his future. Antoine White, Whitey for short. In other places, Whitey's nickname might be less than politically correct, but in the Glades, names were just names and overthinking a luxury best left to others with more time on their hands and money in the bank. In reality, Whitey was not white. Like Ozz, he was some kind of interracial stew. Nor was Whitey slow. He ran the hundred flat faster than Ozz. But this burning field was no racetrack. This was about to be a desperate sprint across scorched earth for both man and rabbit.

Coach spat the toothpick on the ground. "You know what they say, don't ya?" He smirked. "You get one chance to make a first impression, you hear me? When them scouts come huntin' for the next best thing to rise up outta this here swamp, you better be on your A game. And to be on the A team, you gotta catch you some critters today."

Coach raised his stopwatch. "You boys ready?"

Ozz sucked in as much air as he could, until his chest felt as if it would burst. He needed to get out ahead of Whitey fast, make it to the rows of cane first. He needed to be the one to choose the line he wanted, the one he needed.

"You got fifteen minutes 'til I blow this thing again. After that, we count those that gave their lives." Coach stuck the whistle between his sun-cracked lips.

Ozz gripped the thick stick in his right hand, a burlap sack in his left. He hated clubbing defenseless creatures to death, but if that's what it took, he'd do it. He'd done it. He'd do it again so he wouldn't have to scratch and claw for the rest of his days.

At the wail of the whistle, Ozz sprinted toward the rows of charred cane, knees like pistons, the caustic fumes singeing his lungs. Summoning all his power, he bolted ahead of Whitey and headed for the row of cane on the far left. Counting his strides, surrounded by stalks much taller than him, he sidestepped several rabbits that would have been easy to bag, instead keeping his eyes focused straight ahead. At a count of fifty strides, he glanced back through the cane to see Whitey slinging a bloody rabbit into his sack by its gangling back legs.

Ozz counted another fifty strides and cut left at the red painted rock holding down the neck of a sack. The sack under the rock was identical to the one in Ozz's hand, but it contained the dozen dead rabbits he'd bagged earlier, a chore which had taken more than an hour. He exchanged the sacks, and set about batting at the cane with the club to make it seem like he was working hard. At that moment, a cottontail, the holy grail of rabbits, the quickest and most elusive, scurried out of a charred stand. The creature froze, nose twitching, powder puff tail cartoon-like in its downy whiteness. Without a sound, Ozz raised the club above his head. The cottontail's head swiveled, its wide-set shiny, beady eyes on Ozz's. Ozz hesitated a second, then lowered the club and watched the cottontail hop away. Twelve rabbits would be enough. No one had ever bagged more than ten for Coach. And never one cottontail.

Whitey emerged from the cane, chest heaving. "You see that cottontail?" He fixed Ozz with a suspicious stare. "You let that thing get away?"

Ozz shook his head. "Nah. Thing was just too quick for me." He made a show of making a head-first dive toward a marsh rabbit that faked right, then escaped left, launching itself into an irrigation canal.

At the whistle, Ozz and Whitey raced each other back to Coach, limbs flailing, like kids playing sandlot football for nothing more than the joy of the game.

Coach grabbed the sacks and threw them into the bed of his pickup.

Ozz glanced at Whitey's stuffed sack and his heart stopped. He'd thought twelve would be enough.

Coach reached into the cooler at his feet. "Here," he said, holding out two sweating bottles of Gatorade to Ozz and Whitey, who were covered in a ghostly layer of ash.

Ozz cracked open the cap of his, took a gulp, and doubled over, hands on knees, gasping for air.

Whitey collapsed onto his back, the icy bottle pressed against his forehead. "Who won, Coach?"

As Coach took inventory of the fallen with hash marks on a clipboard, Ozz squinted to the west. A hazy ocher curtain was descending on the Everglades, a great blue heron in the center of the frame, the sky awash in pale pink and orange, and his breath caught in his throat. Would he miss this river of grass, the palm fronds swaying, the knee-deep waters, the silent guardians of untold dangers beneath? The creatures hidden deep in its mangroves—alligators, red ants, feral pigs, the brown recluse and black widow spiders, all killers by instinct.?

Whitey's whining voice snapped him back to the present. "Come on, Coach!" Whitey said, his tone one of a child denied candy in the line at the grocery store. "Who bagged the most? Who won? Who gets to start?"

Coach stepped back from the flatbed strewn with bloody corpses and removed his Panthers ball cap. He drew the back of a hand across his forehead, leaving red stripes in its wake. "By my count, it's . . ."

Whitey moaned. "Coach, don't try us like that."

Coach smiled and crossed his arms across his barrel chest. "Whitey," he said, "you got ten." Then he added, "And one squirrel." He shook his head from side to side in disbelief. "I be comin' out here doin' this since I was a Panther—God only knows how long ago that was—and I ain't never seen no one bag a squirrel before."

Ozz suppressed the urge to fall to his knees in relief. Too close. Two rabbits to spare. Thank God the squirrel didn't count. He jabbed Whitey in the ribs with an elbow. "Shit, homie, you don't know the difference between a rabbit and a squirrel?"

"Screw you," Whitey said, advancing on Ozz. "You shoulda bagged that cottontail when you had the chance. But you thought you was gonna beat me anyway, so you let it slide."

Ozz balled his hands into fists and moved toward Whitey.

Coach stepped between them. "Back off, you morons, and mind your language, both of you. You piss me off enough and neither of you gonna be startin' no game." Ozz stepped back and clasped his hands behind his back.

Coach's eyes crinkled at the corners, and his round face, the color of an old penny, broke into a toothy grin. "Wiz," he said, using the nickname Ozz's teammates used for him even though Ozz was short for Osceola, not the Wizard of Oz. "Son, it looks like you still got your startin' job. You bagged you some twelve rabbits and no squirrels."

Ozz closed his eyes and let out the breath he'd been holding for what seemed like forever. "Thank you, Jesus," he whispered.

"Now y'all come over here and bag up your critters and take 'em home for dinner. Y'all be eatin' good tonight. Not one of these needs to go to waste."

Whitey slammed his carcasses back into his sack one at a time, trying not to look at their hollow eyes.

Coach levered his bulk into the pickup and waved goodbye. "See you boys at practice later."

As soon as the truck was out of sight, Ozz held out his sack to Whitey. "Here. You take 'em."

"Nah, they yours. I wasn't fast enough today."

Ozz looked away. He knew that wasn't true. At least, before the chase, he'd feared it wasn't true, but whatever it took was what he needed to do, was what he'd done. "Nah, I don't want 'em." He pushed the sack back into Whitey's chest. "My momma ain't home to cook 'em anyway."

Whitey took the sack. "Goin' for two bucks a pop in town. You sure?"

"Give 'em to your momma, sell 'em, do whatever you want with 'em," he replied, jogging toward the levee that led from the cane fields back to town.

Whitey might have said, "Hey, thanks brother," but Ozz's mind was locked in on getting to work on time. Junior didn't like it if Ozz was even one second late to make his deliveries. And Ozz needed to stay out of trouble, for just a few more months.

3

The anxiety of waiting for a verdict is the legal equivalent of waiting for an abusive spouse to get home. Sometimes you get beat, sometimes you don't, but you can never be sure what's coming.

I stalk back and forth in front of a wall of windows on the twelfth floor of the Federal Courthouse in downtown West Palm Beach, the city spread out below in miniature, its rough edges softened by the high remove. While the name Palm Beach may conjure up waterfront estates hidden behind towering hedgerows to keep the riffraff out and the family secrets in, where ladies lunch with froufrou lap dogs stuffed into ten-thousand-dollar purses, and titans of industry smoke contraband Cohibas, West Palm Beach is the barrier island's ugly stepchild. The ill-conceived patchwork quilt of office towers and half-finished stores and parking structures has a ruined patina thanks to an economic recession that benefited no one except those that didn't need help.

"Jesus, what's taking him so long?" I say to no one.

It's Saturday. The place is deserted except for me and my adversaries, Big Sugar's over-priced posse of attorneys. One of them is banging on the vending machine in a vain attempt to dislodge a candy bar. And then there are my clients, my pickers as I've come to think of them, as if battling Big Sugar for two years gives me some type of ownership in them, an irony given that's exactly what I've been fighting against.

I duck my head into the courtroom and there they are, the pickers, exactly where they've been for three long weeks of torturous testimony and bald-faced lies from Big Sugar's henchmen. Pew after pew, clutching onto each other and their dreams of getting what they're due. The jury came back with its verdict last night, Friday, long after Judge Charles Stillwell had decamped for a very dry martini and a Cuban cigar at the Palm Beach Country Club and I had not yet seen a young man put a bullet in his own chest.

I swallow hard and return to the hallway. I take several deep, useless breaths, but gone is the city. In its place, Ozz Gordon, his body arching back, falling limp onto the food-color green field, his chest a crimson crater, like Sergeant Jones's chest had been when I shoved it aside to get out of the Humvee before it blew.

The putrid smell of burning flesh in the silent, still vacuum.

My fists pounding the glass.

"Miss. Miss! Are you okay?"

A long object threatens me and I back away.

"Miss, can I help you?"

I blink hard to refocus. "What?"

A man holding what I see now is a broom guides me to a bench. "Why don't you rest for a minute?" he says, his voice kind and steady.

I sit and smooth my hair back off my face. "I'm fine."

He peers down at me. "You don't look fine, Miss. Can I get you anything? Call anyone?"

I lean around him and survey the hallway. "All clear."

The man scratches his head and returns to pushing the

broom.

When my phone buzzes, my heart leaps into my throat, but instead of a message from the judge's clerk telling me the jury's back, it's a text from my good friend, Marcus Jackson. "Gay pride parade Sunday?"

"Me?"

"We don't ask, we don't tell, remember?" he replies, which coaxes a weak smile from me, loosening the pressure inside my skull.

Marcus's humor is a welcome relief, a reminder that life does exist outside my purposely circumscribed universe. He's funny, but more important, Marcus is loyal to a fault. He stood by me, one of the few who did, when I turned my life into a slow-motion train wreck and anyone with half a brain told him to get as far away from me as he could, that friends like me ended political careers. As a black man and a standout college football player, not to mention a prosecutor appointed by our Republican governor to head a statewide narcotics task force, coming out had been a gut-wrenching affair for Marcus, one he likened to "committing hara-kiri in the middle of Times Square and then having to come back for more so as not to give the pea-brains the pleasure of having got rid of you."

"Pick you up at 5 PM. Wear something outrageous!"

"Roger that," I type, and slip the phone into my pocket.

I walk back to the wall of windows and turn my gaze to the north end of Palm Beach Island, to Miramar, the Locke family compound, a four-acre oceanfront estate designed in the twenties by Addison Mizner in the Mediterranean Revival style for one of the Henry Flagler heirs. I picture Faith, my mother, drinking tea on the terrace with her mahjong ladies, pinkies crooked, plates of scones left untouched, still slaves to the scale even in their seventies. My father's gone now. He died while I was in jail a while back. All I have left of Percival Locke III are memories. And his British racing green Jaguar E-Type, my only child, as I was his.

Buzz. Another text. "Judge taking the bench."

—

"All rise, the Honorable Charles Stillwell presiding."

Judge Stillwell, a puggish man with the ruddy face of one who likes his whiskey too much, waddles through a pocket door behind the bench and settles himself into a high backed leather chair.

"Madam foreperson, it is my understanding that you have reached a verdict. Is that correct?"

A tweedy woman in the front row of the jury box rises. "Yes, we have, Your Honor," she replies with a slight dip of her head.

I lower my head to cover a blossoming smile. There was never any doubt in my mind that this ample-bosomed woman with eyeglasses hung around her neck on a chain and a tight perm straight out of a fifties sitcom would be the foreperson. Beyond her imposing heft and height—in excess of six feet—she was no less than imperious when answering the judge's questions during *voir dire,* the process by which jurors are accepted or eliminated, adding "of course" to every one of her answers, as if the answer to every question His Honor asked was as obvious as one plus one. It was hard to imagine any of the other jurors resisting her will. Luckily for me, the woman stated she'd never missed a day of work in her life at the Post Office, a quality that makes her perfect for a case about millionaires screwing people out of their hard-earned wages.

"All rise," Judge Stillwell says with the two-handed flourish of a preacher urging his congregation to rise for the benediction.

I stand and steal a sideways glance at Big Sugar's counsel, three male attorneys in dark suits, each of which had to have cost more than any of my pickers makes in a year. They are flanked by Alfonso Tremayne, Big Sugar's chief executive officer and biggest stockholder, a man with black eyes, the color I assume his heart to be. The quartet resembles a cackle of hyenas at a kill, anticipation of a win written all over their smug mugs.

I glance over my shoulder at the pickers in the gallery. Shoulder to shoulder, they hold hands, a human chain who dared to battle the oxymoronically named monster that is Big Sugar. There is nothing about the behemoth sugar conglomerate that is sweet. Black faces, brown faces, white faces, and faces all manner of colors in between, but every single one of the pickers wears the tired look of a person for whom life has gifted little and expected much. Men and women, young and old, united by their status as victims of bald-faced theft. Theft of their paltry wages by the overlords who worked them like slaves, pocketed the fruits of their labors, and then told them to go to hell when payday rolled around. All thirty of them have made the trip from Sugar Bay every day for trial. None have a car, so Hachi arranged for them to be transported to the courthouse in a church bus, a snorting ancient contraption intended for Sunday school outings and senior citizen trips to the casino on the Miccosukee reservation.

The bailiff plucks the verdict form from Madam Foreperson's outstretched hand and walks it to the bench.

Judge Stillwell unfolds the form like a presenter on an awards show, sneaks a quick peek, and waits a couple of theatrical beats before giving it to the clerk for publication.

The clerk reads the case number and the plaintiffs' names one by one, stumbling over several of the Spanish and Creole surnames. Finally, she gets to the "we the jury in the above-entitled action" part. I sense a collective intake of breath behind me and clench my fists in solidarity. If I were one for prayer, now would be a good time. But I'm not, nor have I been for a long time now, so I close my eyes and hope for the best.

"We, the Jury, find the Defendant in the above-entitled action, Sunshine Sugar Industries, liable on all counts and award compensatory damages in the amount of one hundred and fifty-two thousand dollars and eighty-nine cents."

A punch in the gut forces the breath out of me in a blast.

The verdict is the exact amount of the wages owed. Not one

cent extra.

Tremayne's hand goes to his mouth in a failed effort to cover an "I told you" smile.

I choke back the acid rising up my gullet.

"And," the clerk continues, "we award the plaintiffs punitive damages in the amount of five million dollars."

I brace myself against the table, all sensation gone from my body.

Cheering erupts in the gallery. One woman falls to her knees and crosses herself. A man with a tangle of wrinkles for a face, whom I know to be thirty-seven but who looks double that, collapses back onto his seat and cries out, "*Gracias a Diós.*"

Judge Stillwell bangs the gavel. "Order! Order! I will have order in my court!" He keeps banging the damn thing like a rock drummer until a tenuous silence returns. When it does, he coughs, thanks the jurors for their service, and hurries off the bench.

On the way out, I extend a hand to Tremayne. "Nice doing business with you."

He gives me a smile, all mouth no eyes. "This isn't over, Ms. Locke. Not by a long shot."

"Time will tell." I match his condescending expression. "And I've got plenty of that." I point at his trio of suits. "The way I see it, when you get tired of bleeding cash to this crew, you'll wise up and do the right thing."

"Just like you, right? Don't tell me you're in this out of the goodness of your heart, Counselor?"

"That's where you rich folks get it wrong. It's always about the money for you."

Tremayne heads for the door, accompanied by his legal team. "See you in the appellate court, Ms. Locke," he calls back over his shoulder.

"Count on it," I reply.

—

After having my hand shaken, back slapped, and cheeks kissed more times than I can count, I locate my rental car and follow the church bus out of the parking lot.

Through the back window of the bus, I watch the pickers dancing in the aisle and my heart swells with the first tinge of pride I've felt in ages.

I bang my hand on the steering wheel. "I did it. I slew Big Sugar, the Goliath of the Everglades!" I catch myself and add, "For now," so as not to jinx anything. I have a habit of jinxing things. And I've grown superstitious, like my mother, a woman who can't spill salt without throwing more over her shoulder. It can't hurt, can it? Irrational it may be, but I need all the insurance I can get.

I have to say, I do like how this feels, this lightness, this sense that I've done some good in the world, this speaking truth to those with the power to screw the little guy. I've always loved to win, maybe too much sometimes. This feels different, however, from giving a murderer a one-way ticket to the death chamber, or locking up a pedophile with prisoners who will show him no mercy. That kind of winning was about revenge. This win is about justice being done, the sole reason I went to law school after Iraq, where justice was a political slogan promulgated to cover all manner of sins. My clients will now be able to live in better homes—at least ones with real roofs and running water. Their kids will be able to attend better schools, go to the doctor. Maybe they'll buy cars and take family road trips to places they haven't heard of yet. That is, assuming we ever see a dime. Appeals take forever, and the pickers don't have that. Their roofs need fixing now, their kids need shoes now. Now is often the enemy of justice. Needing something now as opposed to much more later is what lets the haves rip off the have-nots.

I trail the bus onto Worth Avenue, an enclave of high-end boutiques and restaurants, where old money and new money, and a certain amount of ill-gotten money, can buy whatever the heart desires. In the shade of coconut palms, skeletal women in Jackie-O shades stroll past Hermes and Tiffany, Birkin bags dangling from crooked elbows. Men in pastel sport coats and Italian loafers greet maître d's in doorways of bistros and are led to their "regular" tables. Not one car parked in the shade of the exquisitely manicured vegetation is anything other than a Bentley or a Maserati, but all are at risk of being side-swiped by the yellow jalopy of a bus as it navigates the narrow street.

Our caravan crosses the bridge over the Intracoastal Waterway to the mainland, leaving the paradise island of Palm Beach behind, a life into which I was born, but of which I am no longer a part.

At a fork in the road, the bus continues west and I turn south, for my real home, where Miranda is waiting behind the door with nothing on her mind but a meaty bone and a walk.

—

I pull into the rutted parking lot in front of *The Hurricane Hotel,* a two-story L-shaped 1950s structure with about as much curb appeal as a steaming pile of doggie doo.

I park my rental in a spot labeled "Guest," except the sign's been vandalized and reads "Gut." As a permanent resident, at least as permanent as anyone can be in a place where it's commonplace for guests not to spend the entire night, I have an assigned space, but it's currently occupied by my Jaguar, a gem I'd never dream of subjecting to the rigors of Florida's highways, where you're about as likely to get impaled by road debris flying through your windshield as you are to catch anyone observing the speed limit.

Around back, I find Vinnie, my landlord, and Miranda perched together on the sea wall like an old married couple. They have no need to speak to be understood. Vinnie knows Miranda loves treats, and Miranda knows Vinnie loves her. If only all relationships were that simple and pure.

Vinnie's head snaps around, eyes vigilant as a shark's. He may be drawing social security, but he hasn't lost his nose for danger, which, in his profession, was around every corner. "Counselor, you're late."

I scrunch down and bury my face in Miranda's dense fur, which smells like a woolen sweater.

"A whole day late."

I stand back, hands on my hips, and talk to the back of his head. "I left a message on your machine."

Vinnie pats the sea wall for me to sit.

I kick off my heels and lower myself down beside him.

He ruffles the fur on Miranda's neck. "Not that I don't like babysitting the mutt or nothin', but still, I worry."

I expel an exaggerated sigh. "Vin, if you got a damn cell phone, it would be easier. I mean, who the hell has an answering machine anymore?"

"That machine works just fine, thank you very much." His back stiffens. "And who the hell would call me anyway, 'cept for you? It'd be a waste."

"Don't you mean who would call that you might want to talk to?"

"There is that." He gives me the look of a naughty child caught red-handed. "You know me too well, sweetheart," he says, his New York accent eclipsing the "r."

"You had no need to worry. I stayed out in Sugar Bay last night, then went straight to West Palm this morning." I moan. "It was terrible."

He pulls back and tilts my chin up with a bony finger. "What? What is it?"

The distress in his voice pushes me over the edge. I drop my head on his shoulder and let my tears soak his T-shirt. There had been nothing to do at the hospital except to hold their hands and repeat the lie that everything would be okay, which it never would be again. Death changes everything.

I squint at him through my tears, his age-spotted skin crimped and paper-thin, but his dark eyes still as sharp as flint. "The football game, there was . . ."

Vinnie folds his hands in prayer over his mouth. "Holy mother of God, Gracie. You were there? *That* was the game you said you was . . . The kid who . . . I saw it on TV. How he . . ."

I bury my face in my hands, visions of Ozz squirming like a hooked fish running in a continuous loop on the inside of my eyelids.

"Jesus, Gracie, what the . . . I mean, I know you said on the message you was goin' to some game out in the boonies with Pocahontas."

I rub my eyes. "Jesus, Vin. A little respect, if you don't mind. The boy was her nephew."

I feign offense, but I know he didn't mean anything by it. It's just his way. And that this old man bound to me by choice not blood would have such concern for me never ceases to amaze me after what I cost him. Vinnie Vicanti may have a smart mouth, but he knows the pain of the loss, the loss of a child to his violent lifestyle and, almost, of his own life. Vinnie might be my landlord now, but he was once a condemned man. Back when I was Assistant State's Attorney Locke, I sent him to death row for murder. And I did it gladly, with a level of pride that comes only before a fall. Later, I found out that he had been set up, and I spent two years pissing off judges and making enemies of cops in an effort to reverse his wrongful conviction. As a result, the old man thinks he owes me. He doesn't, but his way of paying his debt is by giving me a place to stay and taking care of me as he would have his own son, if he'd had the chance. I've threatened to move out unless he starts taking my money for rent, but we'll see. Vinnie's stubborn just like me.

I stare out into the night, a sliver of a moon punched out of the onyx sky like a paper cut-out.

"But you're okay, right? I mean . . ." He pauses, searching for the right word to ask about how I'm dealing with witnessing death, yet again.

I glance at Miranda, up on her haunches, head tilted to the side, locked on our every word. As a former Marine K-9 officer, she's seen death too, and lots of it, but I suppose that's the upside of being a dog—no memories. Or maybe it doesn't work like that. Maybe she hurts deep down inside. Maybe she wishes she had done more for those who didn't come home.

"Can you keep her for tonight?"

He gives me the side-eye.

"No need to worry." I sigh. "Any more than you already do. Midnight meeting at St. Anthony's is all."

His craggy, weathered face brightens, affording me a momentary glimpse into the impish boy he must have been, all pranks and attitude. "How could I forget? You've found your God."

I struggle to my feet, center Oscar, and dust off my pants. "Smart-ass."

He smiles like a proud papa, because we both understand the unspoken—Vinnie's the one who got me to NA to begin with. Except now he thinks I'm taking it a bit too far, going to meetings every day no matter what. That's what you get for being a follower—suspicion.

I nudge him with my elbow. "I won, by the way."

"Won what?" His eyes spring wide in recognition. "Your pickers? You won?"

"Well, they won. I—"

He high-fives me. "You da man, Gracie. You beat them lyin', cheatin', stealin' pieces of—"

I give him a time-out sign. "Let's not get ahead of ourselves. There'll be an appeal. Big Sugar's not going to hand over five million bucks without a fight."

He freezes, eyes like saucers. "Did you say five million smackaroos?" He rests his hands on his skinny hips and swivels. "Well, la di da. If my girl ain't back in the big time."

"Like I said, there'll be an appeal."

"I got all the faith in the world in you, Gracie." His lips harden into a taught line. "It's the system I don't got faith in."

I raise my hand, palm out. "Usually, I'm with you on that

score, but today . . . today justice was done."

"Don't go getting all soft on me now." He knocks my elbow with his this time. "Nice work, kid."

I turn to leave.

"Hey, you hungry? I can rustle you up something fast. Think I got some dawgs around here somewhere."

"Yuck."

"Dawgs too good for ya now, are they? Now you're all caviar and filet mignon."

"Thanks, but no thanks."

"Suit yourself. In that case I need to get my beauty sleep." He grabs Miranda's collar. "Ciao, bella."

He disappears through a sliding glass door into his apartment, Miranda springing along at his heels on three legs, the loss of the back left limb something she seems not to notice. Or, maybe she does but isn't one to bitch. Marines are like that.

With a few minutes to spare before the meeting starts, I cross to the beach side of A1A and stare at the cloudless night sky shot through with stars. I choose one to wish upon, to ask for the courage to change the things I can change, before I head into the darkness in search of the serenity to accept the things I cannot.

4

Fingers shaking, Ozz tied and re-tied his one-size-too-small cleats to avoid looking at the crowded sidelines.

Faces shaded from the infernal sun with glossy programs filled with names and statistics, like bookies at the track. They'd been observing him all morning, scribbling notes, watching the players' every run, every bench press, vertical jump, every cone drill and short shuttle, as if the players were cattle, all of it done with the slickest of smiles. Freaking smiles! Every single one of them was grist for the football industrial complex. The smiles were just window dressing for greedy hearts.

But that's exactly why he was here, wasn't it? To get noticed? To get out? At least that's what he kept saying to himself, right along with his mantra—*means to an end, means to an end.*

Ozz surveyed his competition, a group of wannabes like him from forgotten backwaters with exotic names like Shalimar and Astatula, but where the only evidence of exotica might be a run-down diner with a Moroccan theme or cheerleader called Cleopatra who put out behind the bleachers. And while they'd spent the week on this stage under scrutinous eyes, putting on a show, an athletic beauty pageant, the grand prize was no tiara or a parade on the back of a convertible. No, sir. What was at stake was a ticket out. And for the dozens of top tier college and pro coaches and scouts, and whoever else with a finger in the football pie was here, what was at stake was a shot at big-time talent like Ozz. All of it amounted to a mutually parasitic relationship propelled by big dreams and big bucks.

Ozz had been dreaming about this opportunity since his father, Trey, had thrown him his first pass on a cinder playground with chalk marks for goal posts back when he was five.

"Imagine you're running under the lights at Doak Campbell Stadium up in Tallahassee in front of eighty thousand screaming fans," Trey had said one evening in the dying light as they ran drill after drill. "It's magic." And from that moment on, Ozz's path had been set. Daily practices with Trey, then Pop Warner, Sugar Bay High, and three state championships.

He tucked in his jersey, aware for the first time how revealing white football pants were. The meat market vibe was more than a little weird, the way these men, and they were all men and almost all white, ogled the players' physical stature, their every move, every muscle. But whatever—*means to an end.*

Florida Phenom Camp held every July was free, if you were lucky enough to get a coveted invitation. The whole thing was financed by End Zone Kings, an online website devoted to rating high school football prospects from around the country, not that much of the rest of it mattered. Florida was ground zero for the best talent, and Ozz was the best the Sunshine State had to offer.

The camp was hosted by Dade University, a football powerhouse a mere fifty miles from Sugar Bay, but the camp might as well have been in another galaxy for kids like Ozz. Carpeted locker rooms with flat-screen TVs and individual shower stalls. Restaurant meals every night. Cheerleaders escorting the players around campus like rock stars. And Ozz even had his own private room with cable TV, a video game console, and a fully stocked mini-fridge. If this was what it took, he could put up with being ogled.

And, like it or not, Ozz needed to be seen. Rich kids who had game, even if they were as dumb as shit, had their own avenues into the college game thanks to legacy admissions or fathers who golfed or sailed with influential coaches. As far as legacy was concerned, Trey's was a college career cut short by injury, and as for golfing or fishing, neither was available as an extra-curricular activity in prison.

Ozz did a few run-shuffle-run drills followed by some high knee drills, less to warm up than to calm his nerves. Flashy perks and promises aside, he knew his future had come down to fewer than five seconds—the 40-yard dash. Run the fastest forty he'd ever run and there'd be no doubt. Come fall recruiting season, Ozz Gordon would be the top prospect at running back in the entire state of Florida, about damn guaranteed to get a scholarship to the school of his choice.

But to run his fastest forty ever, that meant besting Flaco Romero, a Dominican kid from Palmetto Grove. Flaco's real name was Ramón, but he got his nickname Flaco, meaning skinny, because he was skinny, at least for a running back.

Ozz looked over at Flaco on the opposite side of the field. Flaco might look all lungs and legs, more built for the track than the gridiron, but Flaco was no joke. From what Ozz had seen in four years of playing against him, what Flaco lacked in bulk, he made up for with strength, speed, and pure athleticism. More than once, Ozz had marveled at how he could hurdle over defensive linemen for touchdowns, Flaco's signature move.

"Next up in the forty is Ramón Romero. Mr. Romero, please report to the timer."

Ozz bounced from foot to foot like a racehorse in the gate.

Flaco stepped to the forty-yard line, head dipped, arms cocked. When the starter's pistol cracked, Flaco drove his lean body forward, arms pumping, accelerating until he reached maximum velocity, at which point his head rose up like a cobra ready to strike. Chest pushed forward, he lunged over the goal line where a laser registered his time and projected it onto a digital clock in the end zone.

Ozz exhaled. 4.51 seconds. Fastest time posted by any player so far—but slower than Ozz's best.

"And our last player for the afternoon is Ozz Gordon, running back for the Sugar Bay Panthers with a personal best time of 4.41. Mr. Gordon, please report to the timer."

Walking onto the field, Ozz caught sight of Coach Wynne pacing the sideline like a caged lion, but as soon as Ozz took his position on the forty, his focus constricted into a bright tunnel of light. No longer was there a passel of coaches and scouts, all eyes fixed on him. No longer a field. Just silence and the way forward.

At the report of the pistol, Ozz sprinted off the forty-yard line, body and mind coalescing into one unified force not to be denied, gliding over hash marks for the thirty-yard line, the twenty-five. At the twenty, he lifted his head for the final charge into the end zone.

Then he caught a toe.

When he opened his eyes, he found himself sprawled out, his teeth full of turf. After a second or two, he struggled to his feet, the scene around him blurry and hushed, as if he were underwater.

He hobbled off the field and collapsed onto the bleachers, face buried in his hands.

Why this one time? Of all the thousands of forties he'd run, he'd never fallen. Not once. Why now, when it mattered most?

"Shit happens."

Ozz panned around for the source of the voice—a man, shaved head, older than Ozz, but not by much if his baby face was anything to go by. Twenty-something, maybe. Khaki pants, golf shirt with the polo player guy on the chest. Basic white guy wear.

As he descended to Ozz's row, the man caught Ozz staring at his black leather high tops with the lightning bolt logo, the kind Ozz yearned for.

"You like those?" the man said.

Ozz looked away.

"You don't mind if I sit, do you?"

Ozz shrugged.

"Folks say you're the Sunshine State's top prospect at running back."

Ozz bit his lip hard enough to taste blood.

"I've heard you're good enough to go pro now, if they'd let you."

Ozz grunted out a laugh. "Not after today I ain't."

The guy stretched his legs out and leaned his elbows back on the row above. "Like I said, shit happens."

Not to Ozz it didn't. Not when it mattered. Or maybe all the shit his folks and Coach had been feeding him all these years about going to college was just that—shit. The dreams of well-meaning folks who didn't know what it took to make it happen. How it wore you down until all the talent in the world couldn't save you from the mistakes mere mortals make in pick-up games.

"I saw you at Junior camp last year, in Tampa," the man said. "You were fastest in the forty there, ain't that right?"

Ozz shot the guy a sideways glance. This guy wasn't the type to use the word "ain't," given his country club clothes and earnest smile. No, this was the kind of guy who only said "ain't" when there was something to be gained, someone to hustle. That much Ozz had learned from Trey. Ozz had been observing his kind hanging around the sidelines since his freshman year. Cozying up to players with promises of the big time, when what they were after behind their big promises and custom suits was a cut of the players' futures.

"They act like pilot fish, acting all like they're just out to help you, but they're bottom feeders at heart, out only to help themselves," Trey said. Trey knew damn all about sea life, but he did know about football, until one hard hit had ended all that.

Ozz stood, unsteady on his feet, his vision still wobbly.

"It's not the end of the world, son."

"I ain't your son," Ozz said, with enough emphasis on the "ain't" that the man's mouth cracked into a brittle smile, revealing a top row of front teeth like the battlements on those medieval castles Ozz read about in history books.

And he meant it. Ozz didn't like people calling him "son," as if they had some proprietary interest in him. "Son" was for folks who cared. Ozz might not have Trey at home, but he had Coach Wynne. Coach was allowed to call him "son." Coach had faith in him like fathers should, like Trey did. Like his mom did. They all said that if he kept playing at the highest level and the Panthers kept winning, he'd have all the college action he could handle. But that was before he'd landed face first in the dirt in front of the ones who held all the cards.

Ozz pulled his shoulders back, his usual confidence wilted like week-old lettuce, but no way he was going to let a stranger see that, especially not one with fish eyes like a used car salesman.

"Shit don't happen to me. Not now. It can't." Ozz looked the man up and down. "Look, I don't mean to be rude, but I don't know who the fuck you are, and even if I did, I ain't in no mood for talking."

The man stuck out a hand. "Ray. Ray Spire."

Ozz kept his hands at his sides.

"Look, forget about what happened. Let it go. Move on, boy."

Ozz narrowed his eyes to slits. "Mister, let's get one thing straight. I ain't your son, and I sure as shit ain't your boy."

Spire put his hand to his mouth. "Sorry, I meant Ozz."

A knowing look flitted across Spire's face, as if the man had wormed into Ozz's brain, seen Trey shuffling into the visitors room every Sunday at 3 p.m., hands and feet shackled.

After a second or two, the salesman smile reappeared. "I'd be willing to bet every last scout and coach out here is more impressed by your numbers over the last three years at Sugar Bay than one stupid forty at the end of a week-long camp."

"Easy for you to say. It wasn't you making a fool of yourself out there." Ozz turned his back on Spire. "Look, I gotta go."

"At least *I'd* be willing to make that bet on you." Spire walked alongside Ozz toward the locker rooms. "And *I'd* be willing to bet that I can help get you to where you need to go. The question is, are *you* willing to bet on yourself?"

Ozz stopped and stuck his face in Spire's. "And, like I said, who the fuck are you?"

"Ray Spire. Just like I said the first time," he replied, his hand extended, again like a dead fish.

A hand clamped down on Ozz's shoulder from behind. "You better be running along now. That bus back to Sugar Bay ain't gonna wait, even for you, son."

Spire flinched.

"And Mr. Spire here is leaving. Ain't that right, now, Mr. Spire?"

Ozz didn't need to look to know who the voice belonged to, a rasp as scratchy as tree branches on a windowpane in a storm, a voice earned from decades of smoking cigarettes and drinking moonshine strong enough to strip paint, a voice that had barked at Ozz for four years, but never once to do anything other than make him the best he could be.

"You hear me, Ozz?" Coach asked, eyes fixed on Spire, Spire's on him.

"Yes sir, Coach," Ozz said. "See you at practice."

—

"Osceola, now you come on out here and help your momma with this."

Ozz sighed and saved the file of math homework on his computer. Work. Work. Work. Chores. Chores. Chores. That's all the woman ever thought about. More chores were the last thing he needed tonight. The camp had left him exhausted, and so behind with schoolwork it would take until the sun came up to get it all finished. No way Coach let schoolwork slip. Failing any test, blowing off any assignment, was a benching crime, and Coach was judge, jury, and executioner on that score too.

"Coming, Momma!" Ozz said, trying to sound like whatever she wanted him to do was exactly what he had in mind.

He found her on the porch and pasted on his best "how can I help you" smile. Like Coach, Sadie didn't take backtalk.

"What is that?" he said, pointing at the large cardboard box by the front door.

"I got no idea, but use your superhuman powers and bring it on inside, why don't you, Mr. Wizard?"

Ozz did as he was told. "Okay, but don't call me that."

"Don't call you what?"

Ozz dropped his eyes. "Wizard. Wiz. Whatever."

Sadie reached up and squeezed his cheek between her thumb and forefinger. "You're right. You're no wizard. To me, you still my baby boy."

Ozz batted away her hand. "Jesus, Momma."

She pointed at him. "I told you already, no cussing in this house."

He bowed his head. "Sorry."

She signaled for Ozz to put the box on the kitchen table and leaned in close to read the label. "It's addressed to you. Says it's from Ray Spire at Spire Management. You know any Ray Spire? I sure as heck don't."

He couldn't say as he did. He'd only been in his presence for a few minutes. Still, the dude was squirrely. "I met him once. At the camp last week."

"Why's Ray Spire sending you a box as big as this damn house?" She covered her mouth with a hand like a guilty child. "Oops."

Ozz covered a smile. "Now we're even."

Sadie reared back and gave him the once-over, hands on her hips. "We ain't never gonna be even."

Ozz pressed his lips together to keep from laughing.

"Who is this Spire, anyway?"

"He's some kind of scout or agent or something."

Her lips pulled tight. "I'm not following you. What's he doin' sending you . . ." She waved a hand at the box. "Sending you whatever's in there. You know there's rules on stuff like that."

He jumped back, away from his mother's reach to avoid the clip to the side of the head he knew was coming. "He told me to forget it. The fall, I mean. To let it go."

"Sounds like good advice to me. No college in their right mind's gonna judge you by one mistake. Not when you's the best damn high school running back in the whole state of Florida." She flashed him a smile so bright he had no trouble seeing why Trey thought the sun rose and set by his momma.

"I think you might be biased," he said, tickling her in the ribs.

She squirmed out of his grasp. "It's true. Even if you are my son." She pulled out a chair and sat. "Ain't you gonna open it?"

He took a knife from the drawer and slit the tape on top of the box. "Holy shit," he said, staring at the variety of shoes, at least a dozen pairs, the likes of which he had drooled over at the mall but never dreamed of owning.

Sadie grabbed her eyeglasses and slid them on. "What is that all for?"

One by one, he took the shoeboxes out and stacked them on the table. Two pairs of high tops, the same kind Ray Spire had been wearing. Two pairs of football cleats, Panther colors—black with gold lightning bolts on the side and black and silver laces. And the rest an assortment of sneakers, all made by Epic, the company that had signed Panther alum Santonio Taylor, Ozz's idol, to a multimillion-dollar endorsement contract.

"And there's a note with your name on it attached to this one." Ozz unfolded the piece of paper. "'For your mother, With Thanks, Ray Spire,' is what it says."

Sadie pulled a pair of silver sneakers studded with "Go

Panthers" in rhinestones from the box. "Woo hoo!" she said, kicking off her flip-flops and stuffing her feet into the shoes.

"You'd be stylin' at my games in those, Momma," he said as she strutted around the kitchen.

The smile disappeared from her face, and she dropped back into the chair. "You know I gotta work nights, Ozz. We need the money."

He squatted beside her. "I know, Momma. I didn't mean it that way."

She tousled his hair. "I know, son." She squared her shoulders. "So, tell me, why is this Spear, Spire, whatever his name is, sending you all these shoes?"

"Maybe there's a note in here for me too," Ozz said, his voice muffled due to the fact he was rummaging around head first in the box. "Here!" He pulled out a business size envelope like a magician pulling a rabbit out of a hat.

"But it's addressed to you, Momma," he said, handing her the envelope.

She tore the envelope open and read.

"What's it say?"

Sadie looked up, her eyes glassy. "He says he'd like to come by. Visit with us for a bit to talk about your future. He thinks he can help you navigate the college process, whatever that means."

He plopped into a chair beside her. "Yeah, that's what he said at the camp. He said he could help me."

"Why didn't you tell me that? Maybe he *can* help. I mean, after what happened, it couldn't hurt to . . ."

Ozz looked away, Trey's words running through his head.

Sadie took his hands in hers. "I know it wasn't your best day out there. But this Mr. Spire is right. It was one mistake. You've got your whole future ahead of you, and way I see it, any help we can get, we should take advantage of it, right?"

"I guess."

"You guess? Wasn't that what that camp was for? To get seen?"

"But remember what Pop . . ."

Sadie's jaw clenched. "You stop right there. Your Pop's not here. It's just you and me now. And we got to do what's best for you and your future."

He nodded.

"Mr. Spire saw you and . . ." She cast her hand out at the pile of shoeboxes. " . . . and it seems that he thinks you've got the talent to go all the way. Says so right here." She stabbed a finger at the letter. "Mr. Spire also says he helped Santonio get the heck out of this lousy, bug-infested town."

"What? Let me see that," he said, grabbing the letter from her hands.

Sadie slumped back. "Look, Osceola, we ain't got much but your talent, and Sugar Bay don't got none of the advantages of those fancy places on the coasts, so when someone comes along willing to—"

Ozz raised a hand. "I hear you, Momma. Maybe there would be no harm in talking to the man. Besides, if he's good enough for ST, he's good enough for me. Only question I got is how Mr. Spire knew our shoe sizes."

Ozz dropped his head onto Sadie's shoulder, and they laughed like they hadn't done since Trey was locked up.

5

I pull off I-95 north of the Palm Beach county line and head west. Within a few miles, the scenery turns from designer shops, custom homes, and polo fields to tract after tract of identical cinder block boxes plopped down onto the once lush tropical landscape. When suburbia runs out, the view reverts back to what this all was before the speculators, the dreamers, and the con men showed up—cane fields and blindingly green sawgrass, like the food coloring used on St. Patrick's Day to turn everything Irish, including my hair when I was seven, although my black hair ended up looking like pond scum.

"Welcome to Sugar Bay, Her Soil is Her Fortune." The sign at the city limits is a bald-faced lie, given whatever fortune there is out here lines three pockets—Big Sugar, the private prison company that runs Glades Correctional where Sadie works, and the drug dealers.

I read the sign out loud, then add, "Except for the five million and change I've managed to pry from those tight-fisted, misanthropic bastards." I quash the thought. I know better than to count my chickens.

Getting to Hachi's place means driving through Little Mexicali, a war zone of a neighborhood, a collection of tenements housing migrant farm workers from Mexico, Haiti, Jamaica, the Dominican Republic, and wherever else working seven days a week in the fields under the scorching sun sounds like a career opportunity. Once pretty tropical pastels, the buildings are now a dark shade of despair. Men in wife-beater shirts perched on beach chairs, playing cards in the parking lot, and women chasing half-naked toddlers away from the street click by like images from the ancient slide projector my parents used for home movies of summers on the Cape. But there's no mistaking it, this tableau zipping by is no vacation destination. This is the land of last resort, one step up from prison, one step closer to an early grave.

The traffic light turns amber, and I stamp down on the accelerator. Slowing down in this part of town, even for a red light, could be a fatal error in judgment.

I park at the curb outside Hachi's place, a faded yellow clapboard ranch house with a well-tended yard located under high-tension power lines. Across the street a bunch of kids play tag in what passes for a park in Sugar Bay—a cracked asphalt lot with a frame of a swing set, no swings, and an overflowing trash can.

I knock once. No answer. I raise my hand to try again when the door creaks open. Hachi squints at me through the safety chain, her eyes hollow.

"It's me," I say, unsure of why she's asked me to come. It was awkward enough at the Glades Bowl, so much time having passed since the last time I'd seen her, a circumstance of my own making. Add to that the specter of Ozz's death, and I'd rather be anywhere else than here.

She releases the chain and stands aside, her body limp, as if grief has liquefied her bones.

I follow her into the living room, where she drops onto the

couch beside Sadie, who is curled into the fetal position, her diminutive frame shrouded in a white nightgown.

Hachi rubs her sister's back. "Sadie, honey, it's Grace."

Sadie attempts to sit up but lists into Hachi, her long black braids like ragged pendulums weighing down her bird-like head.

Words are my stock and trade, but all I manage is a couple of stuttered "ahs" and "I'm sorrys." What is there to say to a woman whose only child is lying in the morgue on a cold slab, a gaping hole where his heart used to be?

I shift my gaze to a windowsill littered with framed photographs—Ozz and Sadie, Ozz and Hachi. Ozz hoisting a huge trophy aloft.

"That was when they won State last year."

Hachi stands and motions with her head in the direction of the kitchen.

Door closed behind us, she leans against the kitchen counter, arms braced across her chest and waits, as if she expects me to speak.

I steel myself against the memory of how I'd turned away when I saw her in the park that night last year. How I'd convinced myself she was one among the many there trying to score their next hit, chugging rotgut liquor, their laughs the throaty rattles of lifelong smokers, their hyena-like rants raging against whatever machine they held responsible for their misfortune.

Of all the moments Hachi could have chosen to look up, she chose the exact one when Manny and I were stopped at a traffic light after an ill-advised dinner date. It had been too soon to attempt to mend the fences I'd long ago bulldozed. All we did was stare at our expensive food and wonder how we'd come to this—one-time best friends with nothing to say, the type of couple we used to mock, back when we had everything, but most of all, each other's back. Hachi saw me see her, ragged and wild-eyed. Then, as if to confirm her belief that she was not worthy of the sober life she'd managed for the better part of a decade, she dashed to the curb and paraded back and forth.

Manny grabbed my hand before I was able to open the car door. "You've left that life behind, Gracie. You don't owe her anything," he said as we sped away, the buttery soft leather of his Porsche's seats cradling me in an illusory embrace. And I'd believed him. But I was wrong. Wrong about him—divorced people get divorced for a reason, and my ready complicity in his lack of compassion should have been my first clue. And about Hachi—I'd always owe her.

"I need you to look into Ozz's death," she says, her voice rough like sandpaper from crying, not from drugs. Her eyes are clear, free of the user's uncontrollable twitchy energy.

I'm not sure what I was expecting. A tongue-lashing? A diatribe of all the things she'd intended to say to me after the Glades Bowl, but didn't get the chance? Whatever it was, it was not this. Not a plea for help where no amount of help will make a difference. Ozz's death was about as certain an end as anyone can have, an end witnessed by five thousand people. And the rest of what I know? Those are secrets I'm bound to take to the grave with me, even if Ozz is already in his.

"I don't understand," I say.

Hachi raises her chin, jaw set. "You owe me this one favor."

I press my lips together.

"That boy had everything to live for. We need to know what would have made him . . ." Her voice cracks right along with her determination to be brave, her words swamped by gut-wrenching sobs. She crumples to the floor, legs splayed out like a discarded marionette.

Putting all my weight on my good leg, I lower myself down beside her.

"Jesus Christ, why? He was . . ." She wipes her nose on her sleeve. "He was going to college. He was going to have a life." She casts her eyes around the tiny kitchen, the appliances dented, the linoleum floor peeling. "A life far away from this."

I pull her head onto my shoulder. "H, sometimes everything seems great on the surface, but underneath it's just not. Trust me, I've been there."

She springs to her feet. "Typical! It's always about you, isn't it? You think because you—" She gives a dismissive wave. "Forget it!"

As I push myself up, Oscar slips and I collapse at her feet, looking up into eyes filled with the fury of the betrayed.

"What, oh *you* need help now? Or maybe I should say, you need help *again?*"

She turns away.

"Wait!" I say, grabbing her ankle.

She shakes me off and stares down at me.

"When I asked you to the game Friday, I thought, maybe, just maybe, we could clear the air. That maybe we could have some fun together, like we used to." She grabs a pack of cigarettes from the kitchen counter and lights up. "But we didn't get the chance, did we?" She takes a deep draw and exhales hard. "Even after what happened, you manage to turn the conversation back to you."

"I didn't mean—"

"All I was asking for was a little help."

Her words land like body blows, leaving me breathless. After several tries, I manage to pull myself to my feet by crawling to the refrigerator and hauling myself up by the handle. "That's not what I meant. I'm sorry if it came out that way."

She waves her cigarette in the air. "Being sorry isn't what you're good at, is it?"

The unmitigated rage in her voice is frightening, but turning grief into anger to drown out pain is a strategy with which I am more than familiar.

She raises her chin and looks down her nose at me. "Grace needs to stay on her path, the right path. If that means she needs to leave you in the gutter on your own, no matter how many times you've helped her up, then so be it." She steps close enough I feel her breath on my cheek. "You and your fucking career. All you can manage is to live in a damn bubble." She tries to slam her fist onto the counter but misses and hits herself in the leg. "Shit," she says and throws herself onto a kitchen chair at the chipped Formica table.

I open my mouth to speak, but gag on the acerbic taste of shame. I sit and take her hands. "I am so sorry. We should have . . . I should have stopped."

She pulls back. "And how is that husband of yours, Mr. City Commissioner Martinez?"

"Ex-husband."

"I forgot, Mr. Grace Locke is no more. All I can say is good riddance."

"I know you never liked him."

She throws her arms in the air. "Like him? I loathed him. He was a bastard to you."

"Yeah, he was. But he was my bastard."

She grunts. "Until he wasn't."

I sense a smile tugging at my lips. "And he didn't like you too much either, my friend," I say, which makes us both dissolve into laughter for a few seconds like teenage girls without a care in the world until the mood turns somber again.

"Look, H, if you think I can help, I'm here to help. You asked and I came." She lets me take her hands this time. "But I have to ask, given how angry you were with me, why even ask me to the game? You could have forgotten I even exist."

A weak smile flickers across her lips. "I don't know, maybe it was my way of saying screw you."

I drop her hands. "What?"

"I asked you because I wanted to show you I can do good too. Like you, I got my life back together. I've got a good job." She sniffs. "I've got things to live for now, just like you. Maybe I wanted you to see that I have people, like Ozz and Sadie, who love me. Or at least I had." She swallows hard.

Her eyes drift out the window, to a snowy egret staring at us, its pale, watery eyes with dark centers like black-eyed peas.

"There has to be more." She wipes her nose on her sleeve.

"You said it yourself, sometimes things aren't as they seem."

I reach in my bag for a tissue and hand it to her. "I did say that, didn't I?"

She blows her nose. "Now you can put your money where your mouth is and help me and Sadie understand what was going on with Ozz. It might . . . I don't know . . . help, you know?"

I nod, but I don't know.

She gets up and grabs two cans of soda from the fridge. "Not anywhere near as good as a cold beer, but it'll have to do."

I pop the top on my can. "Same sound, though. At least there's that."

She smiles. "I'm sorry I got mad. It wasn't your fault what happened to me last year. I made my own choices." She drops her head to her chest. "Bad choices."

I take a swig. "We seem to be good at that."

She nods.

"But I should have been there for you like you were for me," I say.

"You asked why I called?" She looks me in the eye. "Bottom line is I miss you, Grace. Even if you can be a royal pain in the ass."

"Likewise," I say. We clink cans. "Why don't you tell me about Ozz?" I say, as if I know nothing about him at all.

6

The West Palm Beach bus depot reeked—a combination of urine-laced weed overwritten with ammonia.

Ozz always took the bus to make his deliveries. No chance of getting pulled over by the cops for some bogus not-broken tail light in some lily-white enclave where the only brown skin that's acceptable is the kind you overpay for at the tanning salon. Even though he was pale-skinned enough to pass for any number of ethnicities—dark-skinned Caucasian, light-skinned black, Hispanic, maybe even Middle Eastern—he wasn't taking any chances.

Ozz ducked into the men's restroom, averting his eyes from a man passed out, head resting on the J-trap under the filthy sink. He slipped into an empty stall and changed back into jeans and a T-shirt. He always wore sneakers just in case he had to make a run for it. Running he was good at. Running was what would save him.

He folded his white dress shirt and khaki pants and put them in the empty backpack. Sadie would have his head if he showed up for church on Sunday in wrinkled clothes.

Thankfully, this trip, like all the others so far, had been uneventful, which is what you want when your backpack's stuffed with enough Oxycontin to put you away until your hair turns to gray and your dreams to ashes. Just another risk he was willing to take to get the hell out of Sugar Bay.

As always, he had made his weekly deliveries to his usual clients. His favorite stop was the model-pretty receptionist with a tight blonde ponytail and an even tighter skirt at Franklin and Montgomery, a law firm on the penthouse floor of Flagler Point, a pink marble tower with views of the ocean. The manila envelope he handed her bore no name, yet the girl always said, "Thank you. We've been expecting this," and offered Ozz a mint from the silver dish, which he always declined. What he always accepted from her, however, was a business size envelope full of cash.

If Sadie knew what he was up to when she was on the night shift at the prison, she'd have thrown him in there alongside the inmates to teach him a lesson. But she didn't know, didn't need to know. This was his way of investing in his future. His real part-time job at the supermarket stocking shelves didn't leave enough for the college fund he was squirreling away under his mattress.

Ozz stashed today's cash, somewhere in the neighborhood of two thousand dollars in small bills, under his clothes alongside the nine millimeter handgun he prayed he'd never have to use. He tucked the extra hundred in small bills that Mr. Epstein, his final customer of the day, had thrown in as a tip under the elastic band with the rest of the money. Epstein, even if he was buying in enough volume to anesthetize an elephant, knew fifty a tab was a deal, and said Ozz should keep the tip for himself for "his trouble." But Ozz knew better than to short Junior. Like the cops, Junior had a sixth sense for funny business, and Ozz didn't need Junior jamming him up, not when he was so close. A means to an end, that's all this was.

Ozz looked both ways on his way out of the bathroom. You could never be too careful. So far, so good, but you never knew when things were about to turn to shit, when the cops might jump out of nowhere like what had happened to Trey when he was pumping gas into his truck.

Walking the four blocks to Junior's crib from the bus station, Ozz wondered what he'd be doing on Wednesday nights when he got to college. Homework? Hanging with teammates? Watching TV? All of that sounded good, normal even. Whatever it was, it sure as hell wouldn't be skulking around the shadows as a bag man for an albino crackhead with a mean streak and a twitchy trigger finger. No way, no how. A few more Wednesday runs for Junior and he'd be home free, living in a dorm room at the school farthest away from Sugar Bay that gave him a scholarship. As soon as he got settled, he'd move Sadie out too, get her an apartment somewhere nice, somewhere close to him. He would take care of her like she'd taken care of him.

Ozz found Junior and his crew where they always were—squatted down, playing cards atop a milk crate, outside the package store Junior had co-opted as his headquarters, a squat bunker of a building with barred windows.

"You late," Junior said without taking his eyes off his hand. Junior wasn't white, he was whiter than white, with pink eyes, and an uncanny instinct for detecting bullshit. His crew called him the "Human Lie Detector." The cops called him a wanted man. Ozz called him his boss. For now.

"I ain't late. The bus was late," Ozz said with a goofy smile, even though Junior liked jokes as much as blue misery lights in his rear view.

Junior dropped his cards and watched them flutter to the ground like falling leaves. He got to his feet in slow motion and faced Ozz, right hand resting on the butt of a handgun sticking out of his waistband. "If I say you late, you late."

The circle of men kept their eyes glued to their cards.

Ozz bit his lip. *Means to an end. Means to an end.*

"What you got for me, Wiz?" Junior asked, his skin a spooky shade of yellow under the street lights, his bald head a map of veins.

Before Ozz had time to answer, Junior stuck his hand out. "I said what you got for me?"

Ozz reached into the backpack for the cash, his fingers brushing the handgun.

Junior grabbed the cash. An arch of muscle where his eyebrow would be if he had one shot up. "You sure that's all of it? You ain't been skimmin', have you?" he asked, strumming the wad of cash with his thumb.

The circle raised their heads. An icy chill ran the length of Ozz's body.

"Good mama's boy like you, you'd never take what wasn't yours, would you?"

The men's eyes flicked from Junior to Ozz. His heart accelerated, but he willed his face to remain expressionless as he did on the football field, even against defensive tackles the size of dump trucks. To show fear was catnip for Junior, brutality his tool of choice against those who did.

In a split second, Junior closed the space between him and Ozz, and planted his face so close to Ozz's, he could smell the sickly scent of weed wafting off Junior's hoodie. "I said, you sure, boy?"

Ozz held Junior's gaze, trying not to look like the coward he felt, while simultaneously biting back the wave of anger percolating in his gut at being dressed down by a punk who'd be in prison or dead long before Ozz got out of college.

Means to an end.

"It's all there, boss, even the extra Epstein gave me. Said it was a tip."

Junior grunted. "Tip? What he think we runnin' here, one of 'em delis?"

Ozz held his tongue.

After a few seconds, Junior took a step back, but his

bubblegum pink eyes stayed fixed on Ozz. "He ain't never given you a tip before, did he?"

Ozz shook his head.

"You sure, boy?"

Ozz gave a firm nod.

"How's I to know you ain't been keepin' 'em tips for yourself?"

What Ozz wanted to say was, "Because I ain't stupid. Because I'm only doing this crap to get by. To help my mother put food on the table. To stash a few bucks away for a one-way ticket out of this hellhole." Instead, he stood mute. Junior knew he'd been a loyal soldier, and Junior needed loyal soldiers to stay in business.

"Nah, you'd never do dat, would you, Wiz? Hell, yo' daddy Trey kept his mouth shut when he needed to. Ain't that right?"

Ozz did his best to ignore the desire to rush Junior, knock him on his ass like he did anyone who got between him and the end zone.

"We all got those we gotta answer to, right? You sayin' I should trust you?"

"Yes, boss," Ozz said, anger prickling his skin like poison ivy.

Junior pulled on a pair of latex gloves, the kind Ozz hoped to use one day as a doctor. "Give me yo' nine, son."

Ozz dug in the backpack for the nine millimeter and handed it over.

"So, Wiz, to be sure, you sayin' I should trust you?" Junior said again, but his eyes were focused now over Ozz's shoulder.

Ozz glanced back and saw a short Hispanic man approaching, black duffel bag in hand.

Junior swept Ozz out of the way. "'Cause I ain't got patience for people I can't trust." He pointed the gun at the man. "Miguel, why the fuck you late? Ain't I told you before, you late you pay. How is it you Cubanos say it? Give me el dinero?"

Duffel outstretched, eyes wide and pleading, the man opened his mouth to say something, but before he had the chance, he keeled over backward, head hitting the sidewalk with a crack.

The men around the milk crate flinched at the report of the weapon but kept their eyes down on their cards.

Ozz froze, unable to look away from the gaping hole in the middle of the man's forehead, a halo of blood spreading out around his head.

"Mu-er-to is how you Cubanos say it," Junior said, his voice an evil hiss laced with a laugh.

Junior swiveled back around, his top lip contorted into a snarl, the nine millimeter pointing at Ozz's chest. He motioned with the gun. "On yo' knees."

Unable to breathe, Ozz sank to his knees, closed his eyes, and prayed to God. Prayed for a life that, mere seconds before, he hadn't thought worth living unless he got out of Sugar Bay. But with the gun on him, Ozz wanted that life, his life, any life. Just one more second of life, even if it were a life lived in obscurity in this forgotten swamp town. Any of that would be better than being cut down and left to rot in the gutter.

Without warning, Junior smacked Ozz on the side of the head with the butt of the gun. "Open yo' eyes, son. You ain't dead yet."

Petrified to move even an inch, Ozz squinted up at Junior, his eyes dancing in their sockets like neon pinballs.

Junior bent over and spat in Ozz's face. "Fuck, no way I'd go wastin' my best producer, now would I? Hell no! Boy, you can slip right into high society over there on the coast, as if you belong. You's as good as a white, boy. At least one with a good Florida tan." Junior sneered. "What with yo' 'yes sirs' and 'no ma'ams' and yo' chinos and button-downs, all fancy like."

Junior circled Ozz several times, gun still pointed at his head. "Get up!"

Ozz couldn't will his body to move.

Junior blew on the muzzle of the weapon. "Seems like the Wiz here can't get off his knees." Junior kicked Ozz's knees out from under him. "I said get up!"

Legs like jelly, Ozz failed several more times to stand, until

Junior hauled him upright and pulled him over to Miguel, the dead man's eyes as wide as a child's on Christmas morning. "Dat's what them dat's disloyal get," Junior said, kicking the corpse.

"Now, let's get serious here, Osceola. That's your real name, ain't it? I mean, Wizard, that's who you play on TV, right?" He chuckled, his face no more than an inch from Ozz's. "The thing is, I don't know if I believe you always give me every last cent you get from them high rollers, but the thing is, I don't have to. Fact is, you into me now. You hear me? You and me, we bound together. Tighter than a nun's pussy. Now you can't never say you had nothin' to do with dis right here."

Junior poked at the corpse with the toe of his sneaker. "In't that right, Osceola? And, given that state of affairs, I don't have to worry 'bout anyone thinkin' I had nothin' to do with it." He held up his still gloved hands, the pistol dangling from his forefinger.

Junior pointed at the men playing cards. "Now you three gonna help me give Miguel here a decent burial," he said. "And, Osceola, just in case you get to feelin' the need to confess yo' sins, like if you maybe get to feelin' you need to save yo' skin, say you get caught in a jam with the po-po, well, someone . . ." He pointed a finger at himself. " . . . someone gonna be a good citizen and call in a tip that dey's a body buried out somewhere in dem cane fields, and alongside dat body gonna be a gun, this gun, with yo' prints on it."

"Let's call it a guaranty of loyalty." Junior peeled off the gloves and threw them at Ozz. "Your loyalty."

Junior grabbed the duffel Miguel had been carrying and leaned back against the door of the package store and observed Ozz. "We all gotta have some skin in the game, ain't we? And you know all 'bout games, don't you? Everyone gotta play the position they get given." He pointed at Ozz. "I see dat look in yo' eye, boy. The one that says 'I ain't done nothin'. It was all you, Junior.' But you ain't sayin' nothin', are you? 'Cause you don't wanna end up like Miguel over there. But I's here to remind you dat you was as much a part of dis as any of us."

Ozz repressed the urge to vomit.

"You in dis for life. You gonna be doin' what I tell you for as long as I tell you. You hear?" Junior said. "I say you hear me?"

Ozz lowered his head to his chest.

"Or you be doin' life, and that pretty mama of yours, maybe she be getting a booty call from me and the boys here." Junior waved the gun at his crew.

Ozz lunged at Junior, right fist coiled back. When Junior faked left, Ozz collapsed into a heap on the sidewalk.

Junior grunted out a laugh and signaled with the gun for the men to pick up Miguel's body before dropping the gun into the duffel. "One last thing, Osceola. From what I keep hearin', you got you a lot to lose. And, down the road, you gonna have a lot more to share, my man." He rubbed his thumb and forefinger together.

The men loaded the body into the trunk of Junior's Cadillac and drove away, a spray of gravel in their wake.

When they were out of sight, Ozz sunk to his knees and wept.

7

Sadie's house perched on the edge of nowhere, the last house on the last block within the Sugar Bay city limits. Beyond, the Everglades, two million acres of wetlands once a vibrant ecosystem, now on life support thanks to run-off from Big Sugar and willful blindness by the politicians in Tallahassee.

We park on the street under the watchful eyes of a group of teens loitering on the corner.

"Lock your car," Hachi says, confirming the wisdom of leaving the Jaguar back at The Hurricane.

If not for the eight-foot-high chain-link fence, the blue bungalow could be in Anywheresville, USA. Flower boxes overflowing with pink and purple pansies, the edges of the grass trimmed along the walkway, all evidence of someone who is house proud, which can't be easy in Sugar Bay, a town where crime is as common as soul-sucking poverty—thus, chicken wire atop the fence, and a Beware of Dog sign featuring a picture of a pit bull hanging askew on the gate.

Hachi rings the doorbell.

"I don't hear a dog barking," I say.

She shoots me a sideways glance. "Sadie don't got no damn dog, woman. Sign's for show."

She rings again.

We wait some more.

"Maybe it's too soon. Or maybe it's not a good time," I say, retreating a couple of steps, hoping that this is the excuse I need to bow out of this wild goose chase.

"She's here," Hachi says, with an edge in her voice that says, "Oh no you don't!"

She holds her finger down on the bell until Sadie cracks open the door.

"Why can't nobody leave me alone?" Sadie says.

"I told you we were coming," Hachi says, pushing open the door.

We brush by Sadie, who's wearing a bathrobe even though it's three o'clock in the afternoon.

"Damn phone been ringing all day. The newspapers, TV, folks I ain't even heard from in years telling me all how damn sorry they be."

Hachi grabs Sadie by the shoulders and looks into her bloodshot eyes. "Remember, you said I could come take a look around Ozz's room?"

Sadie peers over Hachi's shoulder at me. "I said *you* could. Wasn't so long ago *she* didn't want nothin' to do with you." Sadie swats Hachi back. "Like I said, can't nobody leave me be? What the hell good can it do now, poking around?"

Hachi puffs out her cheeks.

"Yeah, I know you want to understand, whatever the hell that means. You was always like that, for all the good it did you." Sadie whips her long braids back over her shoulder and pads off down the hallway. "But what you never seem to understand is that some things—" Her voice cracks. "Some things don't make no sense. Never will."

Hachi motions me to follow. "Ozz was my kin too, Sadie.

You'd do well to remember that."

Sadie whips around, opens her mouth, then closes it again.

"It won't take long, I promise," Hachi says.

"One damn thing I understand is that nothin' ain't ever gonna bring my son back. Whatever was in his head is gonna be six feet under come tomorrow."

Hachi turns to me, eyes glassy. "I'm sorry."

I wave her off. "No need. Tragedy's no time to judge."

"Better to leave the judging to the higher power, is what I say," Sadie mumbles.

I follow Hachi down the dark hallway. The muggy air smells like compost, as if the trash hasn't been taken out in days. A Do Not Disturb sign hangs on the doorknob of the last room on the left. She pushes the door open and draws a sharp breath as if she's been punched in the gut.

She takes a few deep breaths, panning around the tidy room. She slides her fingertips over the surface of the desk where Ozz did homework with dreams of a better life. A pile of folded laundry sits waiting to be put away on top of a chest of drawers. A book, splayed spine up to save his place for a later that never came. A life preserved in amber.

She points at a box overflowing with Panther football gear in the corner. "Coach Wynne had one of the players bring Ozz's stuff over from his locker. Sadie couldn't stand to look at it, so I put it in there."

"Can I take a look?" I ask, for lack of anything better to do.

"Already did. I thought there might be a note or something." Her voice cracks.

I rest my hand on her shoulder. "Like I said, maybe it's too soon. Maybe we should go."

She shoves me away. "No, let's get this over with."

I nod, but the obvious futility of the task is making it hard to disguise my reluctance. "Okay, but what are we looking for?"

She sinks down onto the bed, her face in her hands. "I dunno. I thought maybe seeing his room would give us some idea of . . .

of . . . what, I don't know of what. Anything."

I point at a poster of a football player in a Miami Dolphins uniform tacked to the wall above the single bed. "Who's that?"

"Santonio Taylor. Graduated a few years back. Went on to college at Alabama on a scholarship. Now he's the best running back in the NFL." She swipes at a tear with the back of her hand. "Ozz got to meet him before the Glades Bowl, before . . ."

I sit on the bed and pull her close.

"Ozz worshiped Santonio. Wanted to be just like him." She stares hard at the image, as if she might find, somewhere in the face of a man who had walked in Ozz's shoes, some inkling, some explanation. "Dammit! Why would he throw everything away like that? We sacrificed so much for him."

I pat her knee. "Sit here while I look around."

I open the closet and marvel at the military precision. Jeans on hangers. Shirts organized by color. Shoes matched in pairs on the floor. If only I'd been this by the book, I might have risen above the rank of specialist, the title given to enlisted soldiers who don't quite fit anywhere else. Not that rank mattered. IEDs don't discriminate.

I thumb through a stack of notebooks and loose-leaf binders on the desk—Math, English, Physics—and run my hand down a tower of library books piled on the desk: *The Divine Comedy, East of Eden . . .*

"Your boy liked to read."

Her eyes widen. "What did you say?"

I point at the books.

Her expression softens. "He went to the library every Saturday. If they didn't have what he wanted in our crap local branch, he'd hound the librarian until she got it for him."

I pick up a thick blue tome—*The Physician's Desk Reference.* "Heavy stuff, for a high schooler."

The light in her eyes dims. "He would've made a fine doctor one day."

I lean against the wall and take in the totality of the space—

barely enough room for a double bed, dresser, nightstand, desk. Bed made complete with hospital corners. A place for everything and everything in its place.

"Now, if I were a teenage boy and I had secrets, where would I hide them?" I say through tight lips.

"What?"

"Nothing."

I point at a laptop in the middle of the desk. "This was Ozz's computer?"

"His prized possession. That and his phone. Saved up for them himself. Bought them secondhand."

I flip up the screen and press the power button. A lock screen appears. "Don't suppose you know his password?"

She shakes her head.

"I didn't see a phone around here, did you?"

I watch her smoothing the comforter on the bed with her hand as if she were stroking a child's head.

I dip my head down to her level.

She flinches. "Did you say something?"

"I said, do you know where Ozz's phone is? Kids these days live much of their lives on their damn phones."

"No clue. It wasn't in the box." She jerks her chin at the box atop of which sits a scarred silver helmet bearing #10 in black lettering.

Without thinking, I pull open the nightstand drawer. I freeze—an empty prescription bottle bears Ozz's name and "Fluoxetine 40mg. 2 tablets per day." Lexapro, a drug without which I might not have found my way back from the abyss.

"Was Ozz depressed?"

Hachi dabs at her eyes with a tissue.

Sadie peeks in. "You two 'bout done in here? You can have more time if you want, but I have to leave. I start work at five."

"Honey, why don't you take another couple of days off?" Hachi says.

Sadie scowls. "Don't work, don't get paid."

"Can I ask you both something?" I say.

Sadie and Hachi nod in unison, a well-practiced motion that amplifies how alike they look.

"Why was Ozz taking Lexapro?" I hold the bottle up like an exhibit in a court case. I regret the prosecutorial tone as soon as the question leaves my lips.

Sadie juts her chin at Hachi. "Why don't you ask *her?*"

Hachi examines her bitten-down fingernails. "Ozz got real quiet over the summer. Stayed in his room a lot. It got worse when school started. Never said much of anything."

I wait for Sadie to chime in, but she's stone-faced. "Teenagers aren't exactly known for their openness, even if you are their favorite auntie," I say.

Hachi's eyes soften. "That's what I thought, but it got so as he wasn't talking hardly at all. When I asked him about it, he blew me off, said something about the pressure of school and not having his dad around."

I glance at the stack of books and files on the desk. "He did have a lot on his plate, what with school and football."

"Had a job too," Hachi says. "Even though I told him it was too much."

Sadie gives Hachi a cautionary stare.

"He did?" I ask.

Sadie pushes herself upright. "When I lost my job a few months back, he got a job baggin' groceries or stackin' shelves or some such nonsense to help out. When I got my new job at the prison, I told him he didn't have to keep working, that he had enough to do what with school and ball. But he was havin' none of it. Said any extra after our bills, he was putting away for his future." The sting of her words hangs in the air, and we all look down.

"Where did he work?"

Sadie hesitates an instant, as if she can't remember. "Over at the convenience store. One on the corner of MLK and Main. Whatever that dump's called."

I look down at the bottle in my hand. The label lists the prescribing physician as Dr. Geraldine Harrison. "He was seeing someone?"

Sadie turns a withering look on Hachi. "Miss Know-It-All here dragged him all the way up to Clewiston to that community mental health center."

Hachi rolls her eyes as if she knows what Sadie is going to say next.

"And that's when things got worse," Sadie says.

Hachi stands, pacing back and forth as she speaks. "I got so worried I took him to a shrink. Up in Clewiston, like she said, because he didn't wanna go here in Sugar Bay. Said he didn't want people to think he was crazy."

"And did the counseling help?"

Hachi gives me the side-eye. "If only. It wasn't real counseling. Like actually talking to someone. We couldn't afford that. All they were able to do was let him see a psychiatrist for a few minutes. She's the one who prescribed the Lexapro."

Sadie's nose twitches. "Girl, you of all people should know that drugs never do you no good." She grabs the bottle from my hand. "You two, coming in here all high and mighty, thinking you can see into my son's head like some kind of mind readers." She drops the bottle back in the drawer and slams it shut. "Look, I gotta get to work."

"I think we should leave," I say, but what I'm thinking is I wish to hell I hadn't come, hadn't let myself be dragged into the middle of this drama. And when it comes down to it, what the hell do I know about their kind of loss? The loss of a child. All I've ever managed is two miscarriages and a divorce. I swallow hard. All I've ever lost has been my own damn fault.

Like a deflating balloon, Sadie wilts onto the bed beside Hachi, rocking back and forth, repeating, "My boy is gone, and ain't nothin' ever gonna bring him back."

Hachi buries her head in Sadie's neck. "Grace is here 'cause I asked her. She wants to help."

"Nobody can ever know why he did what he did 'cept him and his maker," Sadie says, her voice a whisper.

I turn to leave but feel Sadie's eyes on me.

"If you wanna know something about my son, know that he wasn't no punk kid. He wanted to be an orthopedic surgeon. His 'Plan B,' he called it. In case his dream of the pros didn't come true. Now no one's dreams will ever come true again." She struggles to her feet. "I need some air. Fucking pills. I should've known better."

Sadie brushes by me and disappears down the hallway.

"Look, H, I don't want to seem heartless, but Ozz shot himself. He was depressed. Depressed people kill themselves."

Hachi's eyes bore into me. "And some live to tell the tale."

I ignore the remark, fearful of making things about me again. "Kids are impulsive. They make split-second decisions that can't be taken back. Think of the shit we did when we were kids, right? I'm lucky I lived long enough to get blown up in Fallujah," I say, smiling, as if an IED under a Humvee is in the slightest bit humorous.

"Then that rat bastard Wynne had to go and bench Ozz for a game."

"What? Why? I thought he was the team's star player?"

"He was, but he had a few dropped balls. I can't remember what else, but he was benched for the game against Crystal Springs. A bunch of college scouts were there, and Ozz missed a big chance to show off his stuff." Her head drops to her chest. "He was devastated."

"Is Coach Wynne really a rat bastard? Seems like the boys like him—" I say, but stop myself from saying any more.

She wipes her nose with the back of her hand. "He's a great coach, don't get me wrong, but he pushes them boys hard. Day after day. Zero tolerance for error, that's what Ozz used to call it. Just like you military types say."

"Roger that. Being perfect is never easy."

I pull her to her feet.

"You of all people should know that."

I shepherd her to the door. "Like you're one to talk!"

She gives me a crooked smile.

"Another reason we're friends, I guess."

"Look, the autopsy will show he was taking Lexapro, but the cause of death was a gunshot, no matter what. I'm not sure there's much else to look at."

She stiffens. "There's not going to be an autopsy."

"What do you mean there's not going to be an autopsy?"

"The medical examiner already ruled that the cause of death was gunshot wound to the chest. Period. End of story. Just like you said."

I hesitate. I am well aware it's up to the M.E. whether to get an autopsy in suicides. And as far as the authorities are concerned, there's nothing to investigate. But . . .

I hold my breath to stop from rubbing more salt in the wound, but Hachi gives words to what we're both thinking.

"I went to the police, and they didn't want to have nothin' to do with me," she says, her resigned tone fine-tuned by a lifetime of inequitable treatment by those with authority. "Nothing to look into, they said, like you did. Damn cracker cop at the Sheriff's office wouldn't even hear me out. Told me to leave. Made me feel like shit on his shoe. Can they do that? Can . . ." Her voice fades into a mumble. "To the cops, Ozz is nothing more than another loser from the wrong side of the tracks, one less . . ." She looks away. "One less nobody for them to worry about."

I nod. There's no question in my mind, if Ozz had been a trust fund kid from Palm Beach Island, if he'd been me, there would have been an autopsy.

She shrugs and stands. "Forget it. I'm sorry I hauled you all the way back out here. You got a life you gotta get back to."

"It can wait." I turn her by the shoulder to face me. "Is there anything else you can tell me?"

She thinks for a second, then says, "Not that I owe him

shit, but when Trey got locked up, we promised him we'd do everything we could to get Ozz out of Sugar Bay. Maybe he knows what was bothering Ozz."

"Ozz used to visit his father, right?"

Hachi's eyebrows hunch up, a crease emerging on the bridge of her nose. "How d'you know that?"

I feel the blood drain from my face. Attorney-client privilege applies even if you're a dead client, and I don't need any more problems with the Florida Bar. "You told me that, didn't you? I mean, that's not a bad thing, right? He's still his father."

Hachi nails me with a look so venomous, I flinch. "That man got nothin' to say I wanna hear. Not anymore."

"Where'd Ozz get the gun?" I ask, hoping for an accusatory edge in my voice to divert her attention away from my misstep.

"Jesus Christ, woman! Where's anyone get a gun 'round here? Easy to get as the clap from a pay-by-the minute whore."

I stick my tongue in my cheek. "No one would ever accuse you of not calling them like you see them, H."

She turns her palms up. "Things is what they is. Guns on every street corner in these parts."

"Does Sadie keep a gun at home?"

Hachi blurts out a laugh. "Sadie won't even kill a spider. Takes the damn things back outside when she finds them in the house. Someone broke in here, she'd have to hit them over the head with a frying pan to defend herself. I keep tellin' her, she needs protection. Not like this is Palm Beach or anything," she says, and I feel the dig as a punch to the gut.

"Ozz got it from the streets, then."

She gives me a "no shit, Sherlock" look.

I glance up at the clock above Ozz's desk. "It's getting late. I need to get home."

"You can stay the night at my place if you want."

"Thanks, but no. Vinnie's been taking care of Miranda a lot lately. I don't want to—"

She shrugs. "Passed over for a dog. What will you do next?"

I go to speak, but she grips my arm to stop me. "You were right to pass right on by that day. I was no good to anyone at that point, least of all myself." She raises her chin. "I'm good now, though. Been clean for three hundred and thirty-three days."

Sadie sticks her head around the door, her face still blotchy from crying. "I'm leaving. Lock up when you leave."

"Sure," Hachi replies.

"She shouldn't be going back to work," I say.

She gives me a sharp look to signal that I shouldn't be trying to tell everyone what to do.

I hunch my shoulders. "Hey, don't hate on me. You said the same thing yourself!"

"We all got our ways of dealing, Grace, and mine is to make sure my sister is okay." She turns to leave. "You about ready? I'll wait for you outside. I can't stand to be in here any longer."

"Yeah, I'll be with you in a second."

Going through someone's dresser drawers may feel creepy, but we all have to bury our secrets somewhere. Underwear. Socks. A couple of dog-eared Playboy magazines. One box of condoms and a half-eaten Snickers bar.

"Yuck. Who keeps their snacks and their rubbers in the same place?"

T-shirts. Boxers. Socks.

A lock box?

I glance over my shoulder to make sure I'm still alone and pull my key chain from my pocket, from which hangs the tiny lock pick Vinnie gave me when he got sick of replacing the door keys I kept losing.

In a heartbeat, I jimmy the flimsy lock.

"And there we have it," I say to myself at the sight of several dozen round electric blue pills packed in tiny baggies, along with a thick stack of bills bound together by a rubber band. None of it surprises me, but it's nothing anyone else but me needs to know about at this point. No need to throw shade on the dead. Ozz's family has suffered enough, suffering being the unspoken cost of suicide, a seemingly self-destructive act, but also the most selfish, the only thing that stood between me and the trigger one dark night. That and Hachi.

I hear footsteps coming back down the hallway. "Grace, you coming?"

"Coming," I reply, trying to keep my tone neutral while stuffing the drugs and cash back into the drawer. No way I'm taking the chance of getting pulled over and getting caught with enough dope to ensure I spend my golden years locked up. Or enough to tempt me.

I meet Hachi outside and we stand side by side. We watch the sun slip over the horizon, leaving a glittery pink haze in its wake.

"Ozz and me, we used to watch the sunset out here together. That might've been the one thing he'd have missed if he'd gotten out of here."

I knock her shoulder with mine. "Except for his cool auntie."

Her eyes flood with tears.

I pull her in for a hug. "H, please forgive me for being a crap friend."

She observes me, her smile half sad, half conspiratorial. "I will if you say you'll help me. If there's nothing to know, fine. I'll move on."

I pull back. "Are you blackmailing me? You think I owe you because I acted like an asshat?"

She gives me the side-eye. "Crap friend? Maybe. Asshat? I wouldn't go that far, but now that you mention it . . ." She cocks her head. "If it were your kid, I'd do this for you."

I raise an eyebrow. "Now you are working me over, woman."

"Look, it doesn't take a genius to know there's more here than meets the eye. Isn't that what you said?"

I cock my head. "And what did I say?"

"Some shit about under the surface and—"

"Okay, okay." I sigh.

Her eyes light up.

"There may be one thing I can do," I say, knowing I'll regret even considering the notion that my nosing around might bring them some sort of peace, even if not the answers they want.

"Yeah, and what's that?" she replies, doubt back in her tone, or perhaps it's fear, as if to entertain hope would lead to more pain.

"I could speak to the M.E. Ask him to change his mind about the autopsy."

"You could do that?"

"I had a bunch of cases with Dr. Owen back when I was working for who I thought were the good guys."

She puts her hands on her hips. "You mean back when you were working for the Man, honey."

We both laugh, and the sound of us laughing together again sends a jolt of warmth through me.

"Yep, the good guys turned out to be badder than the bad guys." I shrug. "Funny how that happens when there's money on the table."

"But seriously, you think he might change his mind?"

I hesitate, reluctant to get her hopes up. "I can try, that's all I can promise. But if he does, the autopsy will have to be ASAP. The body hasn't been embalmed yet, has it? Internal organs deteriorate, which messes with the tests."

She gives a sharp shake of the head. "My people don't do that. It's against our ways. Besides, everything that gets buried out here comes up sooner or later. We're going to have Ozz cremated." She digs the heels of her hands into her eyes. "After we have the memorial day after tomorrow."

I give it a moment before speaking again, the prospect of having your kin getting sliced and diced and then reduced to ashes in a furnace horrific.

"I'll go see Dr. Owen first thing tomorrow."

She slips her arm around my shoulder. "Thanks."

I rest my head on her shoulder. "It's me who should be thanking you."

She tilts her head, confused.

"The jury in the Big Sugar case came back."

"Jesus, I forgot. The verdict." Her eyes bulge. "And?"

I take a bow. "The jury awarded us five million dollars."

She grabs her throat as if she can't breathe. "Holy crap! Those shitkickers could buy all of Sugar Bay with that kind of money."

"If we ever get it. Appeals can drag on forever."

She sighs. "Nothing ain't ever what it seems, is it?"

I take a last look back at the tidy bungalow.

"Let's go," I say. "It's getting dark."

8

Weighed down by a backpack stuffed with homework and library books, Ozz made his way home after the game, his body spent. Every game was high stakes now, high pressure, the hopes of the entire town on the team's shoulders, on his shoulders. Panther football was religion in Sugar Bay. No matter who or what you prayed to, Panther football was the common faith in town, but in exchange for their devotion, the zealous expected the home team to win each and every game.

Thankfully, the Panthers had delivered again—a thirty-six to seven beatdown of Laketown. True, they always beat Laketown by a country mile, but this game had seemed tougher than usual for Ozz, tougher to see the field, to read the coverages, anticipate the plays. The daily practices and Friday games were all beatdowns. Still, each practice, each play, each game, was one more rung on the ladder up and out of Sugar Bay. Whatever it took was what Ozz needed to do, and he was doing it come hell or high water, the latter not being uncommon in a town built on the flood plain of Lake Okeechobee.

Ozz shoved open the front door with his aching right hand, the fingers and forearm bandaged from the move he'd put on Laketown's brick wall of a defensive end. The dude had held on for dear life, clawing at him, but Ozz left him facedown in the dirt and put six points on the scoreboard in the process, the first of his three touchdowns of the night.

"You da man, son!"

Ozz squinted, his eyes not yet adjusted to the blazing light emitted by the fluorescent strips that reminded him of the lighting under which he saw his father every Sunday.

"Awesome game, son."

Something about the voice sounded familiar.

"Come on in," Sadie said, pulling him into the living room.

He blinked hard until the scene came into focus.

"You remember Mr. Spire?" Sadie said.

Ray Spire extended a hand. "Great to see you again, Ozz."

Ozz dropped his backpack and shook. "Phenom Camp, right?"

"Sure was," Spire said. "And this here is Coach Calhoun."

Ozz followed Spire's gaze to Trey's easy chair, to a ruddy-faced man with a nub of a chin and a gleam in his eyes that confirmed he knew how to get things done, how to win. But the man needed no introduction. Ozz knew all about Coach Calhoun. Calhoun was a legend. And here he was. In the flesh. Fitzgerald "Paddy" Calhoun—the head coach at the University of Southern California.

A surge of adrenaline shot through Ozz's body, as if he had the ball cradled in his arm and an empty field in front of him all the way to the end zone.

"Coach Calhoun, I . . ." he said. "What are you doing . . ."

Sadie smiled ear to ear. "Why don't I get y'all some sweet tea," she said, beating a hasty retreat.

Coach Calhoun laughed, a low rumble from deep within his barrel chest. "Why, I came all the way out here to see you, Ozz. That's what I'm doing," he said, his tone folksy, but his gaze penetrating, as if he were looking right through Ozz's skin, a human X-ray, here to determine if Ozz had the goods Coach was in need of.

"Why don't you come have a seat?" Calhoun said. He patted the arm of the couch adjacent to Trey's chair, exactly where Ozz and Trey used to sit every Sunday afternoon to watch football. Back before they sat at a cracked plastic picnic table and ate stale vending machine snacks.

Ozz fixed on Calhoun's right hand, his fourth finger adorned with a gold NCAA national championship ring.

Calhoun extended the hand to Ozz "You like the looks of that?"

Ozz dropped his eyes, heat rising in his cheeks.

"Maybe you can get you one of these one day too," Calhoun said, fingering the bulbous diamond-encrusted ring.

Sadie returned with a tray of drinks and passed them around. "I'll leave y'all to talk football," she said, backing out of the room as if retreating from royalty.

Not wanting to seem like a blithering idiot, Ozz summoned his courage and spoke the first words that sprang to mind. "Were you at the game tonight, Coach?"

"Sure was. And it was a doozy for you, Ozz." He jerked his chin in Spire's direction. "Mr. Spire and I both liked what we saw tonight. You remember Mr. Spire, don't you, Osceola?"

Ozz winced. He was proud of being the namesake of one of the greatest warriors of all time, *the* greatest if you believed Sadie and Hachi, but still, Osceola sounded like something you might call a cartoon princess.

Calhoun set his Coke down on the end table beside Trey's chair. "I'm sorry, should I call you Ozz?"

Ozz smiled. "Yes please, Coach."

"So, Ozz . . ." Calhoun paused and smiled. "I'd like to talk some business with you, if you don't mind." He leaned in, elbows on knees. "I hear from your mother that you're interested in coming to USC, is that right?"

Ozz hesitated, reluctant to put voice to his dreams, as if to do so might jinx them.

"See, I know a lot of other schools are going to be knocking on your door, but we wanted to be the first to tell you that . . ." Calhoun's tone turned serious. " . . . that if you're interested, there will be a spot for you on scholarship as a Trojan."

Ozz opened his mouth, but the words stuck in his throat.

A knowing grin spread across Calhoun's lips. "When you catch your breath, son, why don't you tell me if that's something you'd consider?"

Ozz nodded, and a few seconds later found himself confessing that going to USC had been his dream for as long as he could remember, how its top-notch football program and academics made it his first choice, how there's no way he could play anywhere cold, how . . . He knew he sounded like a babbling fool, but he couldn't help himself.

Calhoun leaned back and settled his hands on his mound of a belly. "Hell, then I'll take that as a yes."

Ozz covered his face with his hands. "Yes! Yes! Thank you, Coach."

Calhoun motioned to Spire that it was time to go. "We'll get you the paperwork when the time comes, but for now, I'll take your word as your bond, young man."

Ozz stood, legs shaky, and shook Calhoun's hand as hard and as many times as he had ever shaken anyone's hand.

"Welcome to the USC family," Calhoun said.

Ozz liked how that sounded. His USC family. He liked the sound of that. The Panthers would forever be his Sugar Bay family, along with his momma and Auntie Hachi, but it was time to move on and, God willing, up.

At the door, Calhoun turned, finger in the air. "At the Phenom Camp last month . . ."

Ozz dropped his head to his chest.

"Don't be like that, son. We all make mistakes. But if you want to play at the highest level—and you do, don't you?"

Ozz nodded.

"Then, you're going to need to be bigger, stronger, and faster than the next guy, son."

Ozz let the "son" pass this time. What was in a name anyway, especially when the person saying it is someone like Coach Calhoun?

Sadie reappeared. "Coach, he'll do whatever workouts he needs to be doing. You can take my word on that."

Ozz bit his lip. He'd tell her later what a kiss-ass she was being, even though he too sounded like one.

"I'm sure you'll do whatever it takes, Ozz. And we're here to give you all the help you need, whatever that may be, to turn you into the type of NFL prospect we know you are."

"I'll be in touch," Spire said, tapping an envelope on Ozz's shoulder. "In the meantime, why don't you two treat yourselves to a fancy dinner out?" He tossed the envelope on the coffee table and hustled out after Calhoun.

Sadie called from the kitchen. "Come on in here and get you some supper."

"Coming, Momma." Ozz attached the safety chain.

En route to the kitchen, he picked up the envelope and stuck it in his back pocket.

He'd play along, for now.

9

The sign declares, "When God Gives You More Than You Can Stand, Kneel."

"Roger that," I say. Life's brought me to my knees more than a time or two.

I manhandle my rental sedan with the turning radius of a cruise ship into a space opposite a row of windows painted white. "I've spent my share of time in tanks, and they maneuver better than this thing."

Without the sign, I would have thought I was in the wrong place. Mount Olive Baptist Church looks nothing like a church, at least not like the churches of my New England childhood. No centuries-old stone walls. No stained glass windows depicting the four apostles. No bell tower. Mount Olive is a strip mall storefront, wedged between a defunct nail salon with a bright orange eviction notice pasted to the door and Pappy's Pawn Shop, which is, according to the neon sign in the window, "O EN," the "P" obscured by an iron bar.

As I climb out onto the steaming, sticky asphalt, a man with skin the color of saddle leather and a wide smile appears.

"Reverend Mathias, I presume?"

"How'd you know?" He tugs at his dog collar, smiling. "And you would be Miss Grace?"

"How'd you know?"

He points at my briefcase. "Don't get many of those things around here." He encircles my outstretched hand with both of his own, the size of catcher's mitts. "It is indeed good to meet you," he says, his accent tinged with the lilting tones of the Caribbean. "From what I hear, you may be the new savior of some of my parishioners." He winks.

"Hardly, Reverend. But I do hope the verdict will be the first step in getting your people the justice they deserve." I hear the words "your people," Hachi's words and the Reverend's, but coming out of my mouth, they sound condescending, even though I've come to think of the pickers as "my people" after more than two years of fighting for them.

"Thanks for allowing me the use of your church for my meeting, Reverend."

"Not at all, Miss Grace. It is an honor to have you visit my humble sanctuary. Any friend of Miss Hachi's is a friend of Mount Olive's." He shoves open the door and stands aside. "Please, come in."

I step inside and stop in my tracks. All around, everything is white. Not cream, not ivory, but bright white, the kind of white used in paintings of Jesus ascending to heaven through rays of white light. Rows of white folding chairs take up much of the space. The only other furniture is a white lectern up front in the shadow of a rough-hewn pine cross, the one thing in the room not white. A pile of white hymnals sits on a white table in back. Strings of white doves suspended from the rafters by white ribbons flutter above us.

I twirl in circles, taking it all in. "This is not what I expected. Not at all."

Reverend Mathias beams, as if it's not the first time he's got this reaction. "Why would you? After all, it's nothing more than a grim strip mall. But appearances can be deceiving, can they not, Miss Grace?"

"Amen to that, Reverend," I say, blushing, ashamed of my preconceived notion that everything in a town as poor as Sugar Bay would have to be decrepit or on the road to decrepitude. But what was I expecting behind the whited-out windows? A bomb shelter of a church where congregants pray for better days to make the present bearable? Maybe. But whatever it was, it wasn't this haven of peace and beauty. Then again, what do I know about churches? The only time I go near a church nowadays is for NA meetings at St. Anthony's, a bastion of white privilege, whose scions deign to open the doors to a gaggle of drunks and junkies to assuage their upper-class guilt. Hell, I'm one of them, the upper class that is, or at least I was, so who am I to judge others for their judginess? I've judged plenty. Still do, according to Hachi.

Reverend Mathias leads me to the front of the sanctuary. "Sugar Bay is all about the muck, so when I opened this church, I wanted it to be about light and hope, Miss Grace." He eyes me. "Grace. Now that is a good name. We could all use a little of that from time to time."

I raise a hand. "Reverend, please call me Grace, no Miss required. Just plain Grace."

Reverend Mathias's eyes go to the cross. "Any grace at all is a blessing, don't you think?"

He pats the lectern. "I will leave you be, then, Just Plain Grace," he says, and disappears through a door marked Office.

I pull a sheet of paper from my briefcase and place it on the lectern—the notice of appeal filed by Big Sugar's counsel. Harmless enough to look at, short and to the point, something most legal documents most certainly are not, yet the few words are momentous—a single page with the potential to reverse the good fortune of the pickers, not to mention my own. While it's not unexpected, I'm not looking forward to telling my clients that our victory has been put on hold, for now at least, until the appellate court rules. For people who live paycheck to paycheck, the news will be devastating.

I reach back into my briefcase for the case file, my hand brushing over the cool steel of the handgun buried under a mountain of paper. A last-minute call, as my mother, Faith, would say. "Better safe than sorry, dear," although I'm sure she wasn't referring to arming myself with a nine millimeter. More likely, she meant in the way she always says, "Don't swim right after lunch, dear. It might make you ill. Better safe than sorry."

The pickers filter in, some in muddy work boots, others in shapeless uniforms and T-shirts bearing company logos. One by one they fill the rows of chairs, their soiled work clothes looking even dirtier against the brilliant whiteness of their surroundings. A few have children in tow. They sit in silence, motionless, as if one wrong move or word will break the spell, turn them back into paupers. All have eyes that belie their fear, perhaps expectation, that what has been given could be taken away, fear engendered by their belief that they are people upon whom the fates do not smile.

I square my shoulders. "Good evening and thank you for coming." I hesitate, casting around for the right words to cushion the blow. "I know we were all thrilled with the jury's decision, but there's something I must tell you."

A man in the back row stands and removes a battered wide-brimmed straw hat. "Miss Locke, when are we going to get our money?" All heads swivel in his direction.

I swallow hard and look down at the notes I scribbled on an index card to keep me on point. I rehearsed what I was going to say, had it down pat, and, standing alone in front of the mirror in my bathroom, it had all sounded good, reasoned and reasonable, but now those same words fly out the window right along with my composure.

I run my tongue over my dry lips. "That's what I want to discuss. I think you'll remember that I explained to you that, if we won, there was a good chance that Big Sugar would appeal." I pause to gather my thoughts, my resolve to lay out the facts without sugarcoating them weakening second by second. How easy it would be to tell them it's simply a matter of time. That everything will work out in the end. But that would require stretching the truth, would give them false hope that, like all hope, is an illusion, a substitute for the harsh reality that deep pockets are better than empty ones.

"Let me cut to the chase. The fact is, Big Sugar is appealing the jury's decision."

A collective outcry surges through the rows, building in intensity until the wave breaks wide open with everyone speaking at once, rapid-fire, in a host of languages—Spanish, Creole, English, and a couple of others I don't recognize.

A barn-door-sized man in the front row shakes a clenched fist at me. "We want our money."

Following the man's lead, the crowd's roars soon coalesce into a unified chant of "We want our money! We want our money!"

I grab the lectern for support in the face of the onslaught unlike any I've ever experienced as a lawyer, both in kind and ferocity. As a prosecutor, I faced down murderers and rapists, brought them to their knees until they begged for mercy. Back then it was easy to ignore their anger, labeling it as self-inflicted and self-serving. But this is different. These are the victims, people cheated out of what they are owed by an unscrupulous conglomerate that sees them not as humans but as an expendable resource to be depleted and discarded with the trash.

I raise my hands, palms out. "Please, if you would let me finish. I'd be glad to stay all night to answer every last one of your questions."

After a minute or two of talking among themselves, an expectant hush falls over the room.

"What the appeal means is that Big Sugar is challenging what the jury decided, and it'll be up to the—"

Even before the words are out of my mouth, I know they will be cold comfort. Nothing more than legal gibberish. But before I can finish, the man in the front row leaps to his feet, face red with rage. "We need the money now. Not later—now! We want our money now!"

"I understand, sir, but . . . there's going to be a delay."

"For how long?" he asks, an engorged vein protruding from his forehead.

Telling this crowd that most appeals take at least a year, that the district court of appeals is more backed up than a porta-pottyat a rock concert, is likely to incite a riot. I fudge. "Maybe a few months."

Everyone is up now, pointing at me, shouting, chanting, "Money now! Money now!" I can't breathe. I cast around, looking for a safe way to get the hell out of here.

On the verge of bolting, Reverend Mathias appears at my side. "Please, everyone, please stay calm and let Miss Grace speak."

Reverend Mathias positions himself between me and the mob, his arms outstretched in benediction. "Please, let Miss Grace speak. Remember, she is the one who helped you when no one else would."

After a few seconds of grumbling, everyone sits back down, with the exception of the instigator from the front row. He digs a slug of chewing tobacco out of a can and stuffs it in his cheek, crosses his arms, and stares daggers at me.

"Thank you, Reverend," I say, conscious of the man's predatory gaze, his body a tight coil of energy waiting to be unleashed. "I feel certain that you will all get your fair share, but it will take some time."

Wait! What the hell am I saying? There are no guarantees. The appellate court might as easily decide the jury was full of it and overturn the verdict, or that some error or other I made justifies a new trial, or any number of other unimaginables, all of which would have the effect of leaving them empty-handed.

I scan the room. While a few eyes still blaze, many others have started to fill with the look of resignation, the recognition that, as with all dreams, the win was just that, a dream. Even they don't buy my hollow words.

"There may be another option," I say, my tone hesitant, not sure if I believe what I am about to say, given how Big Sugar has dug its heels in every step of the way. "Given the size of the verdict, Big Sugar may be willing to negotiate. I know they weren't before the trial, but now they might agree to drop the appeal if I can get them to agree to a reasonable settlement offer."

"Yeah, and what the hell would reasonable look like to you?" the instigator says, moving toward me.

Reverend Mathias steps into the man's path. "Arturo, please take a seat. Everyone here is in the same boat."

A chastened Arturo drops back into a chair.

I start to explain the negotiation process, but a young woman in the back raises a hand.

I point at her, willing my hand not to shake. "Yes?"

"Would that mean we'd get paid and not have to wait?"

"Yes, that's what negotiating a settlement would mean."

A few heads nod. Others lean into neighbors for a translation.

"But to talk about any settlement, I'll need your go-ahead. All of you." I brace myself and look Arturo in the eye. "Even you, Arturo."

Arturo glares at me, then at the young woman.

The young woman stands. "Maybe we should consider what she's saying," she says, her voice shaky.

Lots of heads bobbing up and down. A scowling Arturo throws his hands in the air in disgust.

"Shall we take a vote about making a settlement offer?" I glance down at Reverend Mathias, who is still holding his ground. "Reverend, maybe you can help me count the votes?"

"Of course," he replies.

"Okay, if you want me to try to get Big Sugar to drop the

appeal and pay you whatever I can negotiate, please raise your hand. Of course, I'll share any offer with you to get your agreement."

Several hands go up, followed by many more, until everyone's hand is raised. All except for Arturo's.

I take a deep breath to calm my nerves. I might have a law degree to fall back on if this all goes south, but I've got a lot at stake here too, and less money now beats maybe nothing later. Trusting three old men in black robes who get campaign contributions from Big Sugar every year is not what I need to be doing.

"I'll even agree to cut my fee down to twenty percent, instead of the thirty we agreed on," I say.

Arturo grunts in the way the powerless do when feigning power is the one and only type of power they have left.

"Our agreement says that whatever the majority of you decide rules. But you do have another option if you're not happy with any agreement I strike with Big Sugar to avoid an appeal. I know this sounds like legal mumbo jumbo and it is, but because each of you is an individual plaintiff and not a member of a class, you can refuse to sign the settlement papers and move forward with the appeal process on your own with another lawyer. It's your choice."

Without warning, Arturo rushes me, but Reverend Mathias blocks him, leaving Arturo sprawled on the floor.

Arturo gets to his feet, spits a bulbous, wet wad of tobacco at me, and heads for the exit, but not before pointing a hand at me, cocked in the shape of a gun.

Shaken, my good leg buckles at the knee and I stumble forward, managing to catch myself on the lectern at the last second.

For several seconds, no one so much as flinches, until a burly young man steps out of the crowd.

"Let me help you," he says, leading me by the arm to a chair in the front row and brushing the wet wad off my sleeve.

I sit, fists clenched in my lap to keep me from going after Arturo. Back in Iraq, I took down men as big as him, put them on their knees begging me not to shoot. But that was back when I was a biped and there was an actual enemy. Despite the rage he leveled at me, Arturo isn't my enemy. While he is frightening, he too is a victim.

"Are you okay, Grace?" Reverend Mathias asks.

I nod. "Nice tackle, Reverend. It would seem that the scriptures were not all you learned in divinity school."

He salutes. "Defensive end, first string, Sugar Bay Panthers at your service."

I manage a smile and let him guide me back to the lectern to finish what I have to say.

I clear my throat and check to make sure Arturo is gone. "I'll discuss a possible settlement with Big Sugar's lawyers tomorrow. All I'm asking for now is that you all go home and think about your options. Let's meet again same time same place next week."

On the way out, I overhear the young man who helped me translating what I said into Creole for an older man I assume to be his father, a man as frail as his son is strong.

Reverend Mathias offers me his arm. "Let me escort you to your car."

I hook my arm through his again. "Thank you, Reverend Defensive End Mathias."

"Better safe than sorry, Miss Grace."

"I couldn't have said it better myself."

10

The locker room reeked of sweat. The throat gagging, nostril burning, hold-your-nose kind of sweat. The kind of sweat born of loss, of pain, the kind that obliterates any memory of the sweet scent of sweat born of victory, the ominous kind that casts into doubt the prospect that victory will ever again be possible.

Ozz yanked on his practice jersey and stole a glance at Whitey. Whitey held his head high. He intended to capitalize on Ozz's mistake last Friday night, intended to leverage the team's loss into an opportunity for himself to become the first-string running back, no damn rabbits required.

And why not? Shit, Ozz would do the same thing in his place. His last-minute goal line fumble had cost the Panthers the win against Sun Coast, a team Sugar Bay had never lost to. Not once, not until last Friday. The Sun Coast Rebels was a misnomer in Ozz's book if he'd ever heard one. The Rebels were a team of trust fund kids from a private school in the Naples suburbs, the type who get cars on their sixteenth birthdays and college funds set up when they're in diapers. The type of kid Ozz might be like on the inside, what with his 4.0 GPA and dreams of being a doctor, but not on the outside.

Ozz told himself to get his game face on. This was no time to show weakness. Whitey was gunning for his starting job sure as the sun would rise tomorrow on Sugar Bay, and sure as the place would still be the same hellhole it had always been. Ozz might have a size advantage on Whitey, but what Whitey had on Ozz was he'd had nothing to do with the loss to the Rebels.

Coach Wynne strode in, clipboard in hand, ever-present stopwatch and whistle hanging from a lanyard around his bull neck. "You slugs be slower than molasses on a winter day. Come on, men! Get them pads on and get out on the field before I deprive your sorry asses of any hope of playing in a Panther uniform again."

A collective groan rose up from the players.

"You heard me. All hands on deck in full battle rattle. And now! And I don't wanna hear another damn word about it. Not after what happened on Friday night. That crap was plain embarrassing."

Ozz stared at the dinged-up helmet in his hands. The prospect of another full-contact practice made his joints ache, but in Coach's world, no-tackle practices were for "sissies." Coach presided over his practices like a symphony conductor, breaking them into three movements. First, calisthenics—push-ups, sit-ups, and jumping jacks supplemented by running laps for those caught slacking off. Next, drills with position coaches, all of it capped off with thirty minutes of full-on mayhem, a "practice" game for Coach to decide the roster for Friday night. Fail to play hard, you'd be benched. Fail to execute, benched. Fail to hurt the opponent, benched. No excuses.

A few more games, that's all Ozz needed, then on to sunny California. With enough credits to graduate early, no way was he hanging around until May, sitting in classes for credits he didn't need taught by teachers who didn't give a shit. No way was he taking his chances on the street, running for Junior any longer than necessary.

Junior. The mere mention of the name had his guts in a knot.

He told himself to calm down. That worrying about what might not happen was a waste of energy. But, what if Junior . . . ?

He slapped himself. Get a grip! One day at a time. Means to an end. For now, all he needed to do was be patient, win games, and do whatever it took to stay in Junior's good graces.

Coach fixed the players with his "don't you try me, boys" stare. "Man up!" he boomed. "Sugar Bay don't raise no sissies, does she?" He waited for the ritual "no sir" from the players, then led them out of the locker room like the Pied Piper of the gridiron.

Ozz said a silent prayer, crossed himself, and fell in line. Coach may have been an old-timer, but he never missed a beat. Every practice. Every play. Every game. Everything counted. No one got a free pass, even if you were a sure shot for a scholarship. The way Coach saw it, you owed him for that chance and you owed it to your teammates to do all you could to make sure they got their chance at a scholarship, too. Everyone, no matter how talented or sought after, had to earn playing time. Coach wouldn't play you if you sucked in practice, dropped the ball, let up on the run before the end zone, no matter how good you'd been the play, the game, the week before.

And scouts, you never knew when they'd be in the stands in your one-stoplight town on game day, shooting film, scribbling notes, to send back to teams with legendary names like the Alabama Crimson Tide and the Notre Dame Fighting Irish, or, in Spire's case, the University of Southern California Trojans. And then there were the agents lurking around in the shadows, the guys with greasy hair and shiny suits who weren't supposed to have any contact with the players or their families, but that was a rule honored in the breach. No one was policing squat out here in the swamp, especially when there was money and reputations involved. Out here, the NCAA stood for Nobody

Cares Athletic Association. Sure, Ozz had his deal sewn up with USC, but it was never too late to change his mind if a better one came along. Dog eat dog was the only rule anyone cared about out here.

Coach pointed at him. "Don't be thinkin' you can get by on your talent. You're only as good as your last game. You gotta execute, son. And from what I saw on Friday, you got executed by Sun Coast's defense."

Ozz fastened his helmet strap and jogged to the huddle. "A few more games, that's all," he repeated to himself as the center snapped the ball and the quarterback handed it off to Ozz for a running play from the twenty-yard line, a play Ozz had completed a thousand times.

Head down, Ozz sprinted upfield, ball nestled in the crook of his arm, shoulder dipped to fend off defenders swarming from all directions.

A force so violent came from behind that hee felt as if he had been hit by a garbage truck. First, his neck ratcheted back. His torso followed, flipping up in an arc before slamming down on the turf.

Then his lights went out.

—

A shape-shifting face, an oozing image like he were looking in a fun house mirror.

An acerbic smell under his nose, a rocket to the brain.

He blinked again and again, trying to assemble the puzzle pieces dancing in front of his eyes.

Finally, Coach Wynne's face came into focus.

He struggled to sit up.

"Relax, son."

He felt all head, no limbs. He was an enormous hammering head, blood pounding in his temples like a river on the verge of breaking its banks.

A circle of faces looking down, their features liquid.

"Everyone stand back. Give him some air." It sounded like Coach, but why was he speaking underwater?

The faces melted away.

Blue sky dotted with puffy clouds.

Tugging on his chin strap. Taking off his helmet.

An open hand dropped down in front of his face. "Nice and easy, okay?"

He pushed himself up onto his elbows and squinted against the caustic sunlight. Once he got to a seated position, he rested his head on his knees atop crossed arms. Each breath required a supreme effort, as if there were a refrigerator on his chest.

He willed his limbs to move until they did. Toes first. Feet next. Legs. Arms.

Pixel by pixel, the hit reassembled itself in his mind's eye.

The ball stuffed into his hands by the quarterback.

Running like the wind.

Then darkness.

A hand waggled in front of his face and he reached for it, missing it the first time like a kitten batting at a length of string, before making contact the second, which required a superhuman concentration that made his head pound even more.

An arm pulled up on his hand, and another grabbed him under his armpits from behind, levering him off the ground like a sack of cement.

He hobbled off the field suspended between two Panther uniforms.

—

"You wanted to see me, Coach?" Ozz said, poking his head around Coach Wynne's door.

Coach continued mapping out a play on a whiteboard with x's and o's and arcing lines. "Come on in, son. Take a seat."

He sat, clutching his ball cap in both hands, sculpting the brim to disguise his shaking hands.

Without saying another word, Coach closed the door.

The pit in Ozz's stomach got larger and larger as he ran through the possible consequences of what had happened the week before against the Rebels. One, benched. Two, benched. Three, benched. There was no way around it. Coach was a man of his word.

Coach propped his feet up on the desk. "How you feelin', son?"

He focused on the whiteboard. "Fine, Coach."

"I coulda sworn you were faster than that Rebel cornerback. You remember him at all, the one who recovered your fumble and ran it in for a touchdown and the win?"

Ozz suppressed the urge to beg for forgiveness. He needed to play. Needed to win. But there was no mistaking it, he'd misread the coverage. And Coach wasn't one for forgiveness. What Coach wanted was results, not explanations.

"I think I am as fast, Coach."

Coach grunted. "Is that so?" He slipped a pencil out from behind his ear and pointed it at him. "Not from where I is, you ain't. And not from where you sat flat on your sorry ass after that simple running play at practice."

Ozz looked at his hands, the brim of his cap now a pointy beak. He should stab that thing into his eye and call it a day. Go home and resign himself to living out the rest of his days cutting cane and dying young.

"Boy, I coulda sworn you had better eyes than to miss that cornerback closing in on you. He wan't movin' that fast." He shook his head hard. "Hell, it wasn't even a game. It was just practice."

Ozz nodded. He'd always had great instincts for who was where, who was behind him, who was down the field, which way to cut, the exact moment to strong-arm the defender. How had he missed Williams? The dude was as big as a freaking dump truck. "I'm sorry, Coach."

"I'm sorry too, son." Coach laced his hands behind his head. "Yes siree. I'm mighty sorry that you won't be playing this Friday.

We sure will miss you." He gave a saccharine smile. "But, if I were a bettin' man, not as much as you'll miss us. Whitey sure will be happy, though."

He opened his mouth to speak, but Coach beat him to it. "And it might be more than this Friday 'less you pick up your game."

He scooted to the edge of his seat. "But, Coach . . ."

"But nothin', son."

Ozz squeezed his eyes shut to block out the image of his future, the one he'd dreamed of every night and every waking hour since he'd put on pads, disappearing.

Coach's eyes softened. "I think you know how important you are to this team. How much the other players, especially the young ones, look up to you, wanna be you."

Various permutations of how sorry he was, how he'd work harder, not make any more mistakes ran through Ozz's mind, all of which he knew were just that—words. He bit his tongue.

"The team needs you, Ozz. You're their captain. I need you. You need you. We all need you to play like I know you can. You took one helluva hit. You seen a doctor?"

"Nah, I'm good, Coach," he said, even though his vision had been blurry ever since.

Coach eyed him for a second. "You ain't got insurance. That it?"

Ozz looked away. Maybe one day he'd be a doctor, but for now, seeing one was not in the cards.

Coach dropped his feet to the floor and leaned in. "Don't you worry about that, son. We got you covered. We're on the same team, remember?"

11

The county morgue is a Quonset hut, a tin can with an even tinnier roof that looks like a hurricane casualty waiting to happen. Yet, the ethereal reflection of the sun off the crenelated aluminum siding, the heat rising like a desert mirage off the asphalt path, gives it an otherworldly aura.

Dr. Owen, an elderly gentleman in a rumpled tweed suit topped by a halo of white hair, greets me the moment I step into the super-refrigerated air.

"Grace Locke. Well, I'll be. How are you?" he says, his voice laced with a disarming Southern drawl, a welcome salve in this grim setting.

He shakes my hand, his grip much firmer than his diminutive stature might suggest. "I must admit, I was surprised to get your call. I thought you'd turned all fancy-pants on us and left the charms of the criminal world behind for greener, and shall we say, richer pastures?"

Owen's self-deprecating humor coaxes a smile onto my lips. The physical uplift brightens my mood, which has vacillated somewhere between anger at myself for having given in to Hachi's pleas and guilt for having abandoned her in her hour of need. Regardless, she twisted my arm, again. So here I am, on a futile errand when I should be doing real work, work that pays, work that has been piling up along with my bills since the Glades Bowl.

"Not a chance, Doctor. Just a short hiatus on the civil side. I'll be back in the criminal saddle soon." I grip his cold hand with both of mine. "It's been too long."

"You mean too long since that last case we worked together? The one with the bodybuilder found naked in a fifty-gallon Rubbermaid container weighed down by a boat chain fit to tie up the Titanic, all courtesy of a jilted girlfriend? I don't think too long would be long enough away from that, how shall I say it, shit show?"

I stifle a smile as he leads me down a dingy hallway, flickering fluorescent lights chirping above us like crickets.

"Thanks for seeing me on such short notice."

"Think nothing of it, my dear. It's always a pleasure to get live visitors," he says with a wink that gives me the briefest of views into him as a young man, the innocent curiosity he surely had and quality he still projects even after a career tending to the dead.

With a wave of his bony hand, he signals for me to take a seat in one of the two mismatched client chairs. "Counselor, tell me. How do you like the more civil side of the law?"

"The truth is, Doc, the money may be better, but more civil it is not. Business types will stab you in the back as fast as look at you. Me, I prefer the full-frontal assault and a little blood to keep me on my toes."

"I agree!"

He lowers himself into a padded chair behind a metal desk, the kind paper pushers in the Army hide behind. "I imagine all that arguing about other people's money gets old." He moves a pile of paperwork to the side to see me better. "And it is always about money, is it not? At least from my experience in civil court it is. I can see how that might make a person wish for some good old blood and guts to spice things up." He pops a chalky peppermint into his mouth and shakes the tin at me until I relent and take one.

"So, dear, what can I do you for?" he asks.

If I hadn't known him for years, I might be offended by the term of endearment in a professional setting, but the man is in his late seventies, wears a pocket watch his great-grandfather had worn in the War Against the States, as progeny of the Old South call the Civil War. I am not about to teach the old dog new manners.

"Doc, I need you to perform an autopsy for me."

He peers at me over his half-glasses as if I were a sample in a petri dish. "Why, you look as alive as alive can be, Miss Locke. Whatever could you want with an autopsy?"

"I see all the years in this dungeon haven't cost you your sense of humor," I say, casting an arm around his cramped office lined with faux wood paneling straight out of a '60s sitcom and a filing cabinet balanced on a brick. Had it not been for Dr. Owen's medical degree from the University of Alabama hanging on the wall next to an autographed picture of him and Bear Bryant, the place could have been a temporary trailer on a construction site.

"Never, never, never lose your sense of humor, is what I say. It should be the last thing to go before your heart gives out." He shifts in his seat. "Tell me about that autopsy you think should have happened."

I settle back into my chair. "I've been retained on a case. By the family of a young man, a football player, who shot himself."

He removes his glasses and rubs the bridge of his nose. "At the Glades Bowl. Yes, I am familiar with the case. A true tragedy. I declined to perform an autopsy in the matter, though." He clears his throat. "But you knew that already, didn't you? And that is why you are here. To ask me to change my mind."

I sense beads of sweat erupting on my brow at the memory of Ozz, prone on the stretcher, arms dangling over the side. I suck in several short breaths.

Dr. Owen leans forward, a look of avuncular concern on his face. "Are you okay, Miss Locke?"

"I'm fine. It's just that . . . that I was there."

His eyes go wide.

I blink hard and try to focus.

He folds his hands in front of him on the desk. "The young man's unfortunate death would seem to be a cut-and-dried death, however. A suicide. What could an autopsy possibly reveal?"

I scoot forward to the edge of my seat. "Dr. Owen, I think you would agree that healthy young men, especially ones with futures to look forward to, don't generally kill themselves, and certainly not in front of five thousand witnesses."

"I would agree with you there."

"But you have the option of requiring an autopsy in cases of suicide, especially if narcotics may have been involved, don't you?"

He nods.

"What if I told you there may have been more going on than met your eye? I mean, why would a talented kid like Ozz Gordon want to kill himself?"

He leans back in his chair, twirling his glasses by a leg. "Miss Locke, I may be a mighty fine forensic pathologist with decades of experience, but no autopsy I have ever done has revealed what was going on in a person's head."

"No, but you can tell what was going on in their blood."

"Whatever do you mean?"

"What if I told you narcotics were found in Ozz's room? The law requires that an autopsy be performed in such circumstances, correct?"

"Drugs are indeed a scourge for our times, especially in some of our poorer communities," he says, a comment that is not only condescending, it doesn't even answer my damn question.

"Nothing can bring the boy back, Miss Locke."

Although I don't disagree with his opinion regarding the futility of my request, what's starting to piss me off is the one thing Hachi and I agree on—that if Ozz had been anything other than a kid from the wrong side of the tracks with a father in prison, an autopsy would have been performed, even if just to give the family "closure," a concept I believe in even less than praying for things to be fine.

"Don't you think the family deserves to know the truth?" I say.

A shadow passes over his face. "Given what you've suggested about possible drug use, I think you would do well to remember that, sometimes, the truth can hurt more than it can help." He looks at his hands. "And, as you know, resources are limited these days."

I motion to a wall covered with photographs of Owen with politicians, all insincere smiles and firm handshakes for the camera. I point to one of him with Governor Stanley Strong, a Republican, handing Dr. Owen an award of some kind.

"I have a sneaking suspicion that if Ozz Gordon had been a white kid from Palm Beach Island, that some of those resources would have been used, no questions asked."

He twists his mouth, then straightens it out again. "The young man would still be dead, though, am I not correct?"

"What if Ozz had some physical ailment? Like a brain tumor?"

He holds his hands up. "You're grasping at straws here, Miss Locke."

I poke my index finger at the state flag on a crooked pole in the corner. "May I remind you, sir, that you are appointed by the governor, who is elected by the people of the Great State of Florida, and that you are paid with their tax dollars. How do you think it will look if word gets out, say someone puts those words in a reporter's ear, that those very same dollars are being used in a way that favors the rich, the less fortunate among us be damned?"

His jaw tightens. "I assure you that no such thing has occurred."

"And I can assure you that I will make whatever public information requests I have to regarding autopsies in cases of suicide, and that I will analyze that data with a fine-tooth comb looking for discrepancies based on socioeconomic status and race."

I sit back and revel in our stare-down. Much like winning, I've always liked to stick my finger in the eye of those in positions of authority a bit more than I should.

He averts his eyes.

"I think you know from your experiences with me in the past that I can be the proverbial dog with a bone."

His bushy white eyebrows hunch together like bat wings over his rheumy eyes. "Perhaps you're being so insistent because you were treated unfairly by the authorities yourself in the past and now you think that we owe you something?"

I bite my lip. He may be an old geezer, but he certainly has my number.

"The boy wasn't your family, was he?"

"That is irrelevant, but for your information, I'm close to his aunt. I'd like her to have some peace, that's all."

"In my experience, as I am sure was the case in yours as a prosecutor, so-called closure is a fantasy."

I flop back in my chair. I thought it was only dead bodies he was good at reading, not minds. "Look. If an autopsy tells us nothing, fine."

I track his gaze to a framed photograph on his desk, a stubby woman with a doughy face and a helmet of gray hair with her arms around a gaggle of squirming children. He tilts his head to the side, his wrinkled face more youthful again, as if the ghost of the young man he once was has made another appearance.

His expression reverts to dead serious. "I will caution you,

Miss Locke, sometimes knowing can be more painful than not. We all should be careful what we wish for, even when we have the best of intentions."

"So, you'll do it?"

He nods.

"If money's the issue, I can—"

"No, money is not the issue." He eyes me over his spectacles. "Even if it were, I have a feeling you would persuade me that it shouldn't be."

"Roger that," I say, with a salute that he returns.

He shifts his gaze to Oscar, in full view today. Recently, I decided I need to wear skirts more often, the stares be damned.

"I was Army too," he says. "Different war, though."

I shake my head. "Same war. They're all the same."

He slaps his palms down on the desk. "Enough talk of the past. Let's get down to brass tacks, shall we? The sooner the better. Organs degrade, and degraded internal organs corrupt the toxicology."

"I seem to remember that," I reply, the image of decomposing organs enough to make me gag. "There's a memorial tomorrow and the cremation right after."

"I'll call the hospital and make arrangements to go out there tomorrow."

"Well, okay," I say, surprised at his transition from dead stop to full speed ahead. There's life left in the old bird yet.

"It's settled, then. Tomorrow it is." He flattens his hands on the desk and looks me in the eye. "One last thing, for the record, however. I would never discriminate against anyone based on how much they have in the bank," he says, reminding me of his humble roots. We worked a case together years back, the murder of a pastor for the collection bag after church. As we waited for the jury's verdict in a stuffy room at the State's Attorney's office, he shared that his late father had been a pastor in the Mississippi Delta, ministering to field hands and sharecroppers.

I look away, ashamed at my outburst, the overzealousness of

which surprised even me. "I'm sorry, Doctor."

He nods. "Apology accepted. We all let our emotions get the better of us from time to time." He rubs his hands together as if to warm them, the age-spotted skin as delicate as tissue paper. "It's when we stop feeling that we should worry."

"Would you like me to drive you out to Sugar Bay?"

He frowns. "Despite the deceptively tranquil name, it's better you drive. An old geezer in a tweed jacket wandering around out in the boondocks might not attract the kind of attention I want."

"No problem. I was planning on going to the memorial anyway. But forewarned is forearmed, Doctor. I've been told I have a lead foot."

He winks. "All the better. I feel the need for speed. The pace of things here is beginning to get to me."

"Beginning? What took you so long? You've been cooped up here for decades."

"Indeed, Counselor, but lately I'm starting to find all the death oppressive."

"I'll pick you up tomorrow at ten a.m.."

"Thank you, Miss Locke."

"And Dr. Owen, please call me Grace." I smile and turn to leave before he changes his mind.

"As you wish, Grace. And you can call me Dr. Owen." He stands and pulls himself up to his full height. "You know, you didn't need to threaten me as you did. Such behavior is conduct unbecoming a good soldier like you."

I drop my head to my chest. "Roger that. And for that I apologize."

12

Ozz fell in line behind the guard, same guy as always, white dude with a shaved head and a balloon gut.

Hands on his gun belt, the guard corralled Ozz and a handful of others into a closet-sized space between a floor-to-ceiling iron gate and the door to the inmate visiting area.

Ozz flinched when the gate clanked shut, a hollow, forbidding sound he hadn't grown used to even after two plus years of coming to the Federal Detention Center in Miami. Its finality, its shrill message, always took his breath away. But Trey Gordon was his father, the only one he would ever have, so Ozz kept on coming, although Sadie would have preferred Ozz forget Trey ever existed.

"You ready for the season to get started again, Wiz?" the guard asked.

Ozz stared at the floor and willed the man to shut up. He didn't need the others staring at him like they were, like they always did when they figured out that the kid in line with them was the one whose photo appeared on the front page of the sports section every Saturday morning.

But, as usual, the guard didn't. "I know you gonna be kicking ass and taking names, isn't that right, son?"

"I ain't your son" were the words on the tip of Ozz's tongue, but he held it. He knew better than to defy authority. Every damn visit, the dude asked some lame question about football, talked to him as if he were his best bud. Always tried to make it look to the other sorry asses in line that he had some kind of stake in Ozz. Ozz had grown used to the bullshit, but it still pissed him off. Shit, maybe the guy was trying to be nice, make him feel special, or at least not as crappy as he felt every time he saw his father in an orange jumpsuit, the same man who'd taught him to throw a spiral, how to block, and how to spin away from defenders with the grace of a ballerina but the power of a Mack truck.

What did this guy from Miami think he knew about Glades football anyway? He might talk a good game, but he didn't know shit about what it took to survive out beyond the city limits. And no one got to call him Wiz, except his teammates, or son, except Trey and Coach. What was that about? The papers called him the Glades Express, but that was lame too. To his friends he might be the Wiz, but to his father, he was a kid with a plan, one they had worked on together since he'd been able to lace up his cleats.

Being singled out in here was the last thing he needed. He dragged himself here once a week for one reason—to spend time with Trey, not to jaw about football. Football was what he did so he didn't ever have to be locked up in one of these places, looking at the sky through chicken wire.

But the truth was, he'd come here today not just to see Trey. A chill ran the length of his spine as he remembered Miguel dead in the gutter, as if the man's life hadn't meant a thing. And it hadn't. Not to Junior. Junior hadn't given a rat's ass that Miguel had a wife and kids, and another on the way. That he'd come on a raft made of sticks from Cuba and nearly died in the process. That he deserved more. They all did. Even if "more" was just to live another day.

The guard selected a key from a bunch on a steel ring as big as a hula hoop and opened the door to the visiting area. "Ain't this your senior year, son?"

Ozz pasted on a tight smile. Shit, maybe he shouldn't be defensive. Answer the guy's questions. Be polite to strangers, like Trey always taught him. But Ozz hadn't been feeling much like himself lately. Didn't even feel like playing video games much anymore. He'd even gotten B's on a couple of tests, not his usual A's, because he couldn't bring himself to remember the right answers even though he knew them. There was no two ways about it, he needed good grades to be pre-med regardless of how many touchdowns he had. He needed to fit in too, to be a team leader, so he made sure to memorize the lyrics to the latest tunes and shot off his mouth about studying being for losers, but he was smart, and he intended to use those smarts. Every last thing Ozz did had a purpose. He wasn't going to be just another jock without an exit plan. The endgame—get out of Sugar Bay. The short game—do it on a football scholarship. Today's game—figure out how to deal with the elephant in his brain, the one that could derail everything. The one called Junior.

The frigid space was large enough for a dozen picnic tables, orange molded-plastic affairs with benches attached, the type meant for mothers to sit together and watch over their kids on the swing set. A row of vending machines loaded with overpriced sodas, candy, and potato chips, delicacies for a population fed the standard incarceration diet of bologna sandwiches and shoe-leather hamburgers, stood at the far end. Four guards patrolled the room, vigilant for any physical contact between inmates and visitors lest contraband be exchanged in the guise of a hug. Every visitor was subject to search upon arrival, and all possessions had to be left in lockers in the entryway, yet, according to Trey, cell phones and drugs were not in short supply.

"Yes, sir. It's my senior year," Ozz replied before making a beeline for their usual table in the far back corner, out of earshot of wives, girlfriends, and baby mamas, and whatever cops, lawyers, or snitches might be listening. A place like this had ears. And Ozz had a story he didn't need anyone hearing—the real reason he was here to see Trey.

A train of inmates shuffled in, hands cuffed in front and attached to waist chains connected to leg chains and ankle irons. The men scanned the room, like kids at school pick-up, trying to look nonchalant, but the twitch in each of their eyes said they were petrified they'd been abandoned once and for all.

Trey nodded at Ozz. His face was drawn, skin ashen. He looked much older than when he'd taken the plea and been convicted of drug trafficking, but he still projected strength, his wiry, muscled body rippling under his jumpsuit.

Trey slid onto the bench, cuffed hands in his lap clasped together as if he were in church. "You look good, son."

Ozz forced a smile and reached into his pocket for a roll of quarters. "Let me know if you want anything from the vending machine, Pop."

Trey looked him in the eye. "School going okay?"

Ozz nodded.

"Good. That's real good."

Ozz stood. "You sure you don't want anything, Pop?"

Trey narrowed one eye. "You okay, son? You seem kinda jumpy. Sit down, why don't you, and tell me what's goin' on."

He dropped back onto the seat, his mind a riot of anxiety and regret. "I'm tired, Pop, that's all. Between schoolwork and practice. And now lots of coaches and scouts coming around. It's a lot of pressure."

Trey fixed him with a caustic stare. "Don't you ever forget that football might be what's gonna get you out of that shithole, but it's school that's your number one priority."

Ozz looked away.

"Look at me! Are you with me?"

He met Trey's gaze. "Yes, sir."

"You gotta have choices in life, son. And rentin' out your body to be beaten up for the enjoyment of others ain't no choice at all. Not when you got brains like you do." Trey's grimace morphed into a proud smile. "Even if you is the best damn high school running back in Florida."

Ozz rolled his eyes. "I know, Pop. I'm doing like we said. Football to get out. School to stay out."

Trey narrowed an eye as if to say, "You better be, or I'll whip your ass."

He reminded himself that Trey wanted the best for him, wanted Ozz not to be like him. Trey had been a Panther too, even had a few scholarship offers his senior year, but a crushed ankle courtesy of a tackle by a player twice his size had left him with broken dreams and a one-way ticket to the cane fields. Ozz had never understood why Trey, who made sure Ozz obeyed every last rule, even down to forbidding him from hanging with his friends at the mall, ended up breaking the law. It was hard to imagine Trey doing what they said he did—stashing three kilos of cocaine in the backyard shed. But he had, and while his confession and plea bargain had saved him from a forty-five year sentence, Trey still ended up looking into the dark abyss of twenty years behind bars. Still, Ozz had seen enough of the streets to know that the choice of making more cash selling dope in one night than he made in a month sweating in the sun or bagging groceries was tempting. Maybe Trey had been tempted too.

"I know when you playing me, son," Trey said, his tone the same one he used when Ozz would say he'd done his homework when he hadn't, back when sneaking out to play ball was his worst crime.

Ozz cut his eyes, made it look as if he were admiring the pretty girl at the next table.

Trey leaned in. "Why you here on a school day, son? You usually come Sundays. Today's Wednesday."

He forced a smile onto his lips. "You been hitting the weight room, Pop? You look good."

"'Bout all there is to do in here except go crazy," Trey replied, his eyes slits now. "Now get to it, boy. Tell me why you're here."

Ozz closed his eyes and took a deep breath, unsure of how to start. "When you got locked up, things got hard, Pop."

"Uh-huh. Things was hard before I got locked up, in case you didn't notice."

"Yeah, but after, Momma lost her job. We couldn't pay the bills. Didn't have enough food. Auntie Hachi helped out some, but it wasn't enough."

Trey grunted. "Yeah, until she started usin' again, ain't that right?"

Without thinking, Ozz was shoving his upper body across the table, his face close enough to Trey's he could feel his breath on his cheek. "From where I sit, you're in no position to be shaming no one."

Trey leaned in. "Put food on the table, didn't I? Provided for my family, didn't I? Even bought you that set of encyclopedias when it took my last cent. But now you're getting all high and mighty with me? If you're so mad at me being inside, why you coming here to see me every week? You ain't missed once, not even after that last hurricane 'bout took your roof off."

Ozz closed his eyes, ashamed at his outburst, a product of his own guilt, not Trey's. "I'm in trouble, Pop," he said, his voice a raspy whisper.

Trey's eyes sprang wide. "Don't tell me! Don't tell me that you—"

"They told me they'd take care of me and Momma, help us out, Pop."

"Who? Who said they'd help?"

He stared at his hands.

"Junior, right?" Trey said, more as a foregone conclusion than a question. "I swear I'll kill that sonofabitch!" He banged his hands on his thighs repeatedly, cuffs and chains jangling so loud heads turned.

"Gordon, keep it down over there," one of the guards said.

Ozz's throat constricted. The words were painful, but he had to get them out. Now more than ever, he needed his father's advice. "He said it would be easy. No street action. Just pills. Said he had a steady supply from a couple of doctors in Lauderdale. All I had to do was make weekly deliveries to some rich folks over in Palm Beach."

"Just pills, huh? Ain't we fancy?" Trey's top lip curled back in a sneer. "Rich people's smack'll put you inside as fast as crack, boy. What's easy 'bout that? Got you popped, didn't it?"

Trey dropped his head to the table, banging it several times. A guard charged over and raised his nightstick. "Sit up, Gordon. Keep your damn head up." The smirk on the guard's face told Ozz that he was a man who enjoyed his work.

"That's not it. I didn't get busted."

Trey raised an eyebrow. "No? What, then?"

Ozz glanced over his shoulder to make sure no one was within earshot. "I made a run for Junior last week. When I went to meet him to turn over the cash, one of his other runners arrived late and—"

Trey squeezed his eyes shut.

"He shot the guy, Pop."

Trey drew in a quick breath as if hearing the shot himself.

"Junior shot the guy with my gun, the one he gave me to take on runs. Said if I ever even thought about ratting him out, he'd—"

Trey swallowed hard. "He said he'd drop a dime and make sure you went down for the murder. His way of making sure you stay loyal and keep your mouth shut."

Ozz jerked back. "Yeah, how'd you know?"

"Seen it before."

"Now I'm screwed. He's got me doin' more and more risky shit." He covered his face with his hands and groaned. "It was supposed to be temporary. To get some extra cash."

Trey shook his head. "That kind of work ain't ever temporary, son. It's not like working at some damn fast food joint."

"Now he wants me to go pick up a big shipment coming into Chokoloskee. I'm scared, Pop."

"Piece of shit," Trey mumbled.

"What am I going to do? I don't want to go," Ozz said, his voice a frantic screech.

Trey's face turned to stone. "You listen to me, son."

Ozz gasped for air, unable to speak another word.

"Get a hold of yourself!" Trey said, his voice like the sound of steam escaping from a radiator.

Ozz tried to steady his breathing, but couldn't, so he held his breath.

"This is what you are going to do." Trey looked from side to side, and kept his voice low. "You remember your auntie's friend? That lawyer woman? Grace Locke?"

"Yeah. She used to come around a lot, but she hasn't been around much lately."

"Call her. She'll keep you out of trouble."

"What? Why?"

"Call her. Tell her what you told me. She can help you figure a way out of this mess you got yourself into."

"Maybe I should come clean with Momma, maybe she—"

"No!"

"Shh, Pop! Keep your voice down!"

Trey bit his lip for a few seconds. "Do not mention this to your mother."

"Why? I—"

"Do I have your word?"

Ozz raised his hands in surrender. "Anything you say, Pop."

"Call Grace Locke, okay?"

"Why would she help me?"

"Because she owes your auntie. Hachi saved her life."

"I'm scared, Pop."

"I know you are, but you need to call her. She used to be a

prosecutor. She'll know who to talk to. What to do."

Ozz laid his head on his hands. "I ain't talkin' to no one! I'll end up in here . . ." He paused. " . . . or worse."

"You ain't got no choice. Call her."

Ozz buried his face in his hands. "I can't. It'll be the end of everything."

Trey panned around the room. "You wanna live or you wanna die? Them's your two choices."

A guard blew a whistle. "Time's up. Everyone out."

Trey stood. "Get out ahead of this thing, son. Sometimes it's the secrets you keep, not the ones you share, that come back to bite you."

Ozz got to his feet. "Yes, sir."

"And one last thing. Tell your auntie to come visit me."

He stuffed the roll of quarters back in his pocket. "Why?"

"Do it, son!" Trey said before shuffling away, back to the cell where he'd remain long after Ozz was reached his age. Long after Ozz would be gone. Or dead.

13

I'm early, one of my few good habits, a holdover from my Army days when being on time meant being late and being late might get someone killed. Ironic, perhaps, but punctuality was what kept my drinking hidden for so long, that and expensive suits, the criminal bar being all about appearances, not what lays beneath the surface. I might have woken up with a head pounding like a tom-tom and a gut full of shame for another night looking at life through the bottom of a bottle, but I was always on time to court and always dressed to the nines.

Apparently, Dr. Owen shares my penchant for timeliness. He's waiting outside the morgue, swinging a black medical bag back and forth, like a kid off on a field trip.

"Need a ride? Sugar Bay Express is ready for departure," I say, leaning across the center console to push open the passenger door.

Dr. Owen lowers his rear end onto the seat, maneuvering his legs in with his arms. "Old age ain't for sissies, Grace."

I eye the medical bag. "I thought only TV doctors carried

those things."

"Them and us old-school types." He pats the bag. "My tools of the trade. I prefer my own things, as I am sure you can understand."

Understand? Not really. Or more accurately, not at all. What would motivate a person to spend a lifetime surrounded by death and decay? But who am I to talk? I enlisted in the Army and went to war instead of taking the cushy Wall Street job my father got me after I graduated from law school. Sometimes decisions get made for reasons other than personal comfort, I suppose.

I drive in silence, perhaps in deference to our mission, or perhaps dwelling on my doubts about what good can come of any of this. Ozz was a kid with promise and problems. His death was a tragedy, yet one of his own making, no matter the immediate cause—depression, teenage angst, an impulsive nature, or whatever other random event may have led to his pulling the trigger. Even if there were a way to have Ozz speak from the grave, he'd still be dead and his family still grieving, perhaps sadder yet for knowing the truth.

But a promise to a friend is just that. So, here we are, me the erstwhile detective with my very own Dr. Watson en route to Sugar Bay, a town all too familiar with death and decay. Come to think of it, perhaps it is a perfect destination for the good doctor after all.

I glance at Dr. Owen, his face expressionless, just another day at the death factory for him. You'd think as a former prosecutor of murders I'd be all good with death, but you'd be wrong. Back then murder was a legal concept, an abstraction without emotional connections, although I did get angry enough a time or two to want to strangle my ex-husband, Manny. I even made a successful career of death. A worthy cause was how I saw my role avenging the victims of the killers I put away. But teenage suicide is not murder, and the victim in this case is not some random stranger. And Manny's still alive and pissing me off, although less often now that I'm sober and he's single. Marriage wasn't good to either of us.

We head west on I-595, an eight-lane expressway designed to shuttle the 9-to-5 masses to and from the suburbia that sprawls west from Fort Lauderdale all the way to the Everglades. Suburbs with cookie-cutter Mediterranean-style homes with two-car garages. Suburbs with parks with jungle gyms, and schools, and big-box stores. Suburbs with gates to keep the undesirables out and the secrets in. Generic suburbs that could be outside Dayton, Ohio, or the town of Springfield in any number of states. Suburbanites around here refer to their neighborhoods as "out west," buoyed by a dreamy illusion of security and the unflagging delusion that middle-class privilege will guarantee their offspring a fine future in similar suburbs where they will produce their own kids, have even more cars in the driveway, and shop in bigger big-box stores.

At the end of suburbia, we hook a right onto US-27, a four-lane north/south chip and seal road that parallels the Everglades to the west. With no median to prevent head-on collisions when drivers are lulled to sleep by the endless nothingness of the pancake-flat landscape, it's the most dangerous stretch of highway in Florida.

"Things change rather quickly out here, don't they?" Dr. Owen says, gazing out at sugar fields as far as the eye can see, the golden cane glimmering like a mirage on a desert highway.

"It may not be pretty, but anything will grow in that muck. It used to be vegetables—'The Summer Vegetable Capital of the World' was what this area was nicknamed before Big Sugar moved in and took over."

"You seem to know a lot about this place."

I shrug. "I do. Learned a lot about it during a not-very-civil lawsuit for a group of pickers."

"Yes, I saw you on the news, the day of your big verdict. I jumped up off the couch and said to Mrs. Owen, 'That's Grace Locke! I used to work on cases with her back when she was a

State's Attorney.'"

I stifle a laugh at his youthful enthusiasm, how a person so steeped in misery every day can emerge so unburdened by it.

"Mrs. Owen said you were 'real pretty.' And I said, 'And she was a damn good prosecutor, too.'"

"You are too kind," I reply, surprised. Most people shy away from any mention of my past life at the State's Attorney's Office, which ended in ignominy.

Dr. Owen turns his gaze back out the window, to the twenty-foot-high berms of dirt. Trucks piled high with cut cane en route to Big Sugar's refinery move along the top of the berms that serve as walls for drainage canals between the cane fields. The water eventually funnels into the New River, flows east through Fort Lauderdale, and out into the Atlantic, leaving the once pristine Glades behind, tainted now by toxic runoff from the sugar mill.

"Look at that! What the heck is that?" he says.

"Beats me."

I track Dr. Owen's pointed finger to a pickup truck waiting to merge onto the highway, its bed piled high with loaves of bread wrapped in plastic. "That explains it." I point to a vast concrete monstrosity to the left surrounded by a chain-link fence topped with razor wire. "There's the reason for all that white bread. That's Glades Correctional, a privatized branch of the prison industrial complex of the Great State of Florida. And the biggest consumer of bologna sandwiches in the entire state."

"We've sent a few folks there, you and I."

"Yes we have."

"Hopefully, they were the ones who got what they deserved," he says, a pleading note in his tone.

I set my jaw. "Most of them deserved that place and more," I reply, and mean it. But the problem is the ones who don't. They are the ones who inhabit my nightmares, their claims of innocence nothing but screams into the void. Until Vinnie's wrongful conviction, I wasn't bothered by the thought that an innocent might slip through the cracks, a cost of doing the business of justice, some would say. But not me. Not anymore.

"Don't get me wrong, Grace. I haven't gone soft in my dotage. I am aware that hardened criminals don't come with a stamp on their foreheads. They may look like you and me, but a lifetime of seeing what people do to each other has proved to me they're not." His tone shifts from righteous to uncertain in an instant. "But to think that many of them will never take a step outside those walls ever again. It's . . ."

"Primitive?"

"Yes, primitive. That's a good word for it." He stares at the guard tower, the tallest structure in the Glades. "If there is a word for such a horror."

I take a sharp turn to the east at a sign that reads "Sugar Bay 2 miles. Royal Palm Beach 32 miles." A mere thirty miles, but worlds apart. Much like our lives and those of the inmates on the other side of that barbed wire fence.

—

I drop Dr. Owen at the hospital where Ozz's body lies in a frigid drawer in the basement, then make my way to Petit's Funeral Home. An imposing structure at the corner of Kennedy Boulevard and Main Street, its ersatz antebellum columns and sweeping veranda are what pass for fine architecture in a town otherwise cobbled together from shotgun shacks and tenement blocks.

Clutches of mourners huddle together outside, some smoking, some with heads buried in others' shoulders, sobbing. An explosion of kids tears around the parking lot trailed by a boy wearing a blindfold, hands outstretched. An old lady wipes her eyes with a linen handkerchief embroidered with spring flowers and joins the back of the line to get inside.

I rummage around in my purse for my sunglasses and slip them on. The stunning brightness of the day doesn't seem right. Shouldn't the sky darken, the wind howl, at least for a moment as some kind of external manifestation of the universe's grief at having lost one of its children, even if he was one who made some bad choices and one fatal one?

I find Hachi alone on the veranda, her eyes swollen from crying, a cigarette dangling from her hand at her side as if it would take too much energy to smoke it.

"Hey," I say.

She doesn't move, tear after tear cascading down her face, soaking her blouse.

"I dropped the M.E. at the hospital."

"How did you get him to agree to the autopsy?"

"Let's say I used my powers of persuasion," I say, but leaving out the part about the pills and the cash she doesn't need to know about.

She stubs out the cigarette. "Watch out for Sadie, by the way. She's pissed as hell."

Before I can ask why, Sadie appears, arms flailing, screaming at the top of her lungs, "Get the fuck away from here! I don't want my boy cut up like a hog!"

Her fingernails strafe my cheek, drawing blood. I grab her arm and twist it behind her back, a move I used more times than I care to remember as a military police officer, a move that was used on me by a real police officer on a night I'd prefer to forget, but never will.

She twists against my grip, spittle splashing my face. "You two, you went behind my back. They said no autopsy, but you couldn't leave well enough alone, could you?" She turns her fire-eyed gaze on Hachi. "You should know better! You know our elders don't approve of such things. Now my boy won't be able to rest in peace."

"I thought it—" Hachi says.

"You thought? That's always your problem, isn't it? And hers too," she says, jerking her chin at me. "You both think too fuckin' much! Nothing will bring my boy back." She falls limp under my grip and sinks to her knees, sobbing.

She stabs her finger up at Hachi. "This is all your fault."

Hachi tries to help her up, but she squirms away and disappears inside.

Hachi and I follow the dregs of the crowd into a reception room, its burgundy flocked wallpaper and gilded sconces less funereal and more bordello. We situate ourselves behind a gigantic arrangement of droopy white lilies for cover in case Sadie decides to lash out again. Mourner after mourner approaches her to pay their respects.

"I'm sorry she acted like that," Hachi says. "It's not like her."

"No need to apologize. Death does funny things to people. I heard that, at my father's funeral, my teetotaler mother got so wasted that she passed out in the bathroom."

Hachi's eyes widen. "Faith? No way!"

"Yes, way." I glance around. "There must be two hundred people here."

The room is filled to capacity, the crowd balkanized by constituency. Teammates clad in Panther jerseys and black armbands bearing Ozz's number 11 in gold. A cluster of teenagers, awkward in their Sunday best. Myriad others of all ages who perhaps knew Ozz, or didn't, but felt the need to pay their respects, all relieved that but for the grace of God go they.

"Everyone loved Ozz," Hachi says between sniffles.

We hang back while the parade offer their condolences to Sadie. The last in line is an albino man with eyes the color of Red Hots and skin like an alien's, sheer like plastic wrap. That alone would distinguish him, but his stance, the way his body is canted forward, shifting from foot to foot, coiled, ready to pounce, is striking too.

I lean in and hear Sadie say, "Thanks for coming, Junior. It means a lot to us."

"Who is that?" I ask.

Hachi's top lip curls back. "No one. That's who that is. No one at all."

14

Ozz spotted Hachi behind the desk in the Welcome Center chickee hut, where she sold wide-eyed tourists tickets for the swamp buggy ride, airboat adventures, and the alligator wrestling shows. In reality, this particular chickee was ersatz, its thatch no longer the palmetto of a traditional Seminole house but long-lasting synthetic, and the frame plywood, not the cypress used before their ancestors had been hunted like animals, removed from their lands, and forcibly marched west.

She waved. "Almost done in here," she said as she herded a few stragglers to the parking lot, toting photos of their excursions and bags full of souvenirs for the folks back home.

He hung back in the shade of a gumbo limbo tree, its copper bark the color of the sunburned tourists' skin. Less than an hour from the tourist hubs of Miami and Fort Lauderdale on the east coast, the Glades Extravaganza on the Big Cypress Seminole Reservation promised a glimpse into the untamed Florida with its snakes and gators, but what it delivered was a sanitized, anemic version, all at a comfortable distance from any real danger.

Hachi pulled him in for a hug, her arms not long enough to reach around his body. "Happy birthday!"

He hugged her back hard for several seconds longer than usual. The pure joy on her face every time they were together always lifted his spirits. Maybe something in him made her feel like a kid again, but whatever it was, Ozz never turned down a chance to hang out with his favorite auntie. And he'd never turn down an opportunity to take an airboat ride through the River of Grass, the grassy slow-moving river that is the Everglades.

"Grab that and let's get the heck out of here," she said.

Ozz lifted the large red-and-white cooler off the picnic table and groaned. "Geez, what you got in here? This thing's heavy."

She motioned him to follow. "Everything we need to celebrate your eighteenth birthday."

He shuffled behind her to the dock, the cooler banging against his knees. "Thanks for doing this for me, Auntie."

She waved him off. "No thanks required. I've been looking forward to this all week too. And don't forget to thank Chief Billy Bowlegs next time you see him for lending us his airboat. He says happy birthday, by the way."

Ozz manhandled the cooler onto the front of the airboat, a flat-bottomed fiberglass skiff powered from behind by a huge caged propeller that made the contraption look like a giant dragonfly. He secured the cooler to a bench seat with bungee cords.

Hachi climbed into the elevated pilot's seat. "Put these on." She handed him a pair of protective earphones and put on her own pair. She reached behind her and cranked the ignition switch. "Off we go!" she said, maneuvering the elongated stick with her left hand to steer.

When they had cleared the dock area, she eased the stick forward and the airboat surged ahead, the noise of the fan deafening even with the earphones on.

"Yeehaw!" she screamed.

Ozz sat back, his arms stretched out over the back of the bench seat, laughing as they bounced over the water, its surface a swirling mirage of sawgrass.

He tilted his face up to the late afternoon sun, submitting himself to the warmth of the day and the spray off the water. For this last time, he'd set his worries aside and bathe in the simple delights of the Glades, commit to memory the great blue herons pecking in the shallows; alligators like spies, their gnarled heads breaching the surface without disturbing the water; and the grassy water itself, nature's filter.

Hachi throttled down and the whir of the fan faded to a whisper. She forced the stick left, and the airboat turned into a hidden waterway, a magical emerald tunnel surrounded by high grasses, the sun's rays angling through the canopy of cypresses overhead, casting shadows on the white deck.

She shut off the engine and let the airboat drift.

Ozz stood and lifted her down from her perch, and they both stood for a moment, drinking in the stillness accompanied by the chirping of crickets.

"Let's get this party started," she said, poking him in the ribs.

She flipped open the cooler and pulled two bottles of orange soda from the ice, followed by a large domed container that she set between them on the bench seat under the pilot's perch. She opened the container and pulled out a chocolate layer cake, careful not to spoil the "Happy Birthday Osceola" frosting or knock over the eighteen candles that formed the number 18.

She pulled a lighter from her pocket, lit the candles, and sang an off-key rendition of "Happy Birthday."

"You're the best." Ozz leaned over and planted a kiss on her cheek. "I wish Momma could have come with us."

She looked away.

He shoveled a huge bite of cake into his mouth. "But at least she has a job again."

"We all pay the piper one way or another."

"What's that mean? Who's the piper?" he said, talking and chewing at the same time.

"Nothing. It's only an expression." She licked frosting from her fingers. "I just meant we all have to find a way to pay the bills, that's all."

She set her plate aside and pulled back to take his full measure. "I can't believe you're eighteen. Seems like yesterday you were a little tyke running all over the place. Now you're a grown man."

He swallowed hard.

"What? What's wrong?"

He forced a smile. "Nothing."

"We're going to miss you so much when you're gone."

He stood and opened his arms, his wingspan wide like a great bird's. "This here, the Glades, this will always be my home no matter how far away I get. No matter where I go."

She stood beside him and, holding hands, they traced the track of the sun until it dipped below the horizon.

"I'm proud of you. You are gonna do great things, Osceola." She pulled out a gold medallion on a chain from her pocket and handed it to him. "This is for you."

Ozz examined the figure carved on the medallion, the face of a man, his features reminiscent of his own, straight nose, deep set eyes, but with long hair framing his distinguished face. "It's him, isn't it?"

"The greatest warrior of all. A leader like you. It belonged to your grandfather."

Ozz slipped the chain over his head and closed his hand over the medallion, tears nipping at his eyes.

She reached for him. "What's wrong?"

"I wish Pop could have been here too."

She dropped her head to her chest. "I know." She put her hand on his heart. "But he's right here."

He bit down hard on his lip to keep from crying. "Which reminds me. When I saw him last week, Pop told me to tell you to go see him."

She pulled her hand back as if she'd touched a hot stove.

He turned to face her. "I know how you feel about him, about what he did. But he's the only father I have, no matter how much you and Momma would rather forget it."

She raised her chin. "I got nothing to say to that man. His kind are leeches, living off the misery of the rest of us. Anyway, why would he want to see me?"

"No idea. But he made me promise to tell you. So, I'm telling you." He swallowed a last bite of cake. "It seemed important, that's all."

She hoisted herself up to the pilot's seat. "It's getting late. We need to go."

He peered up at her, conscious of her anger, but also of his promise to Trey. "Please go see him, Auntie."

"We'll see," she said as the fan roared to life.

15

Sugar Bay High looks more refugee camp than high school. A cluster of portable classrooms, vinyl siding peeling and faded, encircling a windowless concrete bunker of a main building, all penned in by hurricane fences topped with tumbleweeds of barbed wire. A less inspiring institution of learning is hard to imagine. I've been in more uplifting prisons.

What I need now is to be done with playing amateur sleuth on a hopeless case, the outcome of which is already certain. Autopsy? Check, except the results. Talk to Coach? Soon to be checked. After that I will go back to my normal life defending the guilty and getting paid for it.

I quicken my pace to catch Coach Wynne before he goes home to what I imagine is a plateful of fried food and a wife who was once a cheerleader, her glory days but a faded memory and his the stuff of well-worn war stories. Come to think of it, that kind of evening doesn't sound that bad when I compare it to the empty refrigerator and even emptier bed waiting for me at home.

I pass under a gold and black banner emblazoned with "Go Panthers" suspended above the entrance and place my purse on a scanner belt. A uniformed school resource officer, right hand on a taser, waves me through the arch of a metal detector identical to the one at the courthouse, whose purpose, it would seem, is identical—to keep lethal weapons out. A sad state of affairs for a place of learning.

Beep. Beep.

"Anything in your pockets, Miss?"

"No," I say. I add a prophylactic "sir." Better to be an ass-kisser. Resistance is futile in the face of bureaucracy.

The officer rolls back on his heels, thumbs stuck in belt loops, and gives me the once-over. "You sure?"

"Yes, Officer," I say with the sweetest smile I can summon. "Yes, I'm sure. But I do have an underwire in my bra. Does it every time," I say with full knowledge that it's Oscar that set the damn thing off, but I'm in no mood for show and tell today.

A bright pink blush rolls up his cheeks. "You're clear," he says, not meeting my gaze.

I collect my purse from the far side of the belt and cock my head. "Have a great day, Officer," I say with a flick of my hair. Thank you, Lord. That trick works every time.

Rows of dented metal lockers line the hallway, the same kind I had in high school, except those at St. Mark's Preparatory in Greenwich, Connecticut, were painted scarlet and white before every fall semester without fail and bore nameplates appended with Jr. and III.

A bell sounds, pitching my heart rate into overdrive like every other loud noise since Fallujah. Hordes of students spill from classrooms, some laughing and jabbing each other. Others walk alone, arms weighed down by books, eyes focused straight ahead. I recognize that look. I was that kind once, the kind who believed if you studied hard and stayed out of trouble, that no evil would come your way. Little did I know then that the evil that lurks within us can be the most destructive force of all.

The caustic smell of cleaning fluid is overwhelming, and I hold my breath, casting around for the rear exit. On the phone, Coach Wynne said his office was in the field house, part of the athletic complex behind the main building, adjacent to the practice fields. Pushing against traffic, I find my way outside.

I stop in my tracks. "No way!" I say, staring at the plaque above the door: The Alonso Tremayne Athletic Complex. If the main building is a monument to cell block design, this so-called field house is the polar opposite, a hyper-modern steel and glass structure with walls of windows gifted to the school by none other than the king of Big Sugar himself, Alonso Freaking Tremayne.

"Miss Locke, over here."

I look around, over the mile-wide shoulders of a pair of young men flipping tractor-trailer tires as if they were doughnuts, to see Coach Wynne waving his meaty arms back and forth.

"Walter Wynne," he says, extending a meaty paw as I approach.

As if he needed to say his name. A man of Wynne's local renown needs no introduction even if you're not a football fan. His face is all over the papers every fall. The "winningest coach in Florida high school football history," they say. Not to imply that jocks are idiots or anything, but "winningest" is such a corruption of the English language that each time I hear it, I feel the need to report the crime to the language police.

I shake Wynne's hand. Or, more accurately, he crushes mine and I grit my teeth to keep from crying out in pain. Even if his reputation didn't precede him, Wynne would be my first pick in a lineup as a football coach, what with his big head mounted on a neck of equal diameter, a once muscled body gone to flab, track pants, and a polo shirt with an embroidered logo of a panther over his heart.

He leads me inside, the reception area furnished with several overstuffed armchairs and couches, all upholstered with the Panther logo. Glass cases containing dozens of trophies line the walls. Football jerseys the size of bedsheets and pictures of former players annotated with their year of graduation hang from the rafters.

"Some place you got here, Coach."

Wynne smiles the easy smile of a man used to winning, who expects to win, who lets no doubt enter his mind that if he says his team will win, it will. Wynne exudes that enviable single-minded certainty that champions and demagogues are made of.

"Thank you, Miss Locke. Our supporters are most kind."

"And Alonso Tremayne the kindest of all, it would seem."

"Mr. Tremayne's generosity knows no bounds." He flashes a broad smile, his mouth full of chipped and yellowing teeth that say he has no time for anything other than football. Dentist appointments be damned.

"He went to school here, you know."

"Is that so? I had no idea." And I didn't. My one contact with Tremayne was across a conference table when his henchmen spoke for him and all they said was "no" to my offers to settle the pickers' lawsuit.

I smile to myself at the thought that they're the ones sorry now, but Wynne takes it as license to proceed with Tremayne's curriculum vitae.

"Even played for the Panthers. Of course, that was before my time," he says, although I would have put Wynne as a contemporary of Tremayne's, not his junior. Then again, money can do a lot to enhance one's youthful image. And football? From what I've gleaned from going to dozens of games with Marcus, the violence of football has a way of aging a man before his time.

"Mr. T went on to college at the University of Southern California."

"Tremayne sure made it big after he left Sugar Bay," I say, eschewing the temptation to call Tremayne Mr. T, although it does have a certain ring to it.

"Yes he did. Made a lot of money from Big Sugar and from Epic."

"What's Epic?"

Coach lifts a pant leg to show me his sneakers emblazoned with a lightning bolt logo. "Athletic shoes, clothes, all that stuff."

"He owns that, too?"

"No, but he's a big investor from what I understand. He has his hands full already with Big Sugar." A sly smile creeps onto his lips. "And with you too, Miss Locke, from what I read in the papers."

"Coach, are you calling me a handful?" I say, affecting an offended tone.

He releases a booming laugh. "Not at all. I'm a big fan of speaking truth to power, standing up for the little guy, and all that."

"I guess we're both in that business," I say.

His expression shifts from jovial to serious in a heartbeat. "Yes indeed, folks out here in the Glades don't have much power, do they?"

"On that we agree, Coach. Speaking of the powerful, isn't USC where Ozz wanted to go? Same As Tremayne?"

Coach rubs his chin. "Come to think of it, you're right. But USC was one of several schools interested in Ozz. He'd have been a great asset to any team." He drops his eyes. "But he never got the chance."

I point at a tooled silver waist-high trophy shaped like a Grecian urn, mounted on a pedestal under a glass dome. The plaque on the base reads "Florida State Championship."

"And I hear that's not the only one of those you've won," I say, hoping my none-too-subtle attempt at ingratiation will get him to open up when I get to the hard questions I need to ask.

He beams. "It seems as if you've been doing your homework, Miss Locke."

I nod. He's right. I have. Not wanting to seem like a total idiot, I called Marcus, former star for "The U," the University of Miami Hurricanes, on the way here to give me the lowdown on Wynne. It turns out this mountain of a man is the son of an

Alabama sharecropper, who rose to greatness first as a record-setting running back under Bear Bryant at the University of Alabama, and then as a New Orleans Saint. A congenital heart condition forced him out of the game and, while he had several offers to coach in the NFL, he chose Sugar Bay High, a school not unlike the rural, underfunded school he'd attended himself. Six state championships in ten years solidified his status as a legend. And he's still going.

Wynne shepherds me through a rabbit warren of corridors lined with offices, pointing out pictures of some of Sugar Bay's greats as we go. "Do you know that on any given Sunday in the NFL, more than fifty Sugar Bay graduates suit up?"

"I know."

"You a football fan, Miss Locke?"

"I am indeed," I reply, hoping Marcus's tutorial is sufficient to call myself a fan. Marcus often takes me to see the Dolphins play, but I'm no expert when it comes to X's and O's, which is why I picked Marcus's brain until he told me to shut up.

"And please call me Grace, Coach Wynne."

"Whatever you wish, Miss Grace," he says with a wink. "The old South dies hard 'round these parts."

And I have to admit, the southern form of addressing women is something I have come to appreciate, a reminder of more civil times or, at least, a façade of the same.

He unlocks the door to his office and signals for me to take a seat on one of the two chairs opposite his desk. "And you can just call me Coach," he says, with a crooked smile.

While Wynne's charm is unmistakable, I remind myself not to fall prey to the habit of genteel Southerners to skate over the surface of a topic, leaving the less pleasant details unspoken, a habit that has led to my putting faith in the wrong man more times than I'd like to remember.

I settle into a chair and steel myself. I've got some tough questions to ask, like what was going on in Ozz's life beyond yards per carry that might have made him want to take his own life?

"Coach, first let me say thank you for seeing me. This must be a most difficult time for you and your team."

He clasps his hands tight in front of him and sighs. "You're right there, but it must be much worse for Ozz's family, especially his momma and his auntie Hachi."

He sees me perk up at the mention of Hachi's name. "Miss Hachi called to say you're helping them to understand why . . . Thing is, I'm not sure there's much more *to* understand. It's a tragedy plain and simple."

I lose my train of thought for a second. I didn't ask Hachi to call. I wanted to catch Wynne off guard, if that is even possible with a man like him. He seems like the type to map everything out down to the most minute of details. Sloppy preparation doesn't win games. Still, maybe Hachi's call will make him more forthcoming, put him more at ease that he isn't telling personal stories out of school about one of his players.

I glance around the spacious office, the antithesis of Dr. Owen's. Both men from Alabama. One went to med school and ended up working in a claustrophobic den. The other played a game for a living and ended up in an office suited for a CEO. One thing the two men have in common is a photograph with Governor Strong on their walls, except Wynne's hangs alongside four others with past governors and several with former players.

"How can I help?"

I square my shoulders. "Let me start by asking if Ozz had seemed different lately? Upset? Distracted, maybe?"

He tents his fingers in front of his face, giving him the look of a Zen master, albeit a two-hundred-and-fifty-pound one who choreographs sanctioned violence for a living. "Perhaps it would be helpful if I gave you some background, to help you understand Ozz Gordon and what we do here."

I sit back. "I'd appreciate that."

He narrows an eye at me. "Tell me, where'd you go to school, Miss Grace?"

I hesitate. While I am proud of my educational pedigree, one I worked hard for, my Yankee sensibility to avoid self-promotion makes me reluctant to broadcast my Ivy League education, particularly in a setting where it could be read as affecting superiority, which is the last thing I need right now.

"I'm sure it hasn't escaped your notice that Sugar Bay isn't exactly a highfalutin community. People out here are dirt poor, there's no two ways about it. Here at SBH, our students face obstacles far beyond what grades they get." He shakes his head. "Hell, if it wasn't for school lunch, many of 'em wouldn't eat."

"I grew up in Connecticut and I went to a local school," I say, which is true. Yale is a short drive from Greenwich.

The smug smile on Coach's face dampens my inclination to be polite. His presumptuousness about my being unable to empathize is beginning to grate on me, as if poverty were a precondition for understanding the plight of others less fortunate than oneself.

"And once I graduated from that school in Connecticut, I lived in an even more impoverished place than Sugar Bay."

He gives me a half smile. "And where was that?"

"Fallujah. You know, Fallujah, Iraq. It's quite a ways from Sugar Bay in more ways than one."

The smile vanishes.

"Let's say I joined the Army and saw the world, and a lot of it wasn't pretty." I shift in my seat. "Or rich."

He doesn't meet my gaze. "I'm sorry. That was rude of me."

I wait a beat to let him study his hands for a little longer.

"No problem," I say.

"The thing is, Miss Grace, our kids have hard lives. Opportunities for any kind of future are limited, and that's where football comes in. Football offers kids like Ozz hope."

"But only for the talented few, right?"

He gives a reluctant nod. "I wish that weren't the way. I wish every kid could get a fightin' chance at a better life. But, see, I can't go gettin' discouraged by what I can't change."

"Amen to that."

"See, you know what I'm talking about," he says, oblivious to how right he is. I'm still learning that lesson day by day.

"What you're saying is Ozz was one of the chosen few," I say, less a question than a statement of fact.

He leans back, a smile tugging at his lips as if he's seeing Ozz playing in his mind's eye, running, scoring, doing all the things that would get him the hell out of Dodge. "That boy was goin' places. I know a lot of folks think every kid should go to college. To my mind, that's middle-class BS. Half of them kids that do go can't hack it, and when they drop out, they feel let down. Like they got the rug pulled." He shrugs. "I suppose when you got plenty of money, you can afford to waste some."

And while I agree, I can't help but think he's making another less-than-veiled reference to my past. Or maybe it's no more than good old *noblesse oblige* guilt getting the better of me.

"Out here, we can't go wastin' what resources we do got. Out here we got to bet on the favorites, the ones who got the goods to make it."

"And Ozz Gordon was one of those."

His eyes drift to a couple of boys on the football field lying in a pile after one knocked the other on his ass. "Yes indeed. That boy was on his way. Ozz was not only an outstanding student, he was one hell of a football player. He could have punched his ticket out of here either with his brains or his body. But . . ." His voice trails off, and his gaze shifts out the window, to two hulking boys pushing sleds across the practice field toward the setting sun.

After a few seconds, he snaps back. "You asked if Ozz seemed different lately. Exactly what did you mean?"

"Like sad or depressed. Withdrawn?"

He shakes his head. "Ozz wasn't ever the most talkative guy on the team. He was all business. The type who puts his head down and gets the work done." A nostalgic smile creeps onto his lips. "But he did his share of joking around. Hell, on the bus on the way up to Laketown a couple of weeks back, he hid a rubber python in the QB's gear bag. Poor sucker about had a heart attack in the locker room when it flopped out right along with his jock strap." He gives a belly laugh, before his eyes become laser focused again. "But to answer your question, no, he seemed like regular Ozz."

"Safe to say you didn't know he was taking antidepressants?"

His head jerks back. "What? No, I did not know that." His eyebrows, fuzzy like caterpillars, draw together. "We require our players to provide a list of all the medications they're taking on our medical form. In case they get injured and need treatment." He opens a desk drawer and pulls out a manila folder and runs a finger down a document. "No, there's nothing here about no anti-whatever it was you said. Ozz wasn't taking anything according to this."

"How about the other kind of drugs? The illegal kind?"

His eyes bulge. "No siree. Not Ozz. Not ever."

"You sure about that?"

"Yes, ma'am, I am. That boy's daddy went to prison for drugs. No way. No how. Ozz was one of them health nuts. Said he needed his health to get the hell out of Sugar Bay. Wouldn't even eat his mother's fried chicken no more, from what I hear. And that woman makes some delicious fried chicken. Ozz used to bring her chicken to every team dinner. Then he just stopped, started bringin' salads." He grunts. "That did not make him popular with the defensive line."

"How about girls?"

"Ozz had the same girlfriend since freshman year. I heard they broke up over summer break, though."

"How do you know that?"

"She used to come to every one of our home games, sit in the front row all goo-goo-eyed and shit. When she stopped coming, I asked Ozz why. He told me they broke up."

"Did he say why?"

Coach lets loose with another belly laugh. "You're funny. Do

I look like some kinda shrink to you, Miss Grace? I kick those boys' butts up and down the field every day for sport. No way they'd admit no weakness or that some girl hurt their feelings. That shit is for sissies in my boys' minds." He picks up a pen and points it at me. "But I can tell you one thing—he did look mighty sad around then. Even skipped practice a couple of times. Said he was sick, but I didn't believe him. I knew it was the girl. Hell, I was young once too."

"Do you know her name?"

He runs his hand over his mouth. "Paula? Pauline, maybe." He looks up at the ceiling, drumming the pencil on the desk. "Paulette, that's it! That's what he called her."

"You said Ozz said he was sick. With what? Did he say?"

"Said he had headaches or some such things. But if you ask me, what hurt was further south." He points to his heart. "Young love. Pretty young lady like you, you know how that can be."

I shake my head. "I'm not sure about that. It's been a while."

He winks at me. "Yeah, you seem like the all-work-and-no-play type."

"You're an observant man, Coach," I say, half laughing, half wondering how in hell he could tell? Maybe he's a better mind reader than he's saying.

He scoots out from behind his desk. "Let me show you a different kind of love, or maybe hero worship is more accurate." He unhooks a photograph from the wall behind me, a picture of Ozz and Santonio Taylor, the player from the poster. Ozz smiling ear to ear as Santonio presents him with a Dolphins jersey identical to the one he's wearing.

"See that guy right there?" he says, handing the picture to me. "That there was Ozz's hero *numero uno*."

"Santonio Taylor, right?"

"You *do* know your football."

"It's just that I saw a poster of him in Ozz's room."

"Is that a fact?" He takes the photograph from my hand, gently, as if he's handling a rare piece of art, and hangs it back on the wall. "Santonio played right here at SBH. He's gonna be in the Hall of Fame one day. Even told Ozz he'd save him a place."

I study the photo, the look of unadulterated joy on Ozz's face, as if his every dream would come true, a blissful naiveté reserved for the young.

I motion to the collage of player photographs. In every single one of them, the player is looking at Wynne with respect in his eyes. "They're lucky to have you, Coach."

He shakes his head. "The way I see it, it's the other way around."

"I hear you had offers to coach college ball, but came here instead."

He wags a finger at me. "You have been checking me out, young lady, haven't you?"

I give him my best coy look. "Maybe a little. A friend of mine says you're a legend."

He barks out a laugh. "You can tell your friend the check's in the mail." He sits and puts his feet up on the desk. "I like to say that I didn't choose Sugar Bay, but that she chose me. It felt like home around here, you know? And feeling right in a place is about the most a man can hope for."

"Roger that," I say to myself.

"So, here I am. Twelve years and counting. I may have played college ball many moons ago, but I'll always be a small town shitkicker from Alabama. The only difference between where I grew up and Sugar Bay is the crop. Here it's sugar. Back home it was cotton." His eyes lose focus. "Football saved me, Miss Grace. Gave me my life. I wanted the chance to return the favor," he says, his eyes fixed on the photograph of Ozz and Santonio Taylor.

16

Cops and lawyers were to be avoided at all costs. The former had put his pop away. The latter was something Sadie said they couldn't afford, so Trey'd had to settle for court-appointed counsel and a plea bargain for a twenty-year stretch. But for now, Grace Locke was the lesser of two evils.

He walked the mile and a half from the Fort Lauderdale bus depot. On the phone, Grace had warned him that her office was in a "bad part of town," as if that were something new to Ozz. All he knew were the bad parts of Sugar Bay, there being no good ones. In his dreams, however, he bought his momma a house in a nice neighborhood, something far from the acrid smell of burning cane, something with a yard on a piece of land large enough for her to tend to her flowers and sit in the shade of the live oaks. Maybe something up in northern Florida, where their ancestors had lived, at least until their land was stolen and they were herded west of the Mississippi like cattle.

If Ozz could have kicked himself and walked at the same time, he would have. If he'd been smarter, he wouldn't have to be here. He should have known that there was no such thing as easy money. All he'd wanted was to get the hell out of Sugar Bay. Instead, he'd bought himself a one-way ticket to a life of looking over his shoulder. Or a life like his father's, caged like an animal. Or worse. Now, his only way out of Sugar Bay was going to be in cuffs—that is, if Junior didn't feed him to the gators first.

He skirted around a homeless man in a winter coat parked in the middle of the sidewalk. The man kept his jerky eyes on him, as if he were about to take off with the man's shopping cart filled with his hard-earned quarry, a pile of random possessions, including a humidifier and an ironing board, all lashed together with twine.

At first, Grace said she wasn't taking any new clients, but he knew bullshit when he heard it and had pressed on as if his life depended on it, which it did. When he told her he was Hachi's nephew, she softened somewhat, but she still sounded like a hard-ass, telling him she'd give him "thirty minutes, not a minute more."

Auntie Hachi had no clue he was here, however, and he'd make sure Grace Locke didn't breathe a word of it to her either. The truth was, he was only here because Trey had made him promise. That, and because he was scared shitless. Maybe he should be on a bus already to wherever Junior would never find him. It had crossed his mind. But then there was his mother—no way he could take off like a thief in the night without an explanation, and his explanation would kill Sadie. Trey's getting locked up almost had.

"The Law Offices of Grace K. Locke, Esq." was stenciled on the opaque glass door in gold lettering, the only halfway elegant thing about the building, a squat two-story cinder block structure with barred windows that would have fit right in in Sugar Bay.

He tried the door, before seeing the sign above an intercom. "Please ring for service." He pressed the buzzer, igniting a frenzy of barking and scratching on the other side of the door.

A voice crackled out of the speaker. "Ozz? Is that you?"

"Yes," he said, stepping back from the door for a quick getaway in the event whatever rabid beast was back there launched itself at him.

The door creaked open, revealing a tall woman with long raven-black hair and blue eyes the color of a swimming pool at night, and a gigantic wolf-like creature with one brown eye and one blue.

"Come on in," she said, pulling the door back with one hand, the other on the animal's collar. "This is Miranda."

Ozz slipped by Miranda, staying as close to the wall as possible.

"Good girl," she said, motioning him to one of the two chairs in front of the desk and Miranda to a dog bed the size of a flying saucer beside the door.

He perched himself on the edge of the chair but kept his eyes fixed on Miranda.

Ms. Locke dropped into the high-backed leather chair. "I'd say her bark is worse than her bite, but I'd be lying." She threw Miranda a bone, an actual bone that looked to have once been part of a T-bone steak. "Don't worry about her. She's a sweetheart."

He pointed at the dog, drooling as she devoured the bone. "What is she?"

"She's a service dog."

"I mean what kind of . . . She looks like a wolf."

"She's part husky, part German Shepherd. Got her after I got this." She slung her left leg onto the desk and pulled up her pant leg to reveal a fake leg made of metal and skin-toned plastic.

He felt himself staring, but he couldn't help it. A three-legged dog and a one-legged lawyer. This wasn't what he'd expected at all.

She gave him a wide smile. "I promise, Oscar here does not interfere with my ability to provide legal advice."

Miranda emitted a confirmatory bark.

"See? She agrees." Ms. Locke dropped her leg to the floor. "What can I do for you, Ozz? I know you didn't come all the way over here from Sugar Bay to meet Miranda."

He took a deep breath, fear engulfing his insides, and forced himself to speak. "Miss Locke . . . see, the thing is, I play football at Sugar Bay. I have several scholarship offers to go to college."

"Neither of which seem like bad things," she said, chewing on the end of a pen.

"And I sell drugs." The words burned like acid in his mouth.

Her arm, which had been reaching into a drawer for something, froze midair. "What did you say?"

"I make money selling pills."

"Pills? I see." She smirked. "For a moment there, I thought you were saying you worked in a pharmacy."

"To rich people." He cleared his throat. "Not on the street corner or anything."

Her expression hardened. "That makes all the difference in the world, doesn't it? You're a high-class drug dealer."

"That's, that's not what I meant. I . . ." His voice faded along with his courage, and he got to his feet. "Look, I should go."

Miranda lifted her big head and growled, and he sat back down.

"She thinks you should stay too." She gave him a kind smile. "Look, I'm not yanking your chain, I'm just telling you what I know from my and your aunt Hachi's experience. That there is no such thing as a good drug dealer."

He glanced over his shoulder at the door.

"But, in actual fact, selling to rich people is safer than street corners, correct?"

"Used to be."

She drew back. "Used to be? From what I can tell, half of the one-percenters are on something and law enforcement turns a blind eye."

He bit his lip.

She looked him up and down. "You don't seem to have been

arrested because here you are not behind glass at the county jail. And I'm pretty sure you don't have boatloads of bail money sitting around if you're out there hustling for pocket change, so I'm guessing you didn't bond out if you have been arrested. So your problem is what, exactly?"

"I saw someone get killed."

She blinked hard. "Go on."

"I make one delivery a week. To Palm Beach."

He saw a flicker of recognition in her eyes, but of what, he wasn't sure.

"That's it. Once a week. I give some of what I make to my mother to pay bills and save the rest."

She raised an eyebrow.

"For college."

Eyebrow still raised. "Of course."

"For real."

"I believe you," she said, but it didn't sound like she did.

Miranda burped.

"And?"

"And this week, when I got back to Sugar Bay, I went to turn in the cash, and . . ."

"And?"

"And the leader of my crew, he shot a guy. Another runner."

"Why?"

"Because he was late."

She reared back. "What?"

"Not the only reason. See, he—"

"Can we please give this guy, the shooter, a name?"

As he debated whether to tell her Junior's name or not, he couldn't stop himself from thinking about how she showed off Oscar, putting him up on display. He'd never met anyone who named their limbs before. Hell, what was wrong with him? Why was he calling the freaking leg a "him"?

"Look, if you want me to help you, I need to know everything." She held a hand across the desk, palm up. "Give me a dollar."

"Why?"

"Do it! Come on, you're a goddamned drug dealer, aren't you? You've got to have at least a single dollar in your pocket. You guys are like strippers—your pockets are always full of small bills."

He reached into his pocket and came out with a fistful of change from which he extracted three quarters, two dimes, and a nickel.

"Jesus! What kind of drug dealer are you?" She swiped the change into a drawer and held out a hand for him to shake. "Osceola Gordon, you have hired yourself a lawyer, and that dollar bought my silence. Anything you tell me is confidential and cannot be repeated to anyone without your consent."

"Even the cops?"

"Especially the cops."

"Junior," he said. "His name is Junior."

"Last name?"

He shrugged. "Don't know. He's a big, ugly albino dude. Kind of looks like a snowman with red candies for eyes."

"He sounds charming. Now the rest of the story, please." She pulled a yellow legal pad from her briefcase and took notes as he spoke.

—

When he was done, she eyed him for a while, still gnawing on the end of her pen.

"You sure you weren't the one to commit that murder? I need the truth if I'm going to help you climb out of the deep hole you dug for yourself."

He shuddered at the image of his being in a hole, although she was right that it was a hole of his own making. "No, ma'am."

She stifled a smile. .

"Here's the bottom line." She stuck the pen behind her ear. "You've given me two things to work with. First, you know a lot about this Junior guy's business. And second, I'm sure the cops would love to know who killed the dead guy, Miguel." She tilted her head to the side. "Actually, they would love to know if someone told them without them having to do any work. Otherwise, they won't give a shit."

"Junior will kill me if I snitch."

"And the state will kill you with a needle full of a lethal cocktail if Junior snitches on you."

"But I—"

"I know you didn't kill him, but that doesn't matter shit if Junior's in a bind and decides that selling you out to save his own ass is the best option to keep him out of prison for the rest of his miserable life."

He closed his eyes and tried to take deep breaths.

"The way I see it, son, you've left yourself no other choice but to cooperate with the authorities. Unless you want to stay in the swamp and keep doing what you're doing until either the cops get you or Junior does when you're late one night."

Ozz closed his eyes against the vision of a curtain falling on all of his dreams.

"Look, it'll take some time, but let me talk to some of my contacts to see if they know this Junior character and see what we might be able to do."

"But what do I do? I mean now."

"What you've been doing. Act like everything's normal. You have to. Keep making your deliveries and doing whatever you need to do to not get killed, either by the cops or Junior or whoever else has a beef with Junior. We don't need you becoming collateral damage."

"What's that mean?"

She looked at the ceiling. "That means don't get yourself killed running a fool's errand for someone else."

He wasn't sure what that meant either, but her faraway tone told him he shouldn't ask. The woman used a lot of metaphors.

"Yes, ma'am. I'll try not to."

"And son?" she said, leaning in closer to him, eyes burning

into his.

"Yes, ma'am?"

"Don't call me ma'am."

"Okay." He looked her in the eye. "And Miss Locke?"

"Yes?"

"Don't call me 'son.'"

A smile tugged at the corners of her mouth. "Deal."

"I'd like to go now." He pointed at Miranda, afraid to make a move.

She snapped her fingers. "Come, Miranda. No more scaring the clients." The dog trotted to her side, but never taking her eyes off Ozz. "I'll be in touch," Ms. Locke said. "In the meantime, stay in your trench and keep your helmet on."

Ozz slipped out into the twilight. He wasn't sure what she meant by the trench and helmet comment either, but he was willing to do whatever it took to not end up in prison, or worse, as alligator bait, the fate of more than one snitch out in the Glades.

17

I stand at the waterline and drink in the smell of the ocean, the salty tang reminiscent of lazy summers spent wearing nothing but a bikini and a tan. A rosy glow bleeds up from the horizon, turning the water from black to purple, and finally, orange. The appearance of the sun in full, a crimson fireball, is my daily call to action.

I break into an easy jog, my one bare foot gripping the damp sand and propelling my body forward, Oscar 2.0 a beat behind. Oscar's herky-jerky motion serves to remind me that we still have work to do. His predecessor, Oscar 1.0, is somewhere at the bottom of Port Everglades thanks to a cop in whom I put my trust, only to discover he was as crooked as the ones who framed Vinnie. But as with all masks, Sonny's pretty face and smooth demeanor didn't protect him from the truth forever. Or from me.

I relax into my stride and revel in the heat of the sun. While others might have God or kinky sex or booze, running is my escape, my church. The movement clears my mind. After getting out of Walter Reed, I tried everything to calm my mind, to hold the nightmares at bay. Yoga. Pilates. I even tried Buddhism for a while, along with meditation, endeavors ill-suited to a Type A with PTSD, no matter what the acolytes of woo-woo say. If I'd had to pretend I could become mindful, centered, at peace with myself, one more time, I would have lost what was left of my mind. And as for drugs, even the legal ones prescribed by my shrink are no panacea either.

After my medical discharge from the Army, but before Oscar 1.0, I dragged my useless leg around the State's Attorney's Office like a wounded dog in search of a place to die. After five unsuccessful surgeries and enough pain pills to anesthetize the population of a small island nation, I decided to have the damn thing lopped off. When I left the hospital, I buried my Purple Heart deep in my sock drawer and dug a tattered pair of Converse Chuck Taylors from my closet and ditched the right shoe along with my pride. At first, I hobbled around the block on crutches, until the VA got me a futuristic curved titanium blade. I named the thing after Oscar Pistorius, the first amputee to run in the Olympic Games alongside able-bodied athletes, the same one who went on to murder his supermodel girlfriend. At first I ran, or shuffled more like it, a half mile, then a whole one. Then two miles, then five. Manny, my future ex-husband, said I was pushing too hard. "Take it easy. You don't want to hurt yourself," he said with the blithe arrogance of someone who never had to exert himself much beyond lowering his girth into his Ferrari. Every painful step taught me to feel like me again, every painful step taught me more about overcoming than any time I've ever spent with a shrink.

Maybe running works for me *because* the doctors made the mistake of saying, "You'll never run again, Grace." I'm stubborn that way, even when the things I stick with aren't good for me. Telling me "no, you can't" is like waving a red cape in front of a bull. I'll chase what I'm told I can't have until I either get it or die trying, which I've almost done a couple of times. *I will run again, dammit!* became my mantra, and my "pigheadedness," as Faith calls my stubborn streak, had become my most powerful ally.

Heading south on Fort Lauderdale beach, I jog by a few tourists with Arctic white skin setting up beach chairs and umbrellas to protect them from the sun, the same sun that brought them to Florida in the first place. The man in a thong no thicker than dental floss who runs the beach every morning passes and gives me a half wave like the one Queen Elizabeth gives to her subjects. I always wave back, but with eyes averted. He looks like some demented nymph escaped from a water ballet. I'm no prude, but what is he thinking, hanging his privates out like that for all to see?

The sand rakes, Zambonis for the beach, already did their work in the wee hours, the sand scraped into perfect corduroy, which makes running less taxing. To avoid that path of least resistance, I head for the deepest sand, the area behind the sea wall separating A1A from the beach. It hurts to push hard in the deep drifts, but it builds strength and endurance, and the more miles I get under my belt, the more I feel Oscar to be a part of me. Seven weeks left until the Miami Marathon, my first with Oscar, although I did run a few others back when I was a biped. There's no way I'm not getting to that start line. And, even if I have to crawl, I'll get to the finish.

My phone vibrates. I hate bringing the damn thing with me, but I need to hustle. Most of my work starts with a phone call. Missing one means a potential client might go elsewhere right along with my ability to pay the bills. I slip the phone from the waterproof case strapped to my arm and answer on the last ring before it goes to voicemail. "Grace Locke speaking."

"It's H."

"And good morning to you."

"Why are you out of breath, G? You okay?"

"No, I'm running from the po-po," I say, panting.

Silence.

"Kidding! Jesus. When did you lose your sense of humor?"

More silence accompanied by a couple of sniffles.

"I'm sorry. Bad joke. What's wrong?"

"She's . . . throwing his stuff . . . into the Glades . . ." she says, a tremble in her voice that soon becomes an outright sobbing fit.

I lean against the sea wall. "H, take a breath. Who's she?"

"Sadie."

"What?"

"She threw his phone, his books, his . . ."

I raise my voice enough to cut through her wails, loud enough that a couple of fast walkers on A1A throw me dirty looks. "Threw what where?"

"Grace, oh God!"

"Listen to me, woman! Take a second and get a hold of yourself."

I wait as she blows her nose a few times.

"Where are you?"

"In my car."

"Why are—? Never mind. You're not driving, are you?"

"No. I'm parked outside Sadie's place."

"Okay, relax and start at the beginning."

She sucks in a deep breath, a mucous-y rattle in her throat. "I came over here to check on Sadie. Before going to work. And that's when I found her . . ."

The hair bristles on the back of my neck. "Found her?"

"She was out back, throwing Ozz's things in the canal. One by one." She sobs. "Jesus, Grace, she was tossing them into the water!"

"Why?" I yell, drawing more filthy looks from other butt-crack-of-dawn workout freaks like me. I can't say I blame them. Like them, I revel in the serenity of the new day before chaos descends.

"I know it's tradition, but . . ."

I pick at a glob of chewing gum stuck to Oscar. "Shit. People are pigs."

"What? What did you say?"

I toss the wad of gum in a trash can, grossed out by the thought of whose mouth it had been in. "What about tradition?"

"Yeah, tradition," she says in an "of course, you idiot" tone.

"H, I'm not with you here. You're going to need to tell me what the hell you're talking about."

She exhales hard. "I'm sorry. Seminoles believe that holding onto the dead's possessions hinders their journey to the afterlife. That's what the old-timers believe anyway."

"Really?" I say, unable to keep a tone of horror out of my voice. As painful as it was, I returned the personal effects belonging to Jones, Garcia, and the gunner who played "Gangsta's Paradise" nonstop in the Humvee to their wives when I got stateside, hoping they'd provide some solace.

"I don't believe in that voodoo woo-woo, and I didn't think Sadie did either." She blows her nose again. "If I hadn't got there, she would have thrown his computer away, for God's sake! I had to fight her to get it out of her hands." Her voice fades to a whisper. "Everything else of his is gone. Everything."

I wait a few seconds, then say, "Look, Sadie can't be in her right mind right now."

"Dammit! I don't got one single thing left of him now, can you understand that?" I hear her car door slam.

"Wait! Don't hang up."

"Look, I gotta go." Footsteps, then silence.

"You still there?" I ask.

A few more seconds. "I'm here."

"Maybe you want to come stay with me for a couple of days? Get away from things? Vin will give you a room."

"Thanks, but even though I'm as pissed as hell, I shouldn't leave Sadie on her own right now." Hachi grunts. "And the old man would probably give me the one by the ice machine like last time."

I press my lips together to keep from laughing. She's right, the last time she stayed over that's exactly the room he gave her, and now he calls it the Pocahontas Suite, which makes a few of his more adventurous customers think some kinky shit comes included.

"You're a good sister." I sigh. "But . . ."

"Don't worry."

I imagine her walking up the neatly trimmed path.

"I'll call you later, I promise," she says.

I'm reluctant to let her go, but what can I do when I'm sixty miles away? "Roger that."

She gives me a brittle laugh. "You and your military lingo."

"Hard habit to break." I turn for home. I can't be late to the court. I never am. In my mind, a slip like being late once will only open the floodgates to other slippage.

"You hear from Dr. Owen?"

"He said he'd get me the autopsy report in the next couple of days."

"Thanks," she says, her voice stronger now, as if she's preparing herself to be the strong one for Sadie. "But you're probably right. There's probably nothing else *to* know."

I'm glad she's the one to say it, but I can't disagree.

"If it gives you and Sadie closure, I'm glad to have been able to make it happen," I say, disgusted at myself for using that damn word "closure," a euphemism best suited to doors and gates. The truth is, sometimes euphemisms are all we have to put a name to a vain attempt at explaining inexplicable loss.

"See you at St. A's this week?"

"Roger that," I say, and we both laugh—me because I'm comforted by the fact that she's still sober, Hachi because she's still hounding me to keep working the Program and she's enjoying being a thorn in my side, maybe a bit too much. Role reversal is a karmic bitch.

Making sure there's an autopsy for Ozz was the least I could do for a boy who can no longer speak for himself and a family that will never be the same. Perhaps it's also a way to make my amends to my squad's families too, putting my men at risk to go get those damn Easter decorations. That was one fact I didn't share with their families when I returned their possessions.

18

Alonso Tremayne stretched his legs out in front of him, hands laced behind his head, a man at ease, while Ozz felt like a kid going to the dentist, resigned but petrified. Ray Spire, on the other hand, was neither at ease nor resigned. He might be acting like the big man on campus, lounging back in his seat sipping on a drink, but the foot crossed over a knee tap, tap, tapping was a sure sign he knew deep down he had a long way to go to be like Tremayne.

"You ever been in a limo before, Ozz?" Tremayne asked.

"No, sir."

"What do you think? Think you could get used to this?" Spire asked, his tone pressured, as if he wanted Ozz to be impressed, to think Spire traveled in the back of a stretch limo every day and that Ozz would too if he went along with their plan, whatever that was. And there had to be one. This was no joyride.

Ozz studied the long compartment, the glove leather seats, the bar complete with a rack of crystal glasses, the track lighting, the chauffeur hidden behind a retractable screen. He'd seen the inside of limos on TV, but being in one was about as far from his real life as not having to worry about money.

He summoned the most solicitous tone he could manage, like the desperate, impoverished kid from the sticks that Spire thought he was—not easy, given Ozz wasn't prone to kissing ass, except for Junior's, and that was to stay alive. "No way, Mr. Spire. I ain't never been in one of these before. It's real nice."

And it was nice, but Ozz knew nice things had a price, and he was sure he'd be the one paying it, not Tremayne and Spire. Still, he didn't want to do anything to screw up his scholarship from USC. He'd play along, for now.

"So, Ozz, you're going to have to see the doctor just this once. After that I'll be bringing whatever you need by your house," Spire said, eyes gleaming.

He turned his gaze out the window to downtown Miami, a jagged skyline of glass and steel skyscrapers, the same view Trey would see if his cell had a window.

"After your appointment, how about we take you for a steak lunch to celebrate?" Tremayne said. "You like steak, don't you?"

"Celebrate?" Ozz said.

Tremayne slapped a hand on his thigh. "USC, my *alma mater,* getting a great running back. And you getting the hell out of the Glades. I'd say that's plenty reason to celebrate."

He shifted in his seat. "I haven't actually signed the commitment letter yet, Mr. Tremayne."

Tremayne gave a dismissive wave. "A mere formality, kid. You're as good as a Trojan. And we're happy to have you."

He glanced back out the window as they passed a pink marble marker engraved with "Welcome to Coral Gables, the City Beautiful," a moniker so different from Sugar Bay's "Her Soil is Her Fortune" that he had to stifle a laugh. Coral Gables had always been a mythical place in his mind, the home of the University of Miami and its legendary football team, the Hurricanes. Many Panthers had ended up at The U, but Coral Gables was too close to Sugar Bay for his liking. Too close to

Junior.

Tremayne sat forward on the bench seat that ran along the side of the interior, hands clasped. "Which gets me back to why we're here, gentlemen."

Ozz turned his gaze back inside.

Spire picked up the thread for Tremayne. "Consider today the first day of your professional football career, Osceola Gordon. Today is the day Dr. Manley is going to set you up on a regimen of supplements that are going to help you achieve your fullest potential."

Ozz opened his mouth, but shut it again. Whatever he said would make no difference. Men like Tremayne were used to getting what they wanted from kids like him who had dreamed of the fantasy of fame and fortune he was peddling since the first time they laced up their cleats.

"Only the best for our boys, at whatever cost," Tremayne said, as the limo pulled up to a strip mall and parked in front of a bay with blacked-out windows. The sign on the door read "BioGenix Anti-Aging Clinic."

The chauffeur opened the door, and Ozz stepped out, but not before hearing Tremayne say, "And the best ain't cheap," and Spire's reply, "When Ozz and the rest of the Trojans win a national championship dressed in Epic apparel and Epic cleats, you'll be happy, not to mention a lot richer. You can't put a value on all that free advertising, now can you?"

Tremayne slapped Spire on the back. "You did good getting his mother on board, Ray. Real good."

—

Ozz set the two prescriptions Dr. Manley had given him on his desk and flipped to "W" in the index of the *Physician's Desk Reference*. He also opened the browser on his laptop and googled "Winstrol."

He might be green, but he wasn't stupid. The limo ride hadn't been only to get lunch. It had been to get dope. They might wear fancier clothes, but Tremayne and Spire and Manley were no better than Junior. Or him.

Still, his blood ran cold as he read about how Winstrol was an anabolic steroid, a synthetic steroid derivative of testosterone. About how the oral version of the drug, the pills Manley had given him, would take effect in as little as two to three weeks, build lean body mass at a rapid rate, and help him recover faster from hard workouts. The Testosterone Cream was an innocuous blue-and-white jar. The white cream looked like his mother's body lotion but was said to increase muscle strength and size and enhance motivation to work out hard. He shook his head. He didn't need any more damn motivation. What he needed was to get far away.

He had read in the sports pages and magazines about what 'roids did. Even so, the list of side effects froze him to his chair—acne, increased sexual dysfunction, shrinking testicles, enlarged breasts in men, anxiety, paranoia, depression. On and on went the litany of horribles.

He stared at the medications. Maybe he was too uptight. Maybe they would help. It certainly sounded like they would. After all, strength and stamina were prerequisites to playing at a high level, in college and then in the NFL. And if they didn't, he could always stop taking them, couldn't he? After all, it was only for the next three months, until he finished out the season and locked up his scholarship. Also, he'd be helping his team win. Helping himself get the hell out of Sugar Bay.

"Osceola, didn't you hear me?"

He whipped around to see his mother standing in the doorway holding a pizza.

"Jesus, you scared me!" he said, sweeping the bottles into a drawer.

She gave him the evil eye.

"I'm sorry. I know. No taking the Lord's name in vain."

Sadie got up on her toes to see over his shoulder, to see what he was doing. "I thought you'd be hungry."

He was still full from the steak lunch, but he trailed her into the kitchen to get her out of his room.

Sadie set the pizza on the table alongside a couple of plates and silverware. "What's got you all jumpy?"

"Nothing."

Sadie put her hands on her hips. "Right. Nothin'. I know you better than that. What is it?"

He fidgeted with his fork. "I was thinking that, maybe, I might look at other schools."

"Other schools?" Sadie said, a slice hanging from her hands.

"Other than USC."

Sadie dropped the slice onto a plate. "Why? You been wanting to go there as long as I can remember. I mean, that's where Santonio went, isn't it?"

"I know." He took a bite of pizza. "USC might not be the place for me, that's all."

A shadow dimmed the light in her eyes. "Why do you say that?"

"Maybe I'd like the football program somewhere else better. Like, maybe Texas. Or Notre Dame?"

She shook her head from side to side, hard. "Like? What does 'like' have to do with it?"

"I thought—"

Sadie pointed her fork at him. "Stop thinking. You think way too damn much, just like your auntie!"

"What—"

"You got to go to USC, son."

He pushed his plate away. "Why? I got plenty of other options, and they're all great schools. I'll make some calls to follow up on all those letters they've been sending me."

Sadie stood and started to pace back and forth across the tiny kitchen. "Mr. Spire gave me a call earlier."

His stomach turned queasy, the greasy pizza churning in his gut, right alongside the comments he'd overheard getting out of the limo.

"See, after Spire was here with Coach Calhoun, he came back."

"When?"

She turned her back to him and stared out the window. "The next day."

"Why?"

"To give me some money."

He dropped his slice and pushed back from the table. "What?"

"He said he was grateful I was supportive of you goin' to USC. Said you was gonna be a star, win a championship." She flopped onto a chair and buried her head in her hands. "He said there would be more where that came from long as I kept you on track."

He struggled to keep his voice steady. "He paid you to make sure I don't change my mind?"

She nodded. "When he called today, he said if you did, that he'd make sure it got out that I took his money, and that would make you ineligible to play in college."

He squeezed his eyes shut.

She turned, her face scrunched into a knot. "He also said to make sure that you take those pills I saw you drop in your desk drawer. And that if you don't, or if you commit to another school, that he'll make sure they find out about them too."

A loyalty guarantee. Another goddamned loyalty guarantee.

He slammed his fists on his thighs and let out a roar that sounded like an animal in its death throes.

Football might be his means to an end, but it seemed that Spire had his too. And it was Ozz.

19

The inspector's certificate above the control panel alleges the last service was six months ago, a dubious assertion given how the ancient elevator lurches and groans all the way up to the third floor of the courthouse.

I make my way across the bridge from the old wing, a crumbling brick structure held together by mold and a few prayers from local officials who would rather spend money on a new hockey arena than a new courthouse. I cross the walkway into the not-so-old wing, a communist block monstrosity that houses the criminal divisions.

The morning crush is full on. Public Defenders, faces hidden behind stacks of files on the way to another predictable day at the conviction factory. State's Attorneys toting similar stacks, but wearing smirks that say they hold all the cards. Out-of-custody defendants walk with hands clasped behind backs, as if they expect the cuffs to be slapped on at any moment. Mothers tucking their boys' shirts in to make a good impression on juvy judges. The obligatory girlfriends in stripper heels and tube tops, court being the one place they can see their men without a grubby plexiglass wall in between. Like me, they're all still here, and I take comfort in that sameness, even if I'm no longer an insider. These hallways packed with discount suits and worried faces were once upon a time my home away from home when I was Assistant State's Attorney Locke, not just another mouthpiece hustling cases like I am now.

Out of the corner of my eye, I catch a few double takes from former colleagues and adversaries. It's been a while since my fall, but memories last long in a place where schadenfreude is a favorite pastime. I keep my head down, today being no day for reunions, and tardiness not one of Dr. Owen's vices. He's doing me the favor of meeting me in my backyard, said he "needed an outing," as if we're here for a picnic in a park, not a debrief on Ozz's autopsy.

As I scan the cafeteria for an out-of-the-way table, Joshua Jacobs appears, arms flapping. "Grace Locke, how the hell are you?"

I extend a hand to shake, but he pulls me in for his usual hug, ever the showman thanks to his weekly spot on the local news, *Jacobs's Justice*. I can't complain, though. Besides Marcus, Josh was my lifeline in what I've come to call my Dark Times. He saved me a conviction and managed to get me my law license back when my old boss, *the* State's Attorney Robert Britt, wanted to lock me up and make me swallow the key for almost costing him reelection with my much-reported bad behavior. There's nothing like the sound of the overly zealous falling, and I crashed to earth like a jet plane out of fuel.

Jacobs looks me up and down. "What brings you to the other side of the tracks? I hear you've gone uptown, that you're making some good jingle now in civil court."

I feel a blush coming on. "Let's just say I'm doing okay. But arguing about other people's money isn't as much fun as fighting for their freedom."

He winks. "I don't seem to remember you as much of a 'set

my people free' type." He clears his throat. "At least, not until you spent some time on the other side of the fence."

I fake punch him in the arm. "Ancient history, Josh."

His expression turns all business. "My offer still stands, any time you want to join me fighting for those freedoms you speak of, you let me know."

I'm distracted by Dr. Owen motioning from a table in back. "Josh, listen, sorry, I have to go," I say, giving him a quick peck on the cheek.

Jacobs follows me. "Dr. Death, good to see you here in the land of the living," he says before dashing off, his curlicue ponytail bouncing to the beat of the footfalls of his Cuban-heeled cowboy boots.

Dr. Owen raises his bushy white brows.

I shrug. "I'm sure he meant it as a compliment."

He shakes his head. "The man is quite the ringmaster, is he not?"

"Indeed. But the man is quite the lawyer too. He can well afford a little buffoonery to snake the opposition into thinking he's nothing more than a clown."

Dr. Owen points at the paper cup in front of me. "I took the liberty of getting you a cup of tea. It's Earl Grey. I hope you like it." He turns up his nose at the polystyrene cup. "Although, I'm not sure a 'cup' is what you'd call this hideous vessel."

I laugh.

"There's nothing funny about that cup, my dear."

"You sound like my mother, Doctor. Faith would rather poke herself in the eye with a sharp stick than drink tea out of anything other than bone china."

"Your mother is a wise woman."

I grab my legal pad and pen from my bag. "Thanks for meeting me here. I'd have been glad to come to you, you know."

"Truth is, Mr. Jacobs wasn't far off the mark. To be honest, I needed to get out among the living for a change. Even if I am here to talk about the dead." He pulls a file from his briefcase, his expression grim. "This is my report, as promised, but I thought it might be better if we met in person to discuss my findings." He coughs. "Given your close relationship with the young man's family."

"I think you know, Doc, I've seen more autopsy reports than I care to remember. Many of them gruesome. So there's not much that can shock me."

"Yes, of course." He pulls his chair close to the table and rests his palms on top of the file.

I take a sip of my tea, which tastes like bathwater.

"I'm sorry, Grace. Things are as they seem. Cause of death, gunshot wound to the chest at point-blank range. Manner of death, suicide."

As expected. And even if it weren't, if there were mass quantities of drugs in his system or a brain tumor, or any other number of horrors, would it matter? This was always destined to be an exercise in futility designed to delay the inevitable. My head starts to throb. Now it's my job to deliver more bad news. I should have known better than to ignore the old saw about no good deed going unpunished.

"No clues about what was in Ozz's mind, I suppose?"

He mirrors my stiff smile. "Pathological science has not progressed to that level yet, I'm afraid."

I sigh. "And perhaps it never should. As you said, maybe knowing why would cause even more distress."

"We should be careful what we wish for sometimes."

I flop back in my chair. "It's all such a waste, you know?"

He nods, sipping his tea. "Indeed."

"One last question."

He gives me a patient smile.

"What were the results of the toxicological tests?"

He flips open the report to the section labeled "Toxicology," and points at an empty grid.

I stand, trying not to look surprised, which would only lead to questions I don't want to answer. "Thanks, Doc. I know you didn't have to do this."

He struggles to his feet. "'Have to' are weighty words, to be sure. And I know I didn't, but if it were my family . . ." He sets his Panama hat on his head at a jaunty angle. "I bid you a good day."

As he hobbles away, my mind is consumed by why there was no trace of Lexapro in Ozz's system. There had been only two pills left in the prescription bottle. Hachi said he'd been taking it.

I scan the report again. No trace of opioids, either. But there wouldn't be, would there? Ozz was selling, not using. At least as far as I know.

20

Ozz hid in the shadows under an abandoned stilt house, its splintered, weathered boards creaking above him.

He buried his hands in his pockets to keep them from shaking, his eyes fixed on the horizon, but his mind was on the duffel bag at his feet, a bag full of more cash than he'd ever seen. Junior and his crew had dropped him on the causeway across the swamp from Everglades City. Praying to whomever might be listening, he'd walked the rest of the way to Chokoloskee, the only town in Florida's Ten Thousand Islands, a chain of mangrove islets surrounded by nothing but water, smugglers, and all manner of folks up to no good. Like him.

Trey used to bring him out here to Chokoloskee to fish for tarpon. Legend had it that the place was haunted by the ghosts of a Seminole family burned alive in their beds by the U.S. Army during the Seminole Wars. Likely Trey had told him that to scare him, but no matter what, Trey had always made sure they were gone before nightfall.

He walked down the rotting wood dock, its ancient boards

buffeted by the incoming tide. The Colombians had insisted the drop happen at high tide so they could cut the engines and glide to shore to avoid detection. Ozz hadn't wanted the drop to happen at all. He'd even risked trying to persuade Junior it was too risky. But Junior was nothing if not resolute, especially when it wasn't his ass on the line.

"That's exactly why you're going out there and not me," was Junior's response. "It's not like you got a choice, now, do you?"

Rivulets of sweat ran down his back, the heat of the day held in place by heavy cloud cover. He squinted into the pitch dark, lit only by split-second bursts from fireflies on the hunt for mates. The absence of ambient light heightened his other senses to the point that he sensed the rhythmic lapping of the wake against the dock and heard whispers in Spanish long before the cigarette boat slipped through the neck of the channel.

He hung back until a figure leapt onto the dock and tied the bowline to a piling. The man was dressed in all black, long sleeves, long pants, and cap pulled low over his face.

Junior had said there would be two men, but Ozz counted three. One on the dock, one at the helm, one in the rear, the two in the boat holding semi-automatic rifles.

"*Oye,*" the man on the dock shouted into the darkness.

Ozz patted the nine millimeter tucked into his waistband at the small of his back. He stepped forward, duffel bag in hand.

The figure in the back of the boat set down his rifle and heaved a bag the size of a toddler onto the dock.

The man on land pulled a handgun from his waistband and waved it at Ozz. "Coño, que te pasa, hombre? Apúrate, por Diós!"

Ozz had no idea what he was saying, except for the word Diós, which he'd learned from a Dominican kid in junior high when he heard him praying before a game. Ozz assumed whatever was said had to do with the cash, so he kicked the duffel forward.

The man shook his head and signaled with the gun for Ozz to pick up the bag and drop it in the boat. As soon as he complied, the man leapt into the boat and the man at the helm gunned the boat's engine.

Within seconds, the boat was exiting the bay at full speed, skimming over the surface of the water like a rocket, out into the Gulf of Mexico.

He sucked in a deep breath. It had all happened fast, as if in a dream.

But when he stepped forward to grab the bag, he realized his nightmare had only begun.

—

They left him alone in the windowless, frigid room for what seemed like hours without food or water. He wasn't in an actual hole in the ground, but now he understood what Ms. Locke meant by telling him to stay in his trench. But, as Junior said, it wasn't like he'd had a choice. It was do as he was told or go down for a murder he didn't commit.

The side of his face throbbed, his right eye swollen half shut. One moment he'd been about to grab the bag and get the hell out of there, the next he was facedown on the dock, hands cuffed behind his back. Then he was tossed into the back of a black SUV.

He wiped his bloody nose on the shoulder of his T-shirt and bit his lip hard to hold back the tears. They were watching through the two-way mirror. No way he was going to let them see him cry. He'd learned that much from Trey.

When they'd exited I-95 onto NW 5th Street, he'd realized where they were—the Federal Detention Center—and that he was in deeper than deep shit. FDC was a federal correctional facility, the prison where his own father was incarcerated. "The Conviction Factory" was what Trey called the federal system where the government's ninety-eight percent conviction rate was about as sure a thing as existed in the justice system. No slap-on-the-wrist plea bargains, no horse trading for less time. No way. The Feds? They were all about hard time. Trey was proof positive of that.

But, still, why here? This was a place where prisoners like Trey, *convicted* inmates, served their sentences, not a place where they took you for pre-trial detention. That much he knew from seeing what Trey went through when the Feds busted him. They'd held him for a while in another holding facility west of downtown Miami, until he entered his guilty plea. "Something a boy should never have to see his father do," was what the sentencing judge had said as Ozz sobbed in the front row of the gallery, Sadie at his side, stone-faced.

Without warning, three men burst into the room—the two giants who'd taken him down and a mountain of a black man in a navy blue suit and red tie.

The black man yanked the chair opposite Ozz back, the metal legs screeching on the concrete floor like fingernails on a blackboard.

"Osceola Gordon, I'm Marcus Jackson, Head of the South Florida Joint Drug Task Force. I am also chief prosecutor for the Florida Department of Law Enforcement." Jackson pointed at the white giants. "That there is Agent Montgomery of the Federal Bureau of Investigation." He swung his gaze to the other one. "And that there is Detective Rivera of the FDLE." The two giants took up their positions, one on each side of Ozz.

"But I think you've met them already," Jackson said, smiling ear to ear, the whites of his eyes tinted a greenish yellow under the fluorescent lights.

Jackson clasped his hands in front of him on the table, his thick forearms straining against the fabric of his suit coat. "You are the great Ozz Gordon, Wizard of The Glades," he said, giving Ozz the once-over. "I've heard a lot about you."

Ozz bit back the urge to vomit.

"But now what the world will hear about you is that you will be spending much of the rest of your natural life behind iron bars, not on the gridiron."

He forced himself to sit up straight and look Jackson in the eye. "I want my lawyer," Ozz said, conscious his voice sounded otherworldly, as if he were playacting and not doing a very good job of it.

Jackson leaned his chair back on two legs and let out a booming laugh. "*Your* lawyer? *You* have a lawyer?"

He held Jackson's gaze. He in fact did have a lawyer, so this man was not going to get him to back down on this point. On a host of others? Probably. This dude looked like he could bull his way through any defense, legal or football.

"Now that is interesting, Osceola. What kind of kid would need his own lawyer? Especially one on his way to college, where all an athlete like you will need is a strong body, a stronger will, and a high tolerance for alcohol." Jackson widened his eyes in a way that made him look crazy. "That is, if you ever see the inside of a college."

Ozz bit his lip hard enough to split the skin, the taste of blood like iron on his tongue.

Jackson shook a finger at him. "See, where I come from, someone who needs his own lawyer is someone who's up to no good. One who has planned for that rainy day, even if he hopes like hell it will never come. But one who's willing to take his chances." He glanced around the tiny room. "Welcome to your rainy day, Osceola."

Ozz narrowed his eyes, like Trey did when he meant business. "I asked for my lawyer."

"And this alleged lawyer. What might his name be?"

Ozz smirked at how assumptions were inevitable, be they regarding gender, race, religion, or skin color. They simplify a complicated world, to be sure, but that doesn't make them right. "*Her* name," he said.

Jackson grinned. "Nice. And what would this lady lawyer's name be?"

"*Her* name is Grace Locke," Ozz said, still holding Jackson's gaze, which took every last ounce of energy he had. "And I'm not sure she's much of a lady," he added, thinking of how she'd slung her leg up on the desk for him to see.

Jackson's chair came clattering down, and he shot out his cuffs, as if he needed more room for his broad shoulders and thick neck inside his suit coat. He let out a deafening laugh. "I think I'd agree with you on that."

"What?"

"Ozz, it seems as if you and I, we got more in common than you might think."

Ozz slumped down in his chair, his body like a wet noodle. "Yeah, how's that? From where I sit, we don't seem much alike at all."

Jackson leaned in. "I played ball too."

He wasn't surprised given Jackson's build, but he wasn't buying his switch to a good cop routine. He still wanted his lawyer.

"Defensive end. For Miami Northeastern. I'm sure you've heard of it. I played college too, but only because it was a way for me to get out. Any of that sound familiar to you?"

Ozz saw his future receding like a mirage on the highway as Jackson spoke.

"And we got another thing in common, son."

Ozz bristled. Why couldn't people call him by his damn name?

"The way I see it, we can both benefit from your not calling *your* lawyer."

Ozz couldn't help himself. He had to laugh. Trey was right. There were no good cops. Only those who put on a good show, and that was what Jackson was doing.

"You think that's funny?" Jackson said.

He let his gaze travel up to the ceiling and down to Jackson. "Mr. Jackson, I'm betting you know my daddy's locked up in this place. Maybe you're thinking you can get him to lean on me. To get me to spill my guys so I don't end up like him."

Jackson pulled his chair in close to the table. "Now you're talking. I think we are starting to move onto the same page."

The hair on the back of Ozz's neck bristled like it did when he was about to get hit from behind. "I might as well tell you, it ain't gonna work. I got nothing to say to you." He eyed Jackson. "I ain't no snitch, and my daddy ain't one either."

"Shoot. You do talk a good game as well as play one, Osceola Gordon." Jackson chuckled. "But still, just in case things aren't becoming clear in your mind, let me lay it out for you. You were stupid enough to run errands for Junior Williams, and you know what that got for you?"

Ozz sucked on his bleeding lip.

"Forty-five years in here." Jackson rubbed his hands together. "That's what you're looking at."

"*If* I'm convicted," he said, more as a "fuck you" than an actual possibility. He knew what he was facing. He also knew murder brought the needle, like Grace Locke had said.

"Oh, you'll be convicted, all right. We got you dead to rights," Jackson said. "That is, unless you do yourself and us a favor."

He dropped his head to his chest.

"Now that you know those things, let me tell you a few you don't." Jackson stood and started pacing back and forth behind Ozz's chair. "You know that your daddy refused to cooperate, right? Even when it would have meant a lot less time. Or maybe none at all, if he'd given us who we were really after. I mean, he didn't have a record before we found that stash in your shed."

He resisted the urge to twist around and see what Jackson was doing. "Like I said, my father's no snitch."

"No, he wasn't. But the more interesting question is why? Why didn't he help himself when he had the chance?"

Ozz shrugged as if he didn't care. Nothing he could do or say now would help anyway. He was screwed either way. Rat out Junior and he'd die, shanked in the yard, or if he got lucky, he'd live out every last day of his miserable life on death row. Keep his mouth shut and he'd spend decades locked up in Chokoloskee. A classic Catch-22. He'd read the book. But the only things he'd be reading from now on would be the dogeared copies of old crime novels in the prison library and contraband porno magazines.

Jackson leaned in close, his voice a whisper. "Your father didn't snitch because he was protecting your mother."

He twisted around to face Jackson. "What?"

"A real shocker, right? I mean, to you Sadie Gordon's just good ole Mom. Mom who works long hours at the prison to put food on the table."

His heart seized up at the thought of Sadie all alone. Who would take care of her? Hachi, sure, unless she fell off the wagon again.

"We didn't know who was in charge of running most of the dope out in Sugar Bay back then, but we've done a lot of work since."

Ozz opened his mouth to speak, but the words stuck in his throat.

"See, we've been keeping a real close eye on what's been going on out in the Glades since your daddy got locked up. We knew what he told us wasn't the whole story because more and more volume kept running through your hometown. We figured Trey had to be keeping something to himself." Jackson stopped pacing and rested his hands on the table, his face next to Ozz's. "But no way Trey Gordon was gonna budge. Like you said, Trey is a good soldier. A loyal soldier. Trey Gordon ain't no snitch."

"What are you telling me this for?"

"See, that stash we found out in that shed behind your house, turns out it belonged to your mother. But your daddy, he lied to protect her. To protect you. To make sure you grew up with a mother like he didn't."

Jackson shrugged. "Now, I got no way of knowing if he knew Sadie was running the same crew at the time, the one Junior and her run together now, now Trey's out of the picture."

Ozz lowered his head onto the dirty table, the cold metal a shock to his warm skin, skin that felt like it was being peeled from his body layer by layer.

"That's something you are gonna have to ask him." Jackson

stuck his face in Ozz's. "That is, if you decide to help us."

Jackson pushed a glass of water in front of him. "Hang in there, son. There's a few more things we need to talk about, things that might influence your decision to help us out or not."

"What?" Ozz moaned.

Jackson squatted down beside him. "We saw Junior drop you on the causeway. Junior's like your momma. Way too smart to do his own dirty work."

Ozz turned his head to the side and stared, wide-eyed, at Jackson.

"Seems as if you're beginning to get the idea. See, you weren't only working for Junior when you got busted with all that coke last night—you were working for your own mother. The same mother your father went to prison to protect." Jackson shook his head. "Not a happy family story."

Ozz turned away.

"But what I don't get is why? Why would someone like you with so much ahead of you throw it away like that?" Jackson reached across the table and rested a hand on his forearm. "You ain't got nothin' to lose here. The way I see it is you've got no choice but to help us."

"No choice." The same words Trey had used.

He sat back, lightheaded, the room spinning around him. "It was supposed to be a few pills, once a week. I sold them to rich folks in Palm Beach."

Jackson shook his head, harder this time. "That four kilos of coke was no handful of pills. Why take that chance?"

Ozz hesitated, his mind spiraling. To give any explanation was to sign his own death warrant.

"They'll find me wherever I go if I rat. They'll kill me."

Jackson pulled a chair alongside him and leaned in. "No, they won't. We'll make sure of that."

"I've seen 'em do it for a lot less."

Jackson loosened his tie. "Think of it this way. You haven't been charged with anything yet. You've got a clean record and, from what I read in the paper, a 4.0 GPA. No one but those of us in this room knows a thing about what you were up to in your spare time. You got a future, Ozz. I know what that's like, how hard you had to work to get a scholarship. It's so close you can taste it, isn't it? Freedom, I mean."

"For what any of that is worth now," Ozz mumbled.

Jackson rested a hand on his shoulder. "That means the world, Osceola Gordon. That means you know the right thing to do, the only thing, is help us help you."

"But Ms. Locke? I'd like—"

Jackson raised a hand to silence him. "Ms. Locke can wait. You get a pit bull like her involved at this point, and any deal's off the table. Help us and you get to save your life."

Ozz squeezed his eyes shut and forced the words out of his mouth, the few words that might save his life or get him killed. "Okay, what do I have to do?"

—

The split second that had changed his life forever, that had taken up all of his thoughts and dreams for weeks, took less than ten minutes to explain. Under oath, he explained how Junior did business, where he got his inventory, who he sold it to and where, how Ozz had seen Junior kill Miguel as easily as swat a fly, how he used it as leverage to get him to keep taking bigger and bigger risks.

When he was done giving his statement, Jackson and the giants left the room, saying they'd "be back in a few," whatever that meant. A few what? Minutes? Hours? Bile rose up his gullet. Decades, even? He rubbed his hands up and down his arms. All the warmth had gone out of him in the telling.

He slumped back in his chair. It was done. His choices had caught up with him. His heart did feel lighter, less burdened by the secrets, but still, what would any of this mean? Would he actually get to go to college? Ever play football again? Become a doctor? Or was this some kind of game Jackson was playing?

He looked like a good guy, seemed to understand, but Ozz knew that kids from his neighborhood were a dime a dozen, "collateral damage" as Ms. Locke had called them, especially when law enforcement had bigger fish to find.

He covered his face with his hands. Sadie? Could that be true, or a ruse to pump him for information?

"Ozz." Jackson's voice sounded from behind. "There's someone I want you to talk to."

He didn't turn around. Another cop was the last thing he needed.

"Ozz, it's for your own good," Jackson said.

After several deep breaths, he turned.

"Hello, son," Trey said from the doorway.

Ozz could have sworn the world tilted on its axis like a fun house.

"Thank you, Mr. Jackson," Trey said.

The giants unshackled Ozz, and Jackson motioned for Trey to take a seat beside him. "I think you two have some catching up to do," Jackson said. "Take however long you need. We'll be back to explain what has to happen next."

21

Vinnie scowls, his tanned face a tangle of wrinkles, some lines of laughter, some of pain. "You're off again? Back out to that damn swamp?"

Miranda yips and prances in front of him as if to say, "Yippee, another day being spoiled by Grandpa!" I'm starting to think she likes Vinnie better than me.

I hand him the leash. "I have to. But to keep you happy, I'm staying at Hachi's tonight so I don't have to drive back in the dark."

Vinnie signals Miranda to sit and digs a treat from his pocket. "And how is Pocahontas?"

I punch him on the arm. "Vin, that's not nice and you know it. How'd you like it if people called you guinea or goombah?"

He leans against the doorframe, his expression hard to pin down, a look torn between sadness and pride. Vinnie's a survivor, a man of his time and place, but that doesn't mean he doesn't have regrets. Finally, he replies, "I've been called worse."

He stands aside, and Miranda runs into his apartment. She

vaults onto the couch, her huge head held high as if to say, "See, I belong." And I know what she means. Vinnie's is home for both of us.

Vinnie pushes himself up. "You sure you don't want me to go with you? Seemed like things got off the chain with that wiseass last time."

I drop a bag of dog food inside the door along with Miranda's bowl inscribed with "I want to be the person my dog thinks I am." "I'm sure. Thanks for offering to be my knight in shining armor, but they're more than a little suspicious of strange people out there."

He gives me the side-eye. "Hey wait a New York minute! You sayin' I'm strange?"

"You said it, not me, my friend." I pat my backpack. "Besides, I have another friend to protect me."

He scowls. "A gun ain't no good when you get too comfortable with folks. That's when they can take real advantage, as you know."

I drop my eyes. "Let's not mention Sonny again, okay? That's ancient history."

He raises his hands in surrender.

I clear my throat. "Besides, I'm the last friend the pickers have. Without me, they'll have no choice but to go back to picking cane for Tremayne, if he doesn't fire them first."

"Still, I don't like it one bit, you goin' out there all by your lonesome."

"There's nothing to worry about," I say, trying to keep my voice level despite the anxiety bubbling in my chest. Breaking the autopsy news to Sadie and Hachi, and telling the pickers that Big Sugar came in with a lowball settlement offer, is about as appealing as an enema.

"You've made some enemies in your time, Gracie. Watch your back, is all." He goes inside and ruffles Miranda's ears. "Just you and me again, kid."

I give him a peck on the cheek. "I owe you. I hate leaving her alone."

"You kiddin' me? I love having the mutt around."

"And she's a good guard dog, which is helpful given how paranoid you seem."

He sticks his tongue out. "Am not! No reason to be. These days, I'm all about bingo and the early bird special."

"You're not fooling me, Vin. I know you from way back. The moment I'm gone, you're gonna bring in the dancing girls."

He points a crooked finger at me. "You think your job is to keep an eye on me, don't you? *That's* why you don't move out."

"I do not. I think it's the other way around. I don't move out because you keep an eye on me."

"Exactly," he replies, and closes the door, the three deadbolts identical to the ones he's installed on my door snicking into place.

—

I point the car west and drive as if on automatic pilot. This back and forth to Sugar Bay is growing old. I thought once the Big Sugar case was done I'd be back to my comfortable routine. Run. Work. Home. Dog. It may not be glamorous, but it is predictable, and it's a life I like just fine, one that I'm proud of, one that I've grown to rely on. Change used to excite me, but now I avoid change like booze and pills. I can afford better than my one-room efficiency at The Hurricane, but truth is, I like it there and I like the company. Like me, Vinnie keeps to himself most of the time, but in a pinch, he's there with a pan of lasagna and advice gleaned over a lifetime of hard knocks.

I pass through downtown Sugar Bay, which reminds me of Fallujah. Boarded up storefronts line Main Street. A fried chicken joint, pawn shop, and the coin laundry are the only going concerns, and even those look on the verge of collapse, their neon signs unlit for years, the store names spray-painted on the walls. The one newish-looking building is a mega chain drugstore at the intersection of Main Street and Mangrove, where I slow for a red light. I've half a mind to run the damn thing. Nothing good can come of being a stickler for rules in this town.

Out of nowhere, two identical black Cadillac sedans with tinted windows barrel out of the drugstore parking lot, tires screeching, and blast through the red light, nearly clipping my front end. Heart racing, I make sure the doors are locked. I look all around for a cop car, but as with most things in life, they're never there when you need them. All I feel, but cannot see, are eyes on me, the same hair-raising feeling on the back of my neck I had right before the IED went off under our Humvee.

But I'm alone, the street deserted, which does nothing to calm my nerves. Fallujah taught me deserted streets are never empty, they just appear that way. In reality, no one in sight means whoever is out there is better at not being seen than I am at seeing into the shadows.

When the light turns green, I punch the accelerator, but at that exact moment an old man wearing a "Jesus Saves" T-shirt pushing a walker with neon yellow tennis balls at the end of each leg steps off the sidewalk right in front of me. I slam on the brakes. My head bounces off the steering wheel. Rubbing my forehead, which will surely be black and blue by morning, I squint in the rear view and passenger side mirrors and repeat, my head on a manic swivel. Nothing. No one—only the old man hobbling across the street with a Zen look on his face. Maybe Jesus does save.

I exhale hard and floor it all the way to Mount Olive, running each and every red light and stop sign. Better to ask forgiveness than permission.

—

I pull into the strip mall, and even though I'm a few minutes late, I take a few seconds to compose myself. An antsy lawyer is about as good to anyone as tits on a bull. I need to put up a confident front, even if the news I'm about to deliver isn't exactly good.

I close my eyes and attempt to belly breathe, something Dr. Fleming, my psychologist, suggested, but which works about as well as yoga to calm my nerves. It's all too woo-woo for me, but I keep at it. As Faith always says, I'm late to abandon lost causes, like cheating husbands, unwinnable wars, and guilty clients.

Bang! Bang! Bang! A fist on the window.

I slip my hand into my bag on the passenger seat.

Hachi jumps back. "Grace! It's me!"

I fling open the door. "Jesus freaking Christ, woman! Are you trying to scare me to death?" I put my hands on my knees. "I thought you were . . ."

"What?"

I squint up at her and stop breathing. "Never mind." I know the look—the sunken, wild eyes from lack of sleep darting around as if she's being hunted. Her usually tidy braids hang like rats' tails.

"I need to talk to you," she says, grabbing for my sleeve.

I slam the car door and lock it with the key fob. "I don't have time for this now. I'm late."

She steps in front of me to block my way. "Please. There's something I need to tell you."

"The way you look tells me everything I need to know."

"Please," she says, her hollow eyes flooding with tears.

Over her shoulder, Reverend Mathias motions for me to come inside.

"I have to go."

She steps aside. "Of course you do."

The comment cuts, but I really do have to go.

She hangs her head.

"Where's your car?"

"I ran over here."

"Ran?"

She tugs again on my sleeve, harder this time. "I may be high, but I'm not stupid."

"Don't go anywhere, okay?" I shake off her hand. "This shouldn't take more than thirty minutes." I unlock the door. "There's snacks in the glove box if you're hungry."

"I promise I'll wait for you. Until you're done."

I drop the keys in my pocket. No way I'm going to believe any promises a junkie makes. I've made them myself more times than I can count. "Okay, and there's something I have to tell you and Sadie too, about what the M.E. found. Wait for me in the car. We can go over to Sadie's together. We'll talk on the way."

She takes a quick look around, throws herself in the back seat, and hunkers down out of sight.

—

"Two million five hundred thousand dollars is the offer on the table."

The crowd sits in stunned silence. Because the number, any number with a million in it sounds huge, or because it's half of what the jury awarded? I'm not sure.

I scan the room for Arturo, hand on my bag atop the lectern, flap open for easy access. Shooting a gun in a house of worship is the last thing a sinner like me needs to be doing. Still, better safe than dead.

I point at a raised hand and follow it down to the face of the same young man who helped me when Arturo erupted. "Yes?"

"That's half of what the jury awarded, Ms. Locke," he says, perhaps for clarification for the non-native English speakers in the crowd.

I notice the young man's Panthers ball cap.

"And if you all decide to take that offer, Alonso Tremayne, the chief executive officer, promises to cut you all checks within two weeks."

I resist the urge to check again for Arturo, but I've got that same prickling sensation under my skin, the same one I used to get when knocking on doors looking for so-called bad guys in Iraq. As it turned out, there were fewer than the American public were led to believe, but that aura of danger kept us alive on more than one patrol. All but one.

"What do you think we should do, Ms. Locke?" the young man asks.

I grab the lectern with both hands and take a second to think it over. All I've got to lose is a portion of my contingency fee on this one case. For these folks, however, this is their one chance at financial security, not to mention justice. "As your lawyer, I must tell you that appeals take time, and lots of it. Sometimes years."

I let the predictable wave of discontent rumble through the sanctuary.

"Look, haven't I always been honest with you?"

Most nod.

"I am as disappointed in the offer as you are." I pause, expecting Arturo to weigh in, but he's nowhere in sight. "Having said that, two and a half million isn't pennies. It would go a long way to helping each of you. But what I cannot tell you is whether to accept the offer or not. That is for you to decide, each one of you based on what you feel is best for you and your families."

A man in the back row I recognize to be Floyd Pyle, a cane cutter who lost his apartment when he didn't get a paycheck for weeks, stands. "My wife and I . . ." He glances down at a slight woman with a sweet smile. "We would like to take the money. We can't wait." He bows his head. "We've got to get out of the homeless shelter."

"And pay the electric and put food on the table," says a voice from the front row.

One from the middle of the crowd chimes in. "And we've got doctors' bills to pay."

I raise a hand to quiet the crowd. "Here's what we have to do. I've brought copies of the settlement offer. Now, I know it looks like a bunch of legalese, and it is, but it's important legalese. Please read it carefully as best you can, and call me if you have any questions. When you leave, pick up a packet from the back. There's one for each of you. In it is a sheet of paper that asks if you agree with the offer or not, or if you want to go it alone with another lawyer. Attached is a stamped envelope addressed to me for you to send in your choice. Sign and date it and drop it in the mail as soon as possible. I have to give our response to Big Sugar no later than ten days from today. All the documents I've given you are in English, Spanish, and Creole, but if you have any question or concern, or if there's anything you don't understand, please call me at my office collect. My card is stapled to the packet. I look forward to hearing from you." I pick up my briefcase. "Until then, please take care of yourselves and each other."

The young man appears at my side. "Ms. Locke?" he says, a quaver in his voice.

"Yes," I say, more reaction than intention, my thoughts consumed as they are by how to deal with a loaded Hachi hiding in the back seat of my car.

"My name is Whitey Pierre," he says.

"Yes, I remember you from our last meeting."

He glances down at a much smaller, wiry older man standing beside him, who I recognize as one of the pickers. "This is my father, Emmanuel."

"Thanks to you both for coming."

The man dips his head in the way people used to taking orders do.

"Whitey, right?" I ask. If his incongruous name hadn't got my attention, the Panthers hat would have.

"Wilson, but they call me Whitey." He gives me a patient smile. "It's a long story."

"Nice to meet you again, Wilson. And thank you for your help last time."

He tucks his head to his chest, shifting from foot to foot.

"Is there something I can help you with?"

He casts a sideways glance at his father. "It's about Mr. Tremayne. You know who he is, right?"

"Of course. The guy who'll be signing all your checks soon, I hope." I point at his hat. "And I saw his name on your team's facility. He's a real big deal in these parts, from what I can tell."

"He went to SBH way back before he made it rich, is what Coach says."

"You play for the Panthers?"

He nods, but won't meet my gaze.

"*Dis-lui!*" Emmanuel says, poking his son in the ribs, which even I recognize from a few less-than-distinguished years of high school French as "tell her."

"Tremayne thinks if he throws enough money around in town, folks will think he's a good guy."

I glance at Emmanuel, his wizened hands clutching a battered straw hat. "And you think he's not a good guy?"

He chews on his top lip.

"We all know he doesn't treat his workers like your father right. Is that what you mean?"

Emmanuel smacks him in the chest with his hat. "*Dis-lui!*"

He swallows hard. "Look, Tremayne's always bragging about how many kids from Sugar Bay go on to play college ball and then the pros. He even put some of us in his commercials. It makes him look good, I guess."

I sling my bag over my shoulder, growing impatient with what is turning into more of a deposition of a reluctant witness than a conversation with a willing one. "I'm not sure I understand what you're trying to say. I mean, the guy's a lowlife, given how he treats people, but it seems like any money he puts up as a booster for your school and your team would be a bright spot, maybe the only one as far as he's concerned."

He drops his eyes. "That's not all he's doing, Ms. Locke."

Reverend Mathias calls from the back of the sanctuary. "Grace, I need to close up."

"Almost done, Reverend."

I widen my eyes to let Whitey know to get to the point.

"Okay, here's the deal. Tremayne's paying for kids to get

bigger, faster, stronger, to do whatever it takes to win."

I freeze. "What?" I say.

"Look, I'm here because my dad made me come. He found out I was on Tremayne's . . . his program. At least that's what he calls it."

"Program?"

"Steroids, testosterone . . . whatever."

"What?"

"Half the team is taking them. That shit works, but it makes you feel . . ."

"What?" I say, even though I'm aware I sound like a parrot. Yet what he's saying is coming at me out of the blue, and I'm struggling to take it in.

He forges ahead, his words tumbling one on top of the other. "I don't know, kinda nuts sometimes. Other times they make me feel sad. You just can't say how they're going to hit you. They mess with your head is what I'm saying." He crosses his muscular arms across his chest and hunches over as if he's trying to make himself smaller. "And your body too."

I glance at Reverend Mathias by the door, stacking hymnals. "A couple more minutes, Reverend, I promise."

Whitey takes his father by the arm. "Look, I came here with a job to do and I've done it. We need to leave."

"Wait! Tremayne's bankrolling the whole thing?" I say, not sure what that "thing" is.

"There's always college scouts hanging around, trying to recruit us. Tremayne's always acting like the big man on campus with his fancy watch and chauffeur and whatnot."

"Maybe he's a proud alum. I mean, he did build that shrine to football y'all play in every Friday night."

"Ms. Locke, I've seen it with my own eyes."

"Seen what?"

"Tremayne giving the scouts cash."

"What? Why would he do that?"

He smirks. "You're a smart lady, Ms. Locke, but you clearly

don't know much about how football works."

I bite my tongue. Football maybe not so much, but I do know a lot about the Panthers' star player.

"Look, the scouts' game is to get the best kids to go to the schools that will pay them the most. They need the upfront money to give to us players. Sure, they make it seem like they're helping you, but once they got you, you're screwed even worse."

"And why is that?"

"If you don't agree to go to the school they say, they threaten you, say they'll let it be known what you took from them and then no one will give you a scholarship."

"And why would an uber rich man like Alonso Tremayne want anything to do with something shady like that?"

He shrugs. "You should know the answer to that, Ms. Locke."

I open my palms.

"Tremayne likes to be the king of all things in these parts."

"You got that right,' I say.

He shakes his head. "As much as I hate to admit it, he's helped me, got me my ticket out of Sugar Bay and a lot of other kids too."

I resist the urge to ask about Ozz. This boy has enough to worry about.

"Miss Locke, we must go," Reverend Mathias says.

"Coming," I reply, motioning to Whitey and Emmanuel to follow me outside. "Walk with me. Explain to me how this scheme works."

Emmanuel shoots his son a withering look, eyes ordering him to go on.

"They take you to a doctor down in Coral Gables at some place called an 'anti-aging' clinic—you know, the kind of place old guys go to get pills to help them get a boner."

He jerks his head at Emmanuel. "My dad found the pills and the cream." His eyes grow hazy. "My mom died of an overdose a few years back."

I lower my eyes. "I'm sorry."

"He doesn't understand the good some drugs can do. He thinks they're all bad."

I look at Emmanuel, his head bowed in shame.

Whitey looks down at his father, a sad smile contorting his handsome face. "He knows he has to live with it. It was what's best for me. At least, he understands now that I got my scholarship offer from USC."

My heart seizes up like a fist closing deep in my chest.

I thank Reverend Mathias, and we step outside, the smell of scorched cane and night jasmine in the air just as it had been the night Ozz shot himself. "Why are you telling me this?"

"Maybe some good can come of it all." He rests a hand on his father's shoulder. "He made me promise I would. Said you might be able to use the information in some way against Tremayne for the good of all of us."

I study Emmanuel's craggy features made sharp by hunger. He gives me an angelic smile, all the proof I need that Tremayne has underestimated this picker, and likely others whose sons play Panther football.

I look around to make sure no one is listening. "If I'm following you, you're suggesting that if Tremayne doesn't agree to a better settlement offer, *his* big secret might become public knowledge?"

Whitey and his dad nod in unison.

I reel back. "But your dad doesn't speak English? I saw you translating for him earlier."

Whitey's eyes crinkle up at the corners in the same way as Emmanuel's. "He knows the words that matter."

"Don't we all, especially when they have dollar signs attached." I turn to leave, but then remember the toxicology report. "Do you happen to know if Ozz Gordon was on the Program?" I ask, making finger quotes.

Whitey shrugs. "I can't say, but the same scout who was trying to recruit him got me my scholarship after he . . ."

I look over my shoulder and see Hachi is sitting up in the

passenger seat. I need to get to her before she makes a scene.

"One last question. If it came to it, would you be willing to give a sworn statement about what you just told me?"

Whitey's face twists in mock confusion. "What are you talking about, Ms. Locke? I didn't tell you anything."

I roll my eyes. "Ever considered becoming a lawyer, Wilson? Seems like you'd be good at it."

Whitey grins. "Matter of fact, I have." He tilts his head from side to side. "Or maybe a poker player." His smile fades. "But for any of that, I need to get out of Sugar Bay," he says, taking his father's arm and leading him into the darkness.

—

I crank the engine. After checking both ways several times, I ease out of the parking lot and head back toward town.

"What was it you wanted to talk to me about?" I keep my eyes focused straight ahead. I don't need another incident like the one earlier. "Other than the obvious."

"It's not how it seems, Grace."

"Right, of course it's not. Nothing ever is."

"Just look!" She lifts her butt off the seat and digs around for something in the back pocket of her jeans.

I cannot see whatever it is because I am blinded by light.

22

Ozz ran his fingers over the Apple logo on the lid of his laptop, the most basic of images, childlike in its simplicity but beguiling in its promise of a better life, one he would never have now. His beloved laptop was one of the many things in this room, in his life, he would leave behind forever in fewer than six hours, along with his childhood, if he'd ever been able to call it that. It had all been a struggle.

He ran his fingers down the stack of books on his desk, the books he would abandon along with everything else. The thing about books, though, was that they were one of the few things that had never abandoned him. With books, it wasn't the tangible object that mattered, but what they taught, the doors they opened in his mind. Their teachings would be his forever, no matter what. Knowledge was one thing no one would take from him.

He pulled a pad of paper and ballpoint pen from the drawer. The note had to be in his handwriting to leave no room for doubt. What he was about to commit to words were things more than a few people might like to keep secret, and more than a few others might like to use as weapons against the secret keepers.

Most importantly, he needed there to be no question of his intent—to end his life.

The pen felt awkward in his hand, like it did when he'd started to learn to write back in the first grade, when his writing looked more like abstract art than words with meanings. Or maybe the awkwardness was because he hated lying—he'd had enough of lies for a lifetime. And yet, his life, at least what was left of it, from this day forward, his very identity, would be the biggest lie he'd ever told, and the most important.

And so he began. The clock was ticking down to kickoff.

Dear Auntie Hachi:

If you're reading this, I'm already gone.

The reason I've made the choice to end my life as I know it is simple—it's everything. It's all too much for me to ever be able to escape.

For a while now, my world has been dark. I cannot sleep. I cannot concentrate. My head hurts constantly and only becoming nothing will let me rest, give me peace.

Thanks, Auntie for trying to help, but the antidepressants didn't do the job, didn't free me. Nothing can but this end.

If my death can do one good thing, it is to tell the world that there are leeches out there who take advantage of kids who love to play football. Yes, I'm talking about you, Alonso Tremayne, and your buddies, the college scouts, who feed kids like me poison and trap them into making money for them and glory for you. If I can do something to let the world know about what's really happening in the locker room in every high school in America, that's enough for me, for now. But, as far as I'm concerned, it's too late for me. The damage is done.

Time to go. My clock has expired.

With love forever,

Osceola

23

I turn my head to the side, will my eyes to open.

"I knew it! I shouldn't have let you go alone."

Kaleidoscopic parts assembling themselves.

I struggle to push myself up.

"Relax, kid. We got you. You're safe."

We? Safe?

I blink hard. "Vin? Is that you?"

A cold, wet nose nuzzling my palm. "Miranda?"

"We're here, Gracie. We're both here."

I squint.

Focus!

White walls. Beeping machines. "Where's here?"

Vinnie perches on the side of the bed and squeezes my hand. "You're in the hospital. In Sugar Bay. There was an accident."

"Accident?"

"You were T-boned."

"What?" I glance down. A frame holding the sheets off my legs. "No!" I rip the sheets back. "Thank God," I say, rubbing my right leg to make sure it's still there. "But where's Oscar?"

"Let's just say, Oscar got the worst of it. He got crushed on impact. Doctor says you would have lost your leg if you hadn't already. You girls were lucky to survive."

Girls?

"Shit!" I swing my good leg over the side of the bed. "Where's Hachi? I need to see her!"

He grabs my shoulders and pushes me back.

"Vin, tell me! Is she okay?"

He drops his eyes.

"Jesus, is she? Tell me!"

"She's in a coma, Gracie."

I close my eyes. Lights coming fast. Then nothing.

Someone else leans in. "The doc says you're going to be fine. A few bumps and bruises."

"Manny? What the—"

"He did give you something for the pain, though. Before I got here." Manny clears his throat to hide the quaver in his usually steady baritone.

I gesture for him to forget it. "That's the least of my worries right now," I say, but the thought of having taken any narcotic is unsettling. At least this one had a purpose beyond escape.

"How'd you even know I was here?"

"They called me from the E.R.," Manny says. "You still had me listed as your next-of-kin on your car insurance."

"Sorry, I forgot to get that changed."

Manny pats my hand.

I cut my eyes to Vinnie. "And how'd you—"

"Manny came and got me and the mutt." Vinnie's eyes soften, the way they do when we pass babies or puppies on our morning walks. "I mean, it's not like we haven't done this before," he says, referring to the last time I almost died. He flashes me a smile in hopes I'll smile back, but all I can manage is a grunt. Almost dying is one bad habit I'd be happy to forego.

Vinnie pushes a button to adjust the bed into a sitting

position.

"What about the other car? Are they okay?"

"They took off, sweetheart." He levers me forward to puff my pillows. "And it wasn't no car. It was a truck that hit you, at least that's what the cops think."

Arturo's contorted face flashes through my brain, igniting a wave of anger in my chest. "Damn him," I say under my breath.

"What?" Manny says.

"Nothing."

But the thing is, Arturo may not be nothing. Like Vinnie keeps reminding me, it's not that I haven't made more than one enemy in my line of work, but Arturo is the most recent and the most explosive.

Miranda slaps her paw on the bed to get my attention, and I pet the soft fur on her head.

"What were you two doing last night driving around in the middle of freaking nowhere?" Vinnie says.

"I went to speak to the pickers at Mount Olive. Hachi met me there."

Manny's lips crease into a tight slash. The last time he saw Hachi was when we were together in his car, stopped at the traffic light, the night she was as high as she was last night. And I can't say I blame him for his reticence. We've been apart for some time, so it's not like he has any evidence to counter his low opinion of her, even if she has been sober ever since. Until last night, at least. Or so she says. But then, we both know addicts lie.

"She had something she needed to tell me . . ." I sit bolt upright and point at the wheelchair in the corner. "Bring that thing over here!"

—

Miranda and Manny jog alongside my wheelchair.

"Hey, slow down!" Vinnie says, trying to keep up.

"Gracie, at least let me push you. This is embarrassing,"

Manny says, panting.

"She had something in her pocket she wanted to show me," I say, powering down the hallway. This wasn't my first wheelchair rodeo. I gained a lot of arm strength from pushing myself around in a wheelchair at Walter Reed, then more by leaving Oscar in a corner when my stump hurts and going uniped with the aid of crutches.

I slam on the brakes in front of the nurses' station. "Where's the I.C.U.?"

A nurse peers over the counter, checking out Miranda's service dog vest, then motions with a pen. "End of the hall, take a right, then left. Family only, though."

With Vinnie and Manny providing additional horsepower from behind, we're off again. We stop in front of the nurses' station inside the I.C.U.

Vinnie clamps a hand on my shoulder. "I'll handle this, okay? I'll say I'm a family member. Her uncle, maybe."

I twist around. "How do you figure that's going to work?"

He lifts my white arm up to compare it to his tan one. His eyebrows hunch together. "We'll say you're her sister from another mother." He points at the wheelchair. "And we do have the chair for the sympathy factor."

Miranda shakes herself hard, as if to say, "This will never work."

A nurse pops out from behind the counter. "Aren't you . . . ?"

If I had a dollar for every time someone stopped my handsome City Commissioner husband in the street when we were married for some favor or other or for a selfie, or, in our not-so-good days, for his private number, I'd be living on a tropical island with an umbrella drink in my hand. A virgin one, of course.

"Out of the way, you two, before you get us booted out of here," Manny says, pushing in front of me.

After the nurse has fallen for Manny's sob story about our friend, his constituent, how she has given a lot to widows and orphans etc., she points us in the direction of Hachi's glass-fronted room.

"How's she doing?" I ask, my voice raspy from the intubation at the scene of the crash.

The nurse studies me, taking in my blackened eyes and bandaged hand. "You were the one with her in the car, weren't you?"

I swallow hard and nod.

"She's been through a lot. The next forty-eight hours will be critical to see if she's going to come out of the coma." She looks down at a chart. "Five minutes, okay? She's already had enough visitors for today."

I slam on the brakes. "Who? Other family members?" I ask, trying to sound casual.

"The police, not that she was in any state to talk to them. And then her sister." She turns her attention back to a stack of medical charts. "At least, the woman said she was her sister, too," she says, staring me in the eye.

"You did good." Vinnie jerks his head at Manny. "You're a good liar."

Manny almost smiles, catches himself, then smacks Vinnie on the arm. "Asshat!"

I roll my eyes. "I can always count on you two when I need a good con."

"Yes you can, sweetheart," Vinnie says.

I scan the jigsaw puzzle of tubes and wires connected to a bank of beeping monitors on a wheeled cart. My mind flashes back to waking up in the military hospital in Wiesbaden, Germany, surrounded by similar machines that had, I was told, kept me alive for three weeks. "My God."

I park at Hachi's bedside. "I'm sorry, H. All you wanted was to talk to me and . . ." I squeeze her limp hand and remember that hand reaching into her back pocket right before the explosion of light.

I shift my gaze to the closet. "Can you see if her clothes are in there?"

"Why would—" Vinnie replies.

"Do it, please."

He shrugs and slides the door open to reveal jeans and a blouse on hangers and her cowboy boots.

"Pass me the jeans."

He tents his brows but complies, Miranda's nose sniffing the fabric.

I slide my hand into the left back pocket and pull out a pancake-flat package of gum. In the right, I find a piece of paper, folded over several times.

"What is that?" Manny asks.

I unfold the paper and read the words several times before their meaning hits me.

"Holy shit!"

Vinnie leans in, peering at the document. "What? What is it?"

"It's a birth certificate."

Manny peeks over Vinnie's shoulder. "Whose?"

"Ozz's," I say in a whisper, as if to say it out loud would hurt even more.

I roll the wheelchair forward and grab Hachi's hand. "He was your son. Ozz was your son."

"Who's Ozz?" Manny crosses his arms over his chest. "But Hachi doesn't have kids."

Vinnie kneels beside me. "Ozz? The kid who . . ."

I drop my head to my chest.

"Why didn't she tell you? You girls are like sisters." Vinnie wipes a tear from my cheek. "She gave him up? Why?"

I'd like to say I don't know, but I do. I'd never have been able to mother a child when I was using, not that I had the chance. I look to Manny, who turns his face away, eyes clamped shut.

I bite back tears and stare down at Hachi, her body doll-like amid the tangle of machines, her expression serene. "But you, you were stronger. You didn't kill your own child with your own weakness," I say, the image of my stillborn child in the nurse's arms a guilty wound that will never heal.

Manny rests a hand on my back, his warmth radiating through my flimsy hospital gown.

I glance back at the birth certificate, a blank where the father's name should be.

"Miss Locke?"

I raise my head and see two men standing in the doorway. Their set jaws and discount suits are all I need to peg them as plainclothes cops or detectives, if you're one who cares to show respect.

"Miss Locke?" the taller of the two says again, a string bean with a funereal face.

"Yes, I'm Grace Locke."

They fix Vinnie and Manny with questioning stares, as if they're the ones with no right to be here.

I reach for Vinnie's hand. "This is my uncle, Vincent." I nod to Manny. "And this is my ex-husband, City Commissioner Armando Martinez."

They look at each other, then back at us, seemingly confused by our motley trio, not to mention Miranda standing sentry at my side.

"Can I help you?"

An awkward silence fills the room as they take in the scene. Hachi's unconscious form, her face wrapped in bandages, and my stump poking out from beneath my hospital gown.

After a moment, String Bean flashes a gold shield. "I'm Detective Cappas, and this here"—he points at his tight-lipped partner—"is Detective Rinker. Sugar Bay PD." Cappas points at Miranda, now standing up on her three legs, eyeing them as if they were her next meal. "Is she about to—?"

"She's fine," I reply. "She just doesn't care much for cops."

Cappas widens his eyes at Rinker.

"It's one of the many things we have in common."

"Miss Locke," Rinker says, stepping forward. Apparently,

unlike Cappas, he's not afraid of three-legged dogs, or one-legged women. "We've been at the scene of the collision all night."

I brace myself, for what I'm not sure, but the last time Manny, Vinnie, and I were in a hospital room with a couple of cops, I learned that someone had tried to kill me.

"Miss Locke, the collision was no accident. It was an intentional act."

While Rinker recites the reasons for their findings—no skid marks, high rate of speed, white paint chips—I feel a familiar, steely resolve hardening in my chest, the resolve to make sure the guilty pay. Same as I always feel when someone's tried to kill my best friend. And me.

24

Vinnie pulls Carmela, his ancient Crown Vic, curbside. He jumps out and rushes around to the passenger side with the agility of a much younger man, not a senior citizen who remembers the Kennedy administration as if it were yesterday. It's not because he liked JFK much, not at all in fact, but because mobsters of his vintage believe brother Bobby sold them out "after all they'd done for him in Chicago on election day."

He opens the back door for Miranda to leap out. He retrieves my crutches, Oscar 2.0 having gone the way of his predecessor Oscar 1.0—consigned to the junk heap of criminality. I might be the only person on the planet who needs to keep a prosthetist on speed dial.

He shadows me as I hobble my way to the office door. "I'm not a fragile bird, you know. I've used these damn things before."

He throws his hands up. "Excuse the hell out of me, why don't you? I was only tryin' to help."

I pull the keys from my pocket and unlock the three deadbolts on the door, a necessity given my office is in the heart of what some would call the ghetto but what I call a propitious location for attracting my kind of clientele. "You don't have to wait. I'll call you when I'm ready to leave," I say as Miranda trots inside and settles herself at her post. "Besides, I've got the beast. I'll be fine."

"Not a chance. I'm staying no matter what. And Jakie says he can come over too."

I sigh. We went over this back at The Hurricane. Not that it'll matter. Vinnie and Jake, my friend and the owner of my local bar, The Star, they're men made of the same stubborn cloth.

"Do me a favor and tell Jake there's no need. The guy's got a business to run, you know, unlike you retired codgers."

He runs to the kitchen in back and starts filling the coffee maker as if I haven't said a word. "And you better get used to having me around. I'm gonna be driving Miss Gracie, watching Miss Gracie, doing whatever the hell I need to do to keep Miss Gracie safe until we know who tried to run you off the road."

I plop down in the chair behind my desk and turn on my computer. "Maybe you need to get out more. Get yourself a girlfriend or something. Whatever will make you stop bugging the hell out of me."

"Yeah, yeah. Always the asshat." He looks at the ceiling. "Asshat, I like that. I think I'm going to add that to my vocabulary." He grins. "Thank you, Mr. Asshat Commissioner."

"You're incorrigible."

"If I knew what that meant, I might add it to my vocabulary too." He pulls over one of the client chairs and stations it beside Miranda. "Pretend like I'm not here."

I bite my tongue, aware that resistance is futile in the face of his Sicilian recalcitrance and the fact that Vinnie's the only way I can get around until Oscar 3.0 gets built to replace Oscar 2.0, which replaced Oscar 1.0, which was reduced to a mess of crumpled metal and smashed circuitry by a murderer.

I start banging away on the keyboard.

"Why we over here, anyway?" He sits back and folds his

hands in his lap. "Jake says to come over for some chow." He pastes on a goofy smile. "Maybe you're the one who needs getting out more." He tilts his head to one side. "I saw how Manny was looking at you."

I slam my hand down. "Enough already! Been there, done that. Got the divorce decree to prove it."

He sticks out a bottom lip. "You're no fun."

I groan, and Miranda yips in response.

"See, even she agrees. And she's a dog."

I stick my tongue out.

I click on the file containing all the documents I've accumulated during two years of representing the pickers.

"I mean, it's Saturday. A day for college football and . . ."

I shoot him my best withering look. "How can I pretend you're not here when you keep yapping?"

He looks at Miranda, head propped up on her paws. "Doc said she should rest up, and look at where we are." He casts an arm around. "What are we gonna do with your mommy?"

I hammer the enter button to open a file entitled "List of Plaintiffs."

A spreadsheet of each of the pickers' names and contact information fills the screen.

"Been a while since you've seen Jakie."

Another withering look doesn't work either.

"Jake is a nice fellow, maybe you should—"

I slam my fist on the desk again, sending Miranda sprinting into the storage room.

I leap up and hop after her on one leg. I find her whimpering in a corner, ears down, eyes full of fear. I lower myself onto the floor and bury my face in her neck.

"I'm sorry, pretty girl. Mommy doesn't like loud noises either."

After several minutes of stroking her back, she relaxes and plops her head in my lap.

Vinnie pokes his head around the door. "You girls okay?"

I hold out my arms. "Come over here and be useful."

He pulls me up, the feel of his bony, thin-skinned hands familiar in mine. He's helped me up after bad dreams, bad benders, and a bad marriage.

"Thanks," I say.

"For what?"

"For being here." I glance down at Miranda. "For us. I know I can be difficult."

He gives me a crooked smile. "You and me both. We're no good at feeling weak."

With Miranda tight on our heels, he helps me behind the desk and settles himself back into the chair by the door. "I'll be right over here if you need me."

"Roger that."

I scan the spreadsheet for Arturo's name. With dozens of plaintiffs in the case, I know only a few by name, the ones who stood out by serving as translators or leaders for the group, asking questions, helping explain the unexplainable, the unforgivable—why someone would think it's okay to rob another of their due.

Anxious to get out of Mount Olive the night of Arturo's outburst, I'd forgotten to ask Reverend Mathias his last name. Given he'd known Arturo by name, I'd assumed he was one of Mathias's congregants.

I cut my eyes to Vinnie, his eyes on the door, as if the enemy's on the other side. Or maybe he's trying not to make the mistake of disturbing me again.

After several passes, I find no one with the first name "Arturo." I try again, this time misspelling Arturo as "Arthuro," "Arthur," and "Artur."

"Shit! This can't be right. I must have made a mistake when I put this list together. His name's not here."

"Whose name?" Vinnie says in a tentative whisper.

"Arturo's."

"The one who created a scene at your meeting?"

I tap some more. "One and the same. He's the one picker that doesn't want to take Big Sugar's settlement offer. I wanted to give his info to the cops to check him out. He was furious. Maybe he—" I scan the list again. "Why's he not in here, dammit?"

Vinnie clears his throat. "It's obvious, isn't it, sweetheart?"

I stare at the screen, then at Vinnie.

"Why is this Arturo guy not on your client list? Think about it," he says, enunciating every word with precision.

I palm my forehead. "Because he's not one of my pickers."

He keeps staring at the door. "See, there we go. I knew you would figure it out. What with that fancy education and all."

"Arturo's a plant! He was there to stir up trouble, drag everything out, make sure they don't see any money any time soon."

"Or ever," he says. "Like if you were to disappear."

"What, you think . . . ?" Before I can say anything else, my phone vibrates, skittering across the desk. "Grace Locke speaking."

"Grace, it's Marcus."

"Marcus, long time no hear. I was beginning to think you had given me up for a new man," I say, trying to sound chipper, as opposed to freaked out.

"Funny," he says, but his tone is all business. "I've been busy working a big case, which is why I'm calling. I need you to meet me. There's something you need to know."

"Spit it out. You've got my attention."

"No. Not on the phone."

I look down at my stump. "Here's the thing. I was in a car accident. Well, not an accident, a—"

"A hit and run. I know."

"You know? How do you know?"

"Monday, four p.m., my office. I'll explain everything," he says, before the line goes dead.

I throw a balled-up piece of paper at Vinnie to get his attention. "I need a ride."

He throws the paper back at me. "It's getting late, kid. Nothing good happens after the sun goes down. You know that. I'll take you wherever you need to go in the morning."

I grab the crutches and head for the door, Miranda on my heels. "It has to be now. I need to see someone about some information. And I don't have much time."

"And here I was thinking it was time for some shut-eye." He pushes himself out of the chair and yawns. "Where we goin'?"

"The Star."

His eyes brighten. "I'm sure Jakie will be glad to see you."

—

"You should get that thing fixed," I say, jerking my thumb over my shoulder at the broken screen door hanging by one rusty hinge.

"I'll be damned." Jake doesn't raise his head from washing the dishes in the sink behind the bar. "If it's not a voice from another lifetime."

I slap the bar. "Hey, I'm a paying customer. I'd like some service here, if you don't mind," I say, maneuvering myself up onto what used to be my favorite stool back before I thought Jake and I were getting too close.

He doesn't turn around. On the back of his T-shirt du jour is a picture of O.J. Simpson and the quote "If the glove don't fit, you must acquit."

"She doesn't come around for ages, and then she's got the brass ones to get all pissy," Jake says to Vinnie, who is studying the musical selection on the jukebox to keep out of the fray, Miranda sniffing at his pocket for treats.

Jake flips the dish towel over his shoulder and comes out from behind the bar to greet me. "How are . . . Jesus, Grace, where's Oscar?" He flashes a crooked grin, the type that makes rough-around-the-edges guys like Jake look like movie stars. "He didn't leave you for another woman too, did he?"

I snatch the towel and smack him in the chest. "Smart-ass!

You sure haven't got any nicer since I haven't been coming around." I toss the towel back at him and settle onto the red leatherette stool, the kind they used to have in bars before bars got fancy and started charging seven bucks for a beer made with hops massaged by some brewmaster named Chad with a college degree in fermentation science.

Vinnie drops a quarter in the jukebox and Elvis's "Are You Lonesome Tonight" comes crackling through the speakers. He flashes me a shit-eating grin.

Jake perches his butt on the stool to my right, eyebrows drawn together, all pretense of yanking my chain gone. "Grace, what the heck happened to Oscar?"

I lean the crutches on the bar between us. "Car accident."

"Jesus. You okay?"

"Just a few bumps and bruises, otherwise I'm fine. Oscar got the worst of it. Turns out, if I had had a left leg, it would have been crushed when the engine block crashed into the passenger compartment. Funny how dumb luck works."

I lean my elbows on the bar and rest my face in my hands.

His eyes widen. "Don't tell me! Not the Jaguar?"

I look up at the ceiling. "Geez, thanks for the concern, bar boy. And no, it wasn't Percy's Jag." I exhale. "I was driving a rental. Been going back and forth to Sugar Bay and West Palm a lot."

He gives a confirmatory nod. "I saw in the news. Your big win. Congratulations, by the way. Nice payday."

I fill my cheeks with air and blow it out. "If that day ever comes. They've filed an appeal."

"Of course they have. Why pay today when you can put it off until tomorrow?"

"Or until never."

Jake catches me looking at the espresso machine. "Drop shot?"

"Pretty please. It's been a long couple of days."

He slips behind the bar to create my custom concoction—a

shot of espresso accompanied by a pint glass of Coca-Cola. Drop the shot into the glass, wait for the tinkling sound as it hits bottom, and *voilá*—a caffeine addict's dream.

He pulls down hard on the handle of the huge brass Italian espresso machine, Jake's pride and joy, a "gift" he got as payment for his investigative services into a restaurateur/money launderer who wasn't going to need it where he was going.

"So, the accident. What happened?"

I run my tongue over my lips. "Let's just say it was no accident. At least, that's what the cops think."

"Double Jesus."

I lower my head to hide the tears welling in my eyes.

He sets my drink down on a bar napkin. I stare in silence as beads of condensation form and drip onto the paper.

He bends forward and rests his elbows on the bar in front of me. "Oscar can be replaced. You cannot. Otherwise, it seems like you're okay." He winks. "I mean, you're still as full of piss and vinegar as ever."

I glance over my shoulder at the vintage jukebox. "Where's Moose?" I say, asking after Jake's erstwhile handyman and waiter who spends more time spinning old 45s than doing his actual job.

"I let him go early. I was fixing to close when you two walked in."

I smile. "Lawyer and a mobster walk into a bar. Sounds like the beginning of a bad joke."

He nudges me with his elbow. "See, you still got your sense of humor."

I close my eyes. "I wasn't alone. There was someone else in the car with me."

"Who?"

"Hachi."

"Is she okay?"

"She's in a coma. So, no."

He rubs my forearm, the skin on his hand rough and

calloused. "I'm sorry. Your sponsor, right?"

I wipe my drippy nose on my sleeve. "And she was my friend. I mean she *is* my friend."

He squeezes my hands in his, to let me know he's still here for me. Like he has been since I got out of the jail across the street and found myself with no choice but to turn to the dark side, to representing the types of criminals I used to lock up. A while back, we went on a couple of dates, a vain effort to convince ourselves we could lead normal lives with partners and dinners and dreams of babies, but it didn't take. Jake's not one to be tied down, and I'm not one you want to be tied to, so we let it go. But somewhere in there, one night walking down the beach, high on the incandescent beauty of the night sky under a full moon, I told him how, a few years ago, Hachi had found me with a loaded gun in one hand and an empty bottle of Jack Daniel's in the other.

He straightens up to his full height, six feet two inches of muscle and swagger. Jake had once been a cop, but got tempted by the fruits of the crime he was fighting. Or so the story goes. "Why do the cops think it's not an accident?"

"They said there were no skid marks, that whatever hit us kept right on going. All they can say is it was probably a white truck, given the impact and the paint it left behind."

"Bastards!" He rubs his chin the way he does when he's thinking hard, which he does a lot more than his many tattoos and gruff demeanor might suggest. "Any ideas?"

I shrug. "Who knows? I've made more than a few enemies in my time. Could be any number of cons, cops, or jealous girlfriends."

He comes around the bar and sits beside me. We both stare into the mirror behind the array of booze bottles.

"I'm serious," he says.

I swivel to face him. "I am too. Which is why I need you."

He points at his chest.

"Yes, you. I need your finely tuned investigative skills."

"Now you're talking my language, Counselor." He pulls a guest check pad and stub of a pencil out of his back pocket. "One P.I. coming up. Jake O'Brien at your service."

The warmth of his smile comforts me. Maybe Vinnie was right. Maybe I do need to get out more.

"Grace, what is it you need?"

"I need all you can get on Alonso Tremayne."

"Sounds familiar," he says, scribbling down the name.

"Yep, the chief executive officer of Big Sugar and all-around patron saint of Sugar Bay."

He cocks an eyebrow.

"Who knows, maybe there's some skeleton in his closet that can help my clients." *Or more than the one I know about,* is what I would say were I inclined to trust him with the information Whitey gave me. Sometimes, "need to know" is the best policy. Besides, Jake worries about me, and I don't need another shadow following me around. I've already got Vinnie for that.

"Yes, ma'am," he says, saluting me with the pencil.

I sigh.

"What?"

"Why is everyone calling me ma'am all of a sudden? Am I that old?"

"Maybe because you were Army?"

"Enlisted. Only female officers are ma'ams. And those broads are battleaxes, in my experience."

"And what? You're not?"

We share a laugh, which feels good too.

"You played sports, didn't you?" I ask.

"Sure, back in high school. Baseball and football. I still play some pickup basketball every now and again, except the knees ain't what they used to be," he says, rubbing them out of habit much like I rub my stump.

"Tell me, what do you know about performance-enhancing drugs?"

He cocks an eyebrow. "You mean like steroids and whatnot?"

I nod.

"Not much. Why?"

"Curious, that's all."

He stifles a laugh. "Grace, I've known you long enough to know you're a woman of few words, one who doesn't waste them asking questions without a purpose."

I raise my hands in the air. "Busted." I take a quick look over my shoulder, which I realize is paranoid. No way anyone with caviar tastes and a penchant for social climbing like Tremayne would frequent a dive bar like The Star, whose greatest attributes are anonymity for its customers and a mean chili dog.

"I've been told that some of the Sugar Bay Panthers are doping."

"Too bad. That shit is poison."

"Meaning?"

"Meaning it might make you stronger, but it can also make you moody." He wrinkles his nose. "And some PEDs can shrink your testicles and make you grow boobs, at least that's what I heard on ESPN."

"Yikes."

"Yikes is right. You get a big body, but lose your balls. That's what I call a Faustian bargain."

I grin. "You never cease to surprise me, Jake."

"What, you think you're the only one that can read?"

I hop off the stool and give him a peck on the cheek. "I owe you one."

"Grace Kelly Locke, you owe me more than one. Maybe one day I'll collect." He hands me the crutches. "In the meantime, I'll do some digging and see what comes up. I'll be in touch."

"No later than tomorrow morning, okay?" I say. "And tell me where you're doing that digging."

He salutes. "Yes, ma'am."

"I didn't—"

"Yes, you did." He sighs. "Grace, it's late."

I settle the crutches under my armpits. "That's something

else people keep telling me. What difference does late make?"

He holds the broken door open for me. "Always a woman on a mission. You never change."

"Roger that."

25

We gaze up at the shimmering glass tower perched beside the Intracoastal, across the waterway from Palm Beach Island.

"Not bad for a kid from the swamplands," Vinnie says.

"He's not actually *from* Sugar Bay."

"Didn't you say he grew up there?"

"He did, but he was born in Cuba. He came to Florida as a kid. Back in '59."

Vinnie's expression hardens. "I remember '59. Castro screwed my people that year too, when he shut down the casinos."

"Castro screwed a lot of people. Still does. Tremayne's parents got him out on an emergency airlift of children organized by the Catholic Church after Castro took over, and he never saw them again. He was adopted by a family in Sugar Bay, and the rest, as they say, is history," I say.

All this I know because Jake unearthed Tremayne's coming to Florida as part of Operation Pedro Pan in his overnight search, along with a few traffic tickets, hardly what TV cops call a "rap sheet." He attended college at USC, then worked his way through the ranks at Big Sugar all the way to CEO. Hometown boy made good. No scandals. Yet.

"History isn't history—it's not even past. Or something like that," Vinnie says.

I shake my head. "You and Jake, the pair of you are turning into quite the bookworms."

He nods. "Had plenty of time on my hands in the joint."

I look away.

"That rat bastard Fidel, he took that tropical paradise, all those ritzy casinos, beautiful dancing girls, rum that flowed like water, and turned it into a hellhole," he says, his eyes getting a faraway look.

"I take it you've been to Cuba?" I tilt my head from side to side. "Maybe back when some of your people, as you call them, were running the place?"

He puts a finger to his lips.

"Vin, you're quite the international man of mystery. You never cease to amaze."

He gives me a self-satisfied smile as he opens the passenger door for me to get out. "I aim to entertain, madame."

He walks Miranda and me to the entrance, past a marble fountain shaped like cane stalks out of which spritz water droplets like sugar crystals.

"Nice place Tremayne's got here," Vinnie says. "I once had a fountain in my yard in Staten Island. At least, I did until . . ."

I raise a hand. "The less I know the better." I look him in the eye. "I like to think of you as a nice man who grew up on the wrong side of the tracks made good."

He gives me a coy smile. "And I like to think of you thinking of me that way, sweetheart."

"But Tremayne, he's one of the bad guys. He may have grown up in Sugar Bay, but he's Palm Beach money all the way now, which makes squeezing some of it out of him all the sweeter."

Miranda sticks her snout in the fountain for a drink, then looks up at me as if she's gotten away with something.

"Good girl." Vinnie claps his hands. "Like Mommy says, better to ask forgiveness than permission."

"Go wait for us in the car, why don't you?"

"But—"

"This shouldn't take too long. All I could get was fifteen minutes of his time."

Vinnie purses his lips. "If Arturo is Tremayne's guy, you going in there alone isn't the best idea. Remember what happened last time you didn't take my advice?"

I unsling my bag from my shoulder and pat it, the outline of my gun reassuring. "Forewarned is forearmed." I sling the bag back over my shoulder. "Besides, what's Tremayne going to do, whack me in front of a bunch of high-priced suits? You of all people know that's not a good plan."

"I don't like it one bit." He registers his offense with a pout. "And don't talk to me that way in front of your fur child."

Miranda yips and gives him a paw.

"You spoil her."

"So what?"

"So, she's a Marine."

"Retired," he says.

"Marines never retire. Once a Marine—"

"Whatever you say, Gracie," he says, slouching off to wait.

Inside, I find a busty brunette in a skin-tight pencil skirt. "Miss Locke?"

She averts her gaze to Miranda, the corner of her mouth twitching.

"This is Miranda, my service dog."

"We don't allow animals in this building."

I'm tempted to say, "Except for the upper management, who are a breed all their own," but I settle for, "Wherever I go, she goes. It's the law."

She gives me an ingenue shrug, shoulder to ear. "I like dogs.

I have a cockapoo."

"What a shocker," I whisper to myself.

She leads us into a mirrored elevator and presses the Penthouse button. Seconds later, we emerge into a huge room with 360-degree views, Palm Beach Island to the east and the urban sprawl of West Palm Beach and the rest of Palm Beach County to the west, the haves and wanna-haves bifurcated by the Intracoastal Waterway.

"I bet on a clear day you can see Sugar Bay from here," I say.

She gives what I assume would be a frown were it not for the Botox cementing her brow into a flawless veneer. "What's Sugar Bay?"

"Never mind," I say as Tremayne appears from the other elevator, a flock of lawyers trailing behind like ducklings, the same crew from the trial.

With a flick of his wrist, Tremayne dismisses the brunette.

"Good lord, what happened to you, Ms. Locke?" Tremayne says, pointing at the crutches.

"Accident."

"How terrible," he says, his expression inscrutable, the expression of one who wishes to communicate nothing other than the fact that he is in charge. "Please, come sit. I understand you wish to discuss our settlement offer," he says, right arm extended in a welcoming gesture, although in a few short moments, he'll wish he'd never met me.

Miranda emits a deep growl.

"My, that's one large dog," he says, his faux smile cracking.

"She's half wolf," I say. "Like you."

His eyes narrow. "Why don't we take a seat over here?" He points at a marble conference table with a view to the ocean and a chair that would require me to have my back to any escape route.

"I'll stand," I say. "This won't take long."

He rocks back on his heels, hands in his pants pockets, the creases of which are razor sharp. "That's good, because I don't have much time." Smirk. "For you." Another smirk. "Today."

"Or any other day, for that matter. Isn't that the case?"

One of his eyelids flutters, a sure tell for anger brewing.

"What I mean is that delay is about all you've got going for you at this point, isn't it? The more you drag out paying my clients, the longer you keep their money in your bank accounts, the better, correct? Geez, I might even . . ." I snap my fingers, and Miranda sits at attention, eyes glued to Tremayne. "I might even have a terrible accident, and what would that time have given you? That unfortunate accident?" I snap my fingers twice. Miranda freezes. "I am no longer a problem for you, that's what it gets you. Even if it does mean hurting innocents in the process."

"I have no idea what you're talking about, Ms. Locke."

"Oh, but I bet you do, Mr. Tremayne."

I snap my fingers three times, and Miranda moves toward Tremayne.

Tremayne's lead trial counsel, a pale-skinned man in a suit that cost more than Tremayne pays a picker in a year, steps forward, but doesn't get the chance to tell me to tell Miranda to back off because she has already inserted her snout into Tremayne's crotch.

"Good girl," I say, pointing a crutch at her. "She used to be a Marine, you know. Served several tours in Iraq." I look down at where Oscar should be. "Like yours truly."

Tremayne tries to back away, hands in the air.

Miranda emits a rumbling growl from deep within her chest.

"You can lower your hands, Tremayne. That won't stop her from biting you in the balls if I tell her to."

"Get that thing away from me," Tremayne hisses.

"See the thing with dogs is they are highly trainable." I shrug. "But what's hard to do is untrain them. And what she's trained to do is hunt down bad guys."

No one says a word. No one moves an inch, every eye on Miranda.

I step back and lean against the wall by the elevator, keeping the entire group in my line of sight. I too was trained—to trust no one who has a reason to kill you. No one who might have already tried.

"Tremayne, it's my understanding that you grew up in Sugar Bay."

Tremayne gives a tentative nod.

"And you're the Sugar Bay Panthers' biggest booster. Hometown boy makes good and all that?"

More nodding.

"Makes your company seem like a good corporate citizen, giving back to the community from which you take so much. You'd do anything to keep your team winning, correct? I mean, if they started losing, those boys, the sons of the same people you work to death in your fields, they'd stop getting scholarships and their folks would mosey on to some other shit town to pick some other crop, right?"

Tremayne hesitates, eyes flitting around, a cornered rat.

"Right?" I yell.

I snap my fingers, and Miranda nudges his crotch with her snout.

"Yes," he says, but his commanding voice is gone right along with his swagger. He drops his head to his chest. "Ms. Locke, I think we can work this out."

I purse my lips. "Wonderful. Great minds think alike, it seems. See, that is exactly the result I was hoping for."

"What is it you want, Ms. Locke?"

I smirk. "It's what I have that you should want to know about, Mr. Tremayne."

He looks to his henchmen for support, but each of his high-priced lackeys has his hands up and his eyes down.

"For God's sake, boys. My dog is not a cop. Put your damn hands down, but keep them where I can see them. You look like goddamned scarecrows." I turn back to Tremayne. "The thing is, I have evidence you have been getting those Panther boys some extra help. Of the chemical variety."

Tremayne's top lip curls back and then back down. He's struggling not to show fear.

"You do know what I'm talking about. And you know what that help's called in my world, Mr. Tremayne?"

"What's that?" he says, looking back at his posse with a look that says, "This woman is an honest-to-God raving lunatic."

"It's called drug trafficking." I make a tut-tut sound. "And to minors, no less. That alone can put a person behind bars for decades. Trust me, I know. I've put a lot of your kind away in my time. And your kind don't thrive in prison." I look him up and down. "And I don't mean Camp Fed, I mean the real prison, the kind with large tattooed men in search of sex slaves and guards who don't give a fuck when rich shits like you end up shanked in the shower."

He squeezes his eyes shut, and so does everyone else, service staff included, except for Miranda and me.

"Then there's the issue of your friend Arturo."

Eyes widen in confusion.

"Gentlemen, it seems as if your boss here has been keeping secrets from you."

"We had no idea—" the pale intervenor from before says, his face even whiter now.

I raise a crutch. "Let me explain. Mr. Tremayne loses at trial against the pickers, whose meager wages he refused to pay. What does he do? He appeals. Why? Because delay is the criminal's best friend. Of course, he makes a lowball offer to make the whole thing go away, which, by the way, my clients reject."

I take a deep breath. Lying used to come much easier to me. Now, it sticks in my craw along with men like Tremayne with their fancy suits and empty promises.

"The truth is, Mr. Tremayne here understands I'm the one person willing to see things through to the end, which may be years from now. So what, you might ask?" I raise my finger as if testing the direction of the wind. "The thing is, a five-million-dollar potential liability on Big Sugar's books will do all kinds of damage to his company's financial situation, make borrowing money a bigger risk, make getting loans much more expensive. So, what did Tremayne want? He wanted to be done with the whole nightmare, and now. But, why not get rid of the one person who would never give up hounding him for every last red cent he stole from people who need every last cent to put food on their families' tables?"

Tremayne flicks his eyes down to a drooling Miranda.

"Don't even think it. She's staying right there until you give me what I want."

He holds out his hands, palms up. "I don't understand what it is you are so upset about, Ms. Locke."

"Don't act all innocent, Tremayne. You know what I want."

He shrugs as if he has no clue, but his neck turning redder and redder by the second tells me otherwise.

"Every penny you owe my people. That's all I want."

"Five million?" He grunts. "In exchange for what? I'm sure you're aware that half of your clients will be in the wind or dead by the time the appellate courts rule on my appeal."

I mimic his grunt. "You're missing the point here, Tremayne. I'm talking about your paying for my silence." I clear my throat. "And I'm not talking about five million. Double that is what I have in mind."

"That's very funny, Ms. Locke. I'd never take someone like you at your word." He smirks. "You're a trained liar, after all, much like them," he says, pointing at his lawyers. "Your type will say whatever suits her whenever it suits her, no matter how much she's been compensated for keeping her mouth shut."

I mirror his smirk and condescending tone. "Maybe, but your problem is you no longer have the luxury of choice."

He leers at me. "How do you figure that?"

"Let me break it down for you. What Arturo did is done. I'll heal up." His eyes scrunch as if he's confused, but I press on, the *beep beep beep* of the machines in Hachi's room looping through my head. "But my friend, the one Arturo put in a coma, she'll either survive or she won't. Murder or attempted murder. Take your pick. That on top of the PED trafficking, and you're—how is it you Cubans say? *Jodido?*" I turn my gaze to the lawyers. "Fucked, in English, gentlemen, is what your client is, and what you'll be too if I make a report to the Florida Bar about all of this. You may or may not have been involved, but it's the appearance of impropriety that counts, is it not?"

One by one the lawyers slink off for the emergency exit.

"Like rats from a sinking ship. How predictable." I turn my gaze to Tremayne, who is as white as the marble floor he's standing on. "Not that you need their help any longer. All that remains to be done is for you to sign checks totaling ten million. If you don't, or if any of you breathes a word of what went down here today, take my word for it, I can be counted on to turn you in for drug trafficking, which, by the way, carries a minimum mandatory sentence decades longer than you have left."

His shoulders sag.

"And don't worry about me keeping my word. I like my law license a little too much for me to risk any of this getting out."

"And what if I refuse?"

I reach behind me and press the elevator call button. "Then I'll call in the cavalry. I know people who can make what remains of your life a living hell."

When the elevator doors open, I back in and hold my finger on the Door Open button. "It's been nice doing business with you, gentlemen." I pan around. "At least, those of you with the balls to have stayed."

I issue the "stand down" command to Miranda, who extracts her snout from Tremayne's crotch and trots to my side, tail wagging, but looking over her shoulder every second or two. Perhaps she's also having second thoughts and might prefer to eat Tremayne for lunch than give him a second chance to do the right thing.

"You're a girl after my own heart," I say as the doors slide shut.

—

Vinnie bounds around the car to open the passenger side door. "How'd it go, kid?"

I take several deep breaths in an effort to slow the drum beat in my chest.

"You're kinda pale. You okay?"

I hand him the crutches and lower myself onto the seat.

"What did Tremayne say?"

"He didn't say that much, actually. I did most of the talking." I glance at Miranda stretched out in the back. "Or she did, even though she's a woman of very few words."

"Did you get it all worked out like you wanted for the pickers?"

"Yes, we did. Everyone's getting what they deserve. Now, let's go see how H is doing."

—

"It's never easy," the nurse says.

I let go of Hachi's hand and look up at the nurse changing out an empty bag of fluids attached to Hachi's IV drip. "What's never easy?"

"Saying goodbye."

I stand and settle my crutches under my arms. "I'll be back in a couple of days to check on her."

Her hands freeze midair. "You don't know, do you?"

"Don't know what?"

She touches my arm and turns me toward her. "Hachi had an advance directive naming her sister as her medical surrogate. She also had a living will in which she elected not to have any extraordinary measures taken to prolong her life. Because the doctors believe there's no chance Hachi will regain consciousness, her sister has decided to remove her from life support if she's still in a coma forty-eight hours from now."

I've jumped out of more aircraft than I can count, but this is a new kind of free fall. The kind without a parachute. "Wait. Sadie's going to let her die? How can she do that?"

The nurse looks away. "I know it's hard. You can't blame yourself for the accident, Ms. Locke."

I drop the crutches and grip the edge of the bed for support. "It wasn't an accident!"

Vinnie rushes to my side. "Gracie, what's wrong?"

"We need to get over to Sadie's, now!" I say. "I'm not going to let her die!"

26

Vinnie squeezes Carmela between a white sedan and a pickup.

"Wait here," I say.

"Oh no you don't. Not this time." He activates the child locks, but too late. My right leg's out before he's pulled to a complete stop.

"I'm not kidding. Wait here," I say, levering myself out of the car onto my right leg.

Miranda commences yipping in the back seat.

"And you too," I say. "You've both had enough excitement for one day."

"You've got some way of showing your appreciation to a schmuck who's been playing your chauffeur all day."

I lean against the door. "I appreciate your help, Vin, but it's better this way. You have a way of making trouble, and I'm about to make enough of that myself. No way I can let Sadie pull the plug on Hachi."

He lowers his head to the steering wheel in defeat. "How is it I get overruled every time, even when I'm right?"

I grab my crutches from the back. "One, because you have no choice. Two, because the one-legged maniac needs to do this one last thing so she can get the hell out of Sugar Bay once and for all."

Vinnie raises his head and casts a sideways glance at the decrepit playground across the street. "Amen to that."

I lean in to answer, but he's focused on an empty swing drifting back and forth on the breeze.

"A place like this sure could steal a kid's soul," he says.

"A place like this did."

—

Sadie's jaw drops. "Grace, what are you doing here? You're supposed to be in the hospital."

I shove the front door open with a crutch and stride into the living room. "Wrong! I'm alive and kicking, which is what I intend your sister to be for a long time."

"If you insist, come on in," she says, her tone more forceful than I've heard from her before.

She stands aside, smiling. At least, her mouth is. Her eyes pinball from me to the street and back, as if she thinks I might have brought company.

As soon as the door closes behind me, a hand grabs the back of my sweatshirt and a foot sweeps my crutches from under my arms, shoving me onto a chair.

"Get your hands up!" a deep voice says.

I raise my hands above my head and squint into the man's eyes, red like cherries, his skin translucent to the point that the bluish veins in his face and neck are visible.

He grabs me around the neck from behind in a horse-collar, pressing cold steel to my temple. "We were just talking about what to do with you. And, like magic, here you are."

I recognize the man with the gun to my head. He's the one Hachi said was no one. It would appear, however, that he is someone, someone who wants me dead.

And then there's what Marcus told me. As a result, I'm pretty sure I've got it right when I say, "Nice to finally meet you, Junior. I've heard so much about you."

"Don't just stand there, woman, get something to tie her up with!" he shouts to Sadie. He presses the gun deeper into my flesh.

"You're the one from Ozz's funeral," I say.

"That's right," he says, his breath a hideous mix of weed and garlic. "And nice to see you again too." I pull away, but he sticks his face in mine. "Or it would be if you hadn't gone and stuck your nose in places it don't belong."

Sadie returns with what looks to be the belt of the robe she was wearing when I visited with Hachi.

As Junior binds my hands together behind my back and to the chair, cutting off blood flow to my wrists, I will my expression to remain neutral. Not that looking cool will help. It's not the first time I've been tied to a chair. It didn't help then either.

I bite my lip to keep from screaming. Maybe Hachi has been using all along and pretending she's clean. Was Ozz her dealer, too? Was this a family affair? Ozz had seemed sincere when he came to ask for my help, sweet even, a kid out of his depth with people who wouldn't think twice about drowning him. Or was he?

Junior kicks my right leg and I wince. "Hell, I don't have to bother with your legs. It's not like you're goin' anywhere real fast with them wheels."

I glance out the front window, but I made Vinnie park down the street. He's probably taking a nap. Or talking to my damn dog, who he swears understands every word he says. Some security detail I've got. You'd never know I was once military police.

Junior catches me looking and yanks the curtains closed.

I look to Sadie seated on the sofa, arms crossed over her chest.

"Don't go thinking she's gonna help you out." He grins.

"She's the reason you're in this shit. Her and that dumbass sister of hers. But I just couldn't risk that bitch would fuck everything up."

My breath catches in my throat. It hadn't been Arturo. Or Tremayne, for that matter. Jesus, maybe Tremayne will come after me now, after what I put him through.

"Everything was goin' along just fine." He snorts. "But she had to go and see Trey in prison."

I keep moving my head from side to side to avoid being in the line of fire as he waves the gun for emphasis.

"And what did Trey do? He had to spill his guts to her and—"

He stops mid-sentence and smirks. "You got no idea, do you?"

"No idea about what? About who?" I reply, sounding as confused as I am. None of this is making sense. Hachi went to see Ozz's father, that much is clear, but . . .

"He has to go and spill his guts to her. And why? Because his boy was working for us to make some extra coin. And he thinks his 'lil Prince Ozz is too good for that."

I give him a blank stare.

"Trey, you fool. His father." He chuckles. "Well, not his real one, but Trey didn't have much choice but to act like one when that bitch dropped Ozz in her lap." He jerks his chin at Sadie, who averts her eyes.

I keep staring.

"That bitch is Ozz's mother. Or was," he says, and it's the first thing he's saying that I already knew. Ozz is dead. And Hachi is his biological mother.

He dips his face down in front of me. "You're lookin' confused, lawyer lady. Ain't you figured it out yet?"

And I keep staring, because I can't blink, I can't breathe. And I can't think straight. How could Junior know Ozz told me about Junior killing Miguel, about his threats to Ozz? I didn't breathe a word to a soul, and then Ozz killed himself and his secret died with him. Or maybe that's not what he means by "spill his guts."

He turns to Sadie. "Fuckin' fool! Kid made more in one day with us than baggin' groceries for six months."

"Damn straight," Sadie replies. "Until Trey had to go and grow a conscience and spoil it for everyone. I suppose he no longer saw the need to keep covering for me when he found out his precious boy had joined the family business."

My breath catches in my throat. It *was* a family business. Just not the family I thought.

Sadie gets up and takes a wide stance in front of me, hands on her hips. "Shit, you're not that smart after all." She slaps me hard across the mouth.

I lick a trickle of blood from my split bottom lip.

"What is it they say, the apple doesn't fall far from the tree?" She shakes her head. "My sister may be a junkie, but she always has been too much for telling the truth, doing the right thing, and all that shit. Like that boy of hers. Shit, he wouldn't even take them drugs to make him an even better football player when his future depended on it." She rolls her eyes. "He even wanted me to give the damn cash back that one of them scouts gave me."

"As good friends as you and Hachi is, you didn't even know that Ozz was her son?" Junior says.

"Are." I hold Sadie's gaze. "As good friends as we are."

"When she came over a few days back, sayin' she was goin' to the cops with everything about them drugs being mine and my being partners with Junior here, and that if I knew what was good for me, I should get the hell out of town, we had no choice. She had to go."

"Had to?" I say, which buys me another slap, this time from Junior, who gives me a second for good measure.

Junior leans in close, a complacent grin on his face. "Here's another part you might be confused about."

"Enough, Junior," Sadie says.

Junior gives her a dismissive wave. "Hell, it's not like she's gonna be able to tell anyone."

I yank hard against the restraints, but all that does is tighten them.

"Thing is, when the Feds found all them drugs here, in the shed out back, Trey took the fall."

I look to Sadie, who looks quite pleased with herself. "Why?"

She gives me a smug look. "He wanted his boy to have a momma." She pouts. "Even if I wasn't his real one."

I close my eyes, Hachi's unflagging devotion to Ozz now clear.

I feel the air go out of me, all the fight, much as the fight's gone out of Hachi as she lays comatose in a hospital bed for trying to do the right thing, first by giving up her son, then by trying to save the same boy from the one who she'd trusted to keep him safe.

"See, she was in no shape to raise no child in those days, so she asked me. And I did. And praise be to God, did it pay off." She sighs. "I really did love that boy."

Junior snorts. "Was the payday you saw coming that you loved."

Sadie shakes her head, eyes clouded with tears. "And Trey too. Hell, he even wished he was really his daddy." She shakes her head. "But when Hachi was high, she sure wasn't too picky about her boyfriends."

Junior leers at me, his teeth a disgusting yellow against his white skin.

"It was you she was running from that night, wasn't it?" I say, remembering the fear in Hachi's eyes, the desperate insistence in her tone. But I put her off. And for what? My fee on the pickers case, a case she dropped in my lap to help me out when I was trying to get my career back on track?

"Sure was, soon as she saw me coming up the walk. Jumped right over the back fence, fast as a cottontail. By the time I tracked her down, the pair of you was leavin' Mount Olive."

"It was you. You ran us off the road."

Sadie lets out an exaggerated sigh. "Finally, she gets it."

Junior shakes his head. "Her. I ran her off the road. You were . . . what is it they call it when fuckin' nosy people get in the way of other people's business?"

"Collateral damage, you asshole," I say, spitting out the words.

"No way I was gonna take the chance of her flapping her gums to you." He sticks his face in mine. "From what I see, you're that kind."

"And what kind is that?" I ask through clenched teeth.

"Like a dog with a juicy bone. The type that don't let go."

I turn my gaze on Sadie. "You're a miserable piece of shit! You're going to pull the plug so you can go back to your miserable life with this other miserable excuse for a human being." I spit at Junior.

"Perfect solution, ain't it?" Her top lip curls back, giving her a reptilian look. "I got to say, though, it was good of her to give me the chance to run before she spilled her guts to the cops. Sisterly, don't you think?"

I look away, bile rising in my throat at the betrayal.

"But if she thought I was gonna give up my life for one lookin' over my shoulder every minute, she had another thing coming."

"But Trey knows the truth now," I say, but my words are hollow. I know what they'll say. Trusting the word of a convicted felon was never my strong suit either.

"Trey can say whatever the fuck he wants—ain't nobody gonna believe him. He already confessed to his crimes." Junior laughs. "Even if they was ours. Now, don't you worry, Miss Grace. We'll take care of Hachi." Junior stands in front of me and levels the gun at my head. "Like I'm gonna take care of you."

I take one last futile glance at the curtained window.

"Kill, Miranda, kill!"

I open my eyes to the sight of the door bursting open and Miranda erupting out of the darkness, Vinnie's voice commanding her actions.

Miranda launches herself at Junior, clamping her jaws down on his gun hand. Junior tries to shake himself loose, but drops the weapon, which spins around on the tile floor and discharges, hitting Miranda in the torso.

Junior yanks his arm out of Miranda's now slack jaws, her body limp on the ground. He lunges for the gun, but before he can grab it, his chest explodes.

I blink hard to bring Vinnie into focus. He's pointing a .44 Magnum over my shoulder.

Dazed, I twist around to see Sadie, a meat cleaver clutched in both hands, ready to strike.

"I would put that down if I were you, sweetheart," Vinnie says. "Unless you want a hole the size of Lake Okeechobee where your heart never was."

27

String Bean strolls into the interview room and pulls back the chair with practiced ease, a classic technique used by cops to give the impression that they've got it all under control, that they've got you dead to rights, even when they've got nothing.

He grabs the chair opposite me and straddles it, which makes him look even more dorky than he is, as if he's watched one too many crime dramas. "Halliday, Detective Halliday," he says. "I was first on scene."

"I remember," I reply. I make it a practice never to forget a cop's face. On your side or not, cops are people you gotta keep an eye on.

He sits back, fingers laced behind his head.

"Where's my dog? Is she okay?" I ask.

He opens his notebook with a flick of his wrist. "She was shot, Ms. Locke. No, she's not okay."

"Don't be an asshat. I'm asking if there's any news! The EMTs took her to the vet!"

His sharp features soften. "The vet says she will be okay."

I swallow the invective I was about to let loose. A dog lover. He can't be all bad.

"You can go see her as soon as we get your statements, yours and Mr. Vicanti's."

I sit up straight, tell myself to pay attention, that the obfuscation-in-the-name-of-interrogation part of the program is about to commence. "And where is he?"

"Who?" Halliday replies.

I puff out my cheeks. "Let's not play games here, Halliday. Where's Vinnie? He's also my client, by the way, in case you're thinking about trying to take advantage of an old man."

Halliday drums his fingers on the table. "Some old man. Seems to think he's Dirty Harry or something. He's under arrest for possession of a weapon by a convicted felon. And because you asked, and because you're his lawyer, he's next door."

"You're freaking kidding me, right? About charging him? He saved my life!"

Halliday clears his throat. "It seems as if Mr. Vicanti has quite a colorful past. And a rather long felony record."

"No shit, Sherlock. You must be a detective."

He gives me the vacant look cops employ when they think they're on the side of the angels. Even when they're not.

"If not for him, I'd be in the morgue right now. Therefore, the fact that he has a criminal *history* is something for which I shall be eternally grateful," I say. "At least he was able to figure out what was going on before it was too late. Unlike you Keystone Cop types. Cops like you like the badge a bit too much, and the hard work not at all."

"And from what I hear, if not for you, he wouldn't be here—meaning among the living—either." His nose pinches in on itself, as if he's sniffing something malodorous. "You two are made for each other."

I'm tempted to say that but for a few crooked cops, Vinnie would never have lost three years of his life on death row, but I think the better of antagonizing Halliday further. I'm already responsible for creating a mountain of paperwork for the poor sod.

He pushes a small recorder across the table and presses the record button. “Why don’t we start at the beginning, Ms. Locke?” he says, but before we can, there’s a knock at the door.

“Excuse me, Detective. May we come in?”

“Captain. Um, yes, of course.” Halliday leaps to his feet.

The captain, a heavyset man with droopy eyelids and a bad comb-over, enters, followed by two men in black windbreakers stenciled with FDLE and a man in an expensive suit bringing up the rear.

“Marcus, what are you doing here?” I ask.

Marcus flashes a broad smile. “We’re here to get you and that troublemaker of a landlord of yours out of here.”

“Now wait a—” Halliday says.

The captain turns to Halliday. “Detective, these gentlemen are here from FDLE’s joint drug task force with the FBI. They will be taking over the investigation of what transpired this evening.”

Halliday points at his notebook and the digital recorder as if they should make the difference. “I was . . .” he says, but stops, his face puckered up like he’s sucked on a lemon.

Marcus motions for me to get up. “Let’s go, Grace. Vinnie’s already in the car.”

I push back from the table and hop to Marcus. “What? Where are we going? How did you know I was here? Where—”

Marcus turns his palms up. “Grace, have I ever let you down?”

“Never,” I say with certainty. The truth is, Marcus’s loyalty is the one thing I’ve been certain of since I went to the Glades Bowl. That and Vinnie’s and Miranda’s undying devotion, without which I would have been doing the dying.

“Trust me on this. You need to come with me. I’ll explain everything when we get to my office. And I think you might need this.” He offers me his arm for balance, given my crutches are still part of a crime scene.

I link my arm through his. "First I lose my leg. Then I lose my fake leg."

"Twice," Marcus adds.

"Okay, twice." I sigh. "And now I don't even have crutches. Seems as if someone doesn't want me to walk."

Marcus beams. "Whoever that fool is doesn't know who they're dealing with."

—

Marcus installs us in the main conference room at the Florida Department of Law Enforcement's headquarters in downtown Miami, somewhere we both spent more than a few all-nighters when we worked together on the joint narcotics task force. Like all government offices, it's dated, the furniture circa 1960, the carpet threadbare, trod on for decades by cops and lawyers trying to make a difference, and a few bad seeds trying to make a buck under the table at the expense of justice. But unlike other government offices, this one has a forever view over Biscayne Bay to South Beach and beyond to the Atlantic, the endless azure waters glistening under a bluebird sky as if nothing could possibly be wrong in the world.

Vinnie helps me into the chair beside him. "There you go, sweetheart."

"Vin, you doing okay? You haven't said a word since—"

He drops his head to his chest.

I grab his hand, which is ice cold to the touch. "You did what you had to do."

"I know," he says, his voice thin. "But—"

"You and Miranda, you saved my life."

He lifts his head, his eyes glassy. "And how is our girl?"

"The vet says she's going to be okay. We'll go see her when we get out of here."

His fingers curl tight around mine. "That tripod, she's a fighter."

"That she is."

"Just like her mom," he adds, swatting at a tear.

"You two doing okay?" Marcus says, taking a seat opposite us. He unbuttons his suit coat and sits back, settling in for the duration of whatever he has in mind. Whatever it is, he's saved us from String Bean and his notebook.

We nod in unison, still holding hands.

"Can you please tell us what's going on? How did you know about the accident, about what happened at Sadie Gordon's? It's not like the podunk patrol keeps the big boys informed about their provincial comings and goings."

Marcus takes a deep breath. "We've known for a while that Sadie Gordon and Junior Williams have been dealing, that they get deliveries from the Colombians out in the Glades, but we haven't been able to catch them in the act. We have informants who've provided intel on their organization, but we were waiting for an opportunity to take them down once and for all." He cracks his knuckles. "And that was supposed to be today, based on some info we had from a reliable confidential informant."

"Okay?" I say. "And?"

"I knew about the accident and about what happened at the Gordon house because, as podunk as you think Halliday and Cappas are, they've been integral to our investigation."

"Whatever you say, big man." I glance at Vinnie, who seems to have shrunk into the recesses of the big leather chair. That a man so fearless, or perhaps fierce is a better word, should reside in this diminutive body with its twig-like arms and kind face, has always amazed me. But I learned long ago appearances can be deceiving, so I'll buy what Marcus is saying about the Sugar Bay PD.

"Our task force has been working hand in hand with Sugar Bay PD for some time to take them down," he says, and I feel a moment of pride for having once been part of what Marcus still is—a force for good against evil.

"Jesus," I say, my mind flooding with how the people Marcus

has been chasing for ages were the people who tried to kill me and Hachi, one of whom she trusted with her child. People out in the light but working in the shadows, the most dangerous kind.

"Roger that, as you say. Maybe even double Jesus," Marcus says, trying to keep the mood light. "What we didn't count on was you and Mr. Vicanti here getting mixed up in things."

Vinnie shoots Marcus a "What, me?" grin.

"Maybe you can explain something to me, Grace. What were you doing in the company of two known drug dealers? And why did they want to kill you?"

I hesitate. The answer should be straightforward, an accounting of who did what to whom and why, but emotions have a way of clouding facts, so I take a moment to organize my thoughts. I want to give Marcus the plain truth as best I can tell it. I owe him that.

"I've been going back and forth to Sugar Bay recently because I've been representing a bunch of cane pickers in a class action against Alonso Tremayne and Big Sugar. I've also been looking into the suicide of the Panthers' star player, Ozz Gordon, to get the family whatever closure they can get, which turns out to be none. Or perhaps worse than none, given what happened to Hachi."

"And you," Vinnie adds, squeezing my hand.

Marcus narrows an eye. "Ozz Gordon, the football star? Sadie Gordon's boy?"

"Not exactly. But I'll get to that."

"Grace, quit hiding the ball, okay? Why were you at Sadie Gordon's place, and why did a man end up dead thanks to Mr. Vicanti?" He raises his hands in surrender. "Besides saving your life, of course. What I need to understand from you is how all of this happened, and what exactly all of this is."

"Okay, here's the deal. A few nights ago, after I met with my picker clients, my friend Hachi, the dead kid's aunt—his mom, in fact . . ." I sigh. "Like I said, I'll get to that later. Anyway, we were run off the road, and Hachi was badly injured. I'm okay, just a few bumps and bruises. But she's in a coma. I suspected Tremayne was behind it."

"Because of the pickers' verdict."

"Roger that."

"You mean to say he wanted you dead because you won a lawsuit against his company?"

"With no one to fight for them, Tremayne wouldn't ever have to pay the pickers the five million dollars the jury awarded. Or at least he could stall long enough to pay them a lot less," I say, leaving out the fact that I may have threatened Tremayne about trafficking drugs to kids and tried to extort ten million dollars out of him. Such a disclosure at this point would serve no purpose, given I seem to have been mistaken about Tremayne.

Marcus lets out an ear-piercing whistle. "Five mil is mucho moola!"

"But I was wrong."

Marcus raises an eyebrow.

"It was Junior who ran us off the road. He said so himself. Before Vinnie shot him. He told me he did it because Hachi found out about his and Sadie's operation, the one you've had your eye on, the one Trey went to prison for. They couldn't take the chance Hachi would go to the cops."

"But why would Sadie sell out her own sister? Or did she?"

I take a deep breath. "That's where this all gets complicated."

Marcus shifts his bulk in his seat. "You're right about that."

"Listen up, okay? Ozz is . . . *was* Hachi's son."

"Okay, and . . . ?"

I lean in. "Hachi gave Ozz to Sadie to raise when he was small because she was way too far gone on drugs at the time to give him any kind of life. A couple of days ago, Trey Gordon, Ozz's father, told Hachi he had taken the fall for Sadie."

"Why would he do that? He got twenty years."

"Because he wanted Ozz to grow up with a mother, even if she wasn't his actual mother. And he told Hachi the truth because Ozz told him he was working for Junior and Junior threatened to turn him in for murder."

He raises a hand to stop me from saying anything else. I don't blame him. My head is spinning too, what with the machinations. And I'm glad because I have to choose my words carefully, given the attorney-client privilege is the reason I'm not telling Marcus the whole story about Ozz.

"Long story long, Trey told Hachi about Junior and Sadie. Then, Hachi told Sadie to get the hell out of town before she turned Junior in as the actual perpetrator of what they locked Trey up for."

"And Sadie?" Marcus asks.

"No, apparently Hachi gave Sadie a sisterly pass for raising Ozz."

Marcus slumps back in his chair.

"It's ironic, isn't it? The very drugs Hachi was trying to stay off were right there under her nose, in her sister's backyard shed."

Marcus frowns. "Hachi owed Sadie, so she gave her a pass. Guilt is a powerful force."

I look away. "Tell me about it."

After a few seconds, Marcus's frown morphs into a wide grin.

"Marcus Jackson, why are you nodding?"

"Because I pretty much knew all of that." He slaps his hand on the table. "And it seems I got it right." He bows toward me. "Nice work, Counselor."

"How do you—did you—"

"Because Mr. Gordon told me. When he found out from Hachi that Sadie was running drugs with Junior all along, he had no reason to keep his false confession a secret any longer. He was furious Junior had recruited Ozz, after he'd sacrificed himself for Sadie on the promise that she would take good care of his son. More important to him than anything else was saving the boy from being held responsible for a murder he didn't commit, which, I believe, is something Ozz shared with you."

I push back from the table. "Wait! How do you know that? And why were you talking to Trey? How did you put all of this together? Christ, Ozz is dead."

Marcus raises a finger to silence me. "You should know we busted Ozz picking up a shipment of cocaine out in Chokoloskee."

"Damn drugs." Vinnie turns to me. "Damn shame. That Pocahontas, she tried to do the right thing, but ended up getting screwed by her own sister. Mr. Gordon too. And them's years he'll never get back." Vinnie clenches and unclenches his fists in his lap.

"Sound familiar, Mr. Vicanti?" Marcus asks.

"Sure does," Vinnie says, eyes blazing.

Marcus pulls his chair in tight and focuses on Vinnie. "Which is why we're going to turn a blind eye to the fact that you were in possession of a weapon, Mr. Vicanti."

Vinnie's face slackens in relief. "Thank you, Mr. Jackson."

Marcus shakes his head. "No, thank you, Mr. Vicanti. For saving my best friend."

"Both of our best friend," Vinnie says, one eye narrowed.

Marcus gives a definitive nod. "Agreed. Or perhaps I should say, thanks for saving our best friend *again*, Mr. Vicanti."

Vinnie beams. "You know what? Saving Grace seems to be becoming a habit for us two."

I poke him in the ribs. "Asshat."

As Marcus gathers his paperwork, my gaze drifts to the cruise port in the distance jammed with mega-ships destined for ports of call Ozz Gordon will never see, his bright future extinguished in one impulsive moment. "It's all such a tragedy. Ozz had such a future ahead of him. So many things to experience outside of that damn town."

"Maybe it's not such a tragedy, Grace." Marcus strides to the door and yanks it open with a flourish, like a magician pulling back a curtain. "Ozz, Trey, you can come in now."

I feel as if I'm hallucinating. I can't move, or breathe. The only thing I'm seeing is a ghost, the ghost of the young man I met in my office a few weeks ago. The one who went on to shoot himself in front of five thousand witnesses.

But wait! This ghost's expression is hopeful, not fearful. This ghost is alive, not lying dead in a pool of blood.

"Ms. Locke," Ozz says, extending a hand.

I'd shake it if I were able to move, but only manage a dropped jaw.

"Take a seat, guys," Marcus says. "And let's give Grace a minute to catch her breath, shall we? She's usually not at a loss for words, but it seems as if we have rendered her speechless."

I blink hard, half expecting Ozz to disappear. "How? You are supposed to be . . . I saw you . . ."

Vinnie looks to me, then Marcus, then back at me. "Wait! He's Ozz? But Ozz is dead!"

Marcus smiles. "Appearances can be deceiving."

"No shit," Vinnie and I say in unison.

Marcus holds my gaze with purpose, as if I might pass out if he looks away. "Remember I mentioned we had informants?"

I nod.

"Ozz and his father are those informants."

Piece by piece, the picture starts to reassemble itself into a totally different configuration. "Let me get this straight, Mr. Jackson. You guys bust Ozz out in Chokoloskee and he flips?" I smile. "It takes a bottom-of-the-totem-pole dealer to make that case you've been spending tens of thousands of taxpayer dollars on for untold months?" I shake my head. "Hell, you all about got us all killed by your taking so long."

Marcus smiles.

I shoot Ozz a dirty look. "And don't you look so happy either, my friend. Didn't I tell you to keep your head down and stay out of trouble?"

"So, you two *do* know each other?" Marcus gives a self-satisfied smile. "The one thing I couldn't figure out was how Hachi found out about Junior and Sadie, which she passed on to Trey."

"Long story." I look away. "One I can't tell you—attorney-client privilege and all that."

"Which you *will* share with me, Ms. Locke," Marcus says, shaking a scolding finger.

Ozz sits forward. "It's okay, Ms. Locke." He turns to Marcus. "Mr. Jackson, I didn't want to go to Chokoloskee that night, but Junior made me. He said if I didn't, he'd pin Miguel's murder on me."

"Douchebag," Vinnie says under his breath. "Only a coward sends a kid to do a man's work."

Ozz turns to look at Vinnie. "Who's he?"

"I call him my investigator," I reply, at which Vinnie raises his chin and smiles proudly.

Marcus nods. "Ozz, you got scared, and Grace, your aunt's friend, was the only lawyer you knew, right?"

I cough. "I like to think I'm the *best* lawyer he knew," I say, and we all share a moment of laughter.

After we've settled down, I get back to business, to make sure I know exactly how and why I almost got myself killed. "Let me get this straight. You faked Ozz's suicide?"

Marcus bows his head. "We had to. Junior and Sadie's network is widespread. They would have got to Ozz no matter where he was once they found out he'd cooperated. But—" Marcus snaps his fingers. "If there were no more Ozz, there would be no one to look for." He looks at Ozz. "To be fair, we had no idea Hachi was his mother."

"He's right," Ozz says. "When I found out who was working with Junior, I realized Sadie had been lying to me my whole life."

I sigh. "And your father paid for her sins."

Trey closes his eyes as if in prayer.

"Pieces of shit," Vinnie says under his breath.

"There never was an autopsy? Dr. Owen was in on it?" I ask.

Marcus nods.

"Devious old bird."

"That devious old bird was the one who helped us make Ozz's suicide look real."

I suck in a breath.

Marcus looks into my eyes. "I know it was traumatic, Grace, but we had to—"

"And the medics who took Ozz off the field? All fake?"

"All FDLE," Marcus says.

My hand goes to my chest, but words fail me.

"The blood was fake. Ozz wore a bulletproof vest under his Panther jersey and the bullet was a blank."

Ozz leans in. "Leaving behind my old life was the only way they'd never be able to come after me." Ozz glances at Trey. "Or my pop."

"But your family?" I say.

Ozz's expression turns to one of deep sadness. "Did you know Auntie H was my mom, Miss Locke?"

"Not until I saw your birth certificate. That was what she was trying to show me the night we were in the accident. Did Mr. Jackson tell you about that?"

Ozz drops his head to his chest. "Is my mom going to make it?"

"Time will tell. She's hanging in there."

He bows his head. "That's the hardest part of all this. Now I might never get to know her. I mean as my mom."

I reach for his hand across the table. "She'll pull through. Hachi's one tough lady."

Marcus nods in agreement. "When Trey found out what was going on, and that the very same people he was covering for threatened his son with Miguel Ruiz's murder, Trey saw no more need to keep up the charade. He told Hachi the truth about Sadie and Junior, she confronted her sister, and they argued, which resulted in your two getting run off the road. It was just dumb luck that you blamed it on Tremayne's guy."

"Oops," I say.

Marcus stands. "We've arranged for Ozz to relocate to an unnamed location under a new identity. He has to leave today. We're taking down the rest of Junior's network in locations throughout the South tonight."

I flinch. "Witness protection? Leave everything and everyone behind? Including his mom?"

Marcus nods. "Except for Trey."

"What?" I ask, ready in my mind for a fight, but Marcus short-circuits my ire.

"I know what you're going to say. That Trey's innocent, and he is. You'll get no argument from me on that."

I glance at Vinnie, who won't meet my gaze. He was innocent too when I convinced a jury he wasn't. Sometimes, it takes more than innocence to keep you out of prison, and all too often only one powerful person to keep you in.

"Trey's in danger too, now the truth's out. I got a court order to move him to another prison under another name for now—"

I open my mouth to speak.

"Let me finish, Grace! For once, have a little faith you're not the only one in the room on the side of the angels."

I press my lips together.

"As soon as I can, I will present all the evidence we have to the Attorney General's Office and, once they petition the court to vacate his plea, Trey will join Ozz."

Out of the corner of my eye, I see Vinnie shaking his head.

"How do you know they—"

"They will. I'll make sure of it." Marcus follows my gaze to Vinnie. "Like you did for Mr. Vicanti a while back."

Vinnie closes his eyes. "Amen to that, Mr. Jackson. But for Gracie here, I'd have left that place feet first."

I turn to Ozz. "But what about football? College?"

Marcus rests a hand on Ozz's shoulder. "Ozz will never be able to play professional football as himself, but he will attend university in an unnamed place, a stellar institution, under a new name. And if he does well, he'll be able to go on to medical school like he wanted all along."

"Football to get out. School to stay out. Right, son?" Trey says.

Ozz and Trey bump fists. "Right on, Pop."

"You seem to have thought of everything, Marcus. But I have one question. Why did you suspect Ozz and I knew each other?"

Marcus raises his eyes to the ceiling, an innocent look that might work on others, but not on one who has sat in more than one good cop/bad cop interrogation with him.

"Ozz didn't happen to ask for counsel, did he? Like, *before* you convinced him to flip?"

Marcus straightens his tie. "He signed a waiver. It was all by the book."

"Sure it was. I remember that book. I haven't been gone from the State's Attorney's Office so long I've forgotten how the game is played."

Ozz raises a hand. "It's okay, Ms. Locke."

"It may be with you, but Mr. Jackson here knows the rules." I skewer Marcus with a hard stare. "I need to talk to my client alone, Mr. Jackson."

Marcus waves me off. "No way! We're short on time here. He has to fly out of Miami tonight."

"Way, or I'm making an ethics complaint to the Florida Bar about how you denied my client his Sixth Amendment right to counsel."

Marcus shrugs. "It would never stick."

I shrug back. "Maybe, maybe not, but it would be on your permanent record."

"You'd do that to me?"

"You always said I was a stickler for the rules."

Marcus scoots his chair back. "Ten minutes. We've got to get him out of here. The car's waiting downstairs."

Vinnie and Trey follow Marcus out.

"I'll be right outside if you need me," Vinnie says.

"I have no doubt," I reply.

28

Ozz stares into space, his mind a chaotic storm of fear, regret, and relief. "I can't believe this is happening. It's all happening so fast."

Grace pulls back and takes him in, eyes wide, as if she's seeing him for the first time—which she is, after a fashion. At least, the resurrected version of himself.

"*You* can't? *I* can't believe you're alive," she says.

"Thanks to Mr. Jackson. He saved me. I was going to be locked up for a long time. And even if I'd left town after I cooperated, they'd have got to me sooner or later. I had no choice."

"I understand."

"You wouldn't do that to Mr. Jackson, would you?"

She cocks her head. "Do what?"

"File whatever you said? I mean, that didn't sound good."

"Not a chance. Marcus is a good man, a great lawyer, and an even better friend. I was just bustin' his chops."

It's the first time he's seen her smile, really smile, her electric blue eyes twinkling like the stars he loves to count at night, lying on his back in the yard, the cicadas chirping all around, the type of carefree night in the Glades he would never experience again.

He looks at his hands, turning them over and back, as if they belong to someone else, which, in a way, they do. He's no longer the old Ozz, the Wiz. He'll be whatever they tell him to be from now on.

"You have your whole life ahead of you now, Ozz, even without football. You'll be a doctor, helping people."

He bites back the tears nipping at his eyes. "Things will never be the same."

She reaches down and rubs her leg, not Oscar, but the right one. God knows where Oscar is.

"Sometimes, we don't appreciate what we've got until it's gone. The trick is to find a new path."

He can't help himself. "What happened to Oscar?"

She draws her hand away from her thigh fast, as if she's been burned. "He was destroyed in the accident I was in with your mom."

"I can't believe I . . ." he says, his voice cracking. "That I was working for them and they tried to kill my mother. That the person I knew as my mother tried to kill my real mother. And you." He bangs his fists on the table. "I bet she even knew all about what happened with Miguel and how Junior threatened me."

"I bet she did."

"Why? Why did she do that to me? She was supposed to take care of me!"

"Some people will do anything for money, kid."

She leans toward him and rests her elbows on her knees. "But you made some pretty bad choices too, you know?"

"I know. And now I'm paying for them." He rubs his eyes. "I need to tell you something."

She sits back. "Sure, but make it quick."

"I left a note. A suicide note."

Her face twists in confusion. “What? We didn’t find a note.”

“I figured, because there was nothing about it in the news.” He sucks in a deep breath. “Have you ever heard about PEDs?”

She runs her tongue over her lips but says nothing.

“PEDs, performance-enhancing drugs, help athletes build more lean body mass fast and also allow them to recover from workouts faster.” He looks at his hands again. “Alonso Tremayne works with the scouts who have their sights on the outstanding players, and he gets them that stuff.”

Her eyes turn from bright blue to black. “I’ve heard.”

“PEDs are poison—they can have all kinds of side effects. I played along and made it seem like I was taking them, but no way I was gonna take that shit.” A wave of sadness passes through him. “But some of the other players believed they had to, to get a scholarship and stuff. To have a better future.”

“And the note?”

“I left a note. I’d been taking Lexapro. I’d been depressed over the summer, which would make people think that was why I killed myself, but in the note I said how I’d been taking PEDs, and I described what Tremayne was doing and that they had made me feel even worse. They do when you’re depressed, but I wasn’t taking them.”

“Wow, you did do your homework.”

He gives a sad smile.

“Ozz, where did you leave the note?”

“In my friend Whitey’s locker with instructions for him to give it to the Miami Herald. I guess he never found it.”

“Why’d you leave it for Whitey?”

His eyes lose focus. “We’ve always been friends. We competed hard against each other, but he was my closest friend on the team. Also, I knew he’d never take any of that shit. He didn’t need to.”

“So, Mr. Jackson knows about this stuff?”

“No, he has no clue. I left the note right before the Glades Bowl.”

He tries to smile, but can't. "I kinda called an audible. I thought if I had no choice but to go away forever, then I might as well do something good on my way out."

She looks confused, so he adds, "An audible means you change the planned play."

"Oh, okay."

"I wanted to tell you now in case it ever comes out. Maybe ask Whitey?"

"I will."

"The scouts, Tremayne, all of them, they're leeches. I wanted to make sure they didn't take advantage of any more guys." He frowns. "But that won't happen now."

"Don't worry, I'll take care of all that."

"You about done, Grace?" Mr. Jackson says, poking his head around the door.

She outs a finger in the air. "Just one more minute, Marcus" She turns back to Ozz. "When your mom comes out of the coma, and she will, what do you want me to tell her?"

"Tell her I'm sorry for getting involved with Junior." He swallows hard. "Tell her I'm sorry. Tell her I'm proud of her for getting clean, for doing the right thing by me. Tell her I'm sorry I have to go away."

"She'll understand," she says, squeezing his hands. "Sometimes, we have to do whatever it takes to survive, even if it's hard."

"I wish I could see her before I go." He closes his eyes. "Tell her I love her." He chokes back a sob. "Tell her I know she did what she thought was best."

"That's all any of us can do, kid."

Mr. Jackson bangs hard on the door. "Time's up!"

She leans close to Ozz's ear. "You remember my office number?"

"Yes, I memorized it. Burned it into my brain. Just in case."

She stands. "Call me any time to get news of your mom and to tell me yours so I can pass it along. You can't see or contact her directly, but maybe one day . . ."

The door flies open, causing her to reel back in her chair.

"I mean it. Day or night. And call collect," she mouths, drawing a finger across her lips.

"Time to go, Ozz," Mr. Jackson says.

He wipes his face on his shirt. "At least I'll have my dad with me. I know some people think he's bad, but he gave up everything for me, even his freedom. He's the best father in the world."

"Yes he is," she replies.

29

Vinnie flips a burger patty high in the air and catches it on a bun.

"You got skills there, Vin," I say, setting the picnic table behind The Hurricane.

He takes a deep bow. "Once upon a time, I owned a burger joint. On Richmond Road in Staten Island."

"You owned a burger joint?"

"What? You sayin' my people should own pizza parlors? That sounds racist to me," he says, lips pursed in mock insult.

"You don't seem the customer service type. I see you more as a man of action."

He sniffs. "Even a man of action has to put his cash somewhere for safekeeping, far away from prying eyes," he says, straight-faced.

I glance at Miranda in her doggie bed, wrapped in bandages like a mummy, slack-jawed on pain medication. Sad to say, I know the look. "He's a piece of work, isn't he, pretty girl?"

Out of habit, we both wait for her standard confirmatory

yip, but she's still too weak.

I sit beside her. "If not for you, Junior would have taken me down."

Vinnie beams like a proud parent. "You see how she flew off the ground like that flying squirrel in the cartoon?"

I stroke her head. "It's all such a blur. What command did you give her? I haven't had much time to train her."

Vinnie throws his arms up. "What d'ya think?"

"You got me."

"Kill!"

I salute. "Oorah! I should have known that. She was a United States Marine, after all."

He reaches a hand down for me, and I use him for balance to hobble to the table.

"There was no stoppin' her, soon as she saw that slimeball with a gun pointed at you."

Miranda turns her head to look at us, eyelids droopy.

"She's one tough war dog, even on only three legs," I say, my heart swelling in my chest.

He sets our plates down. "You both are, sweetheart. And speaking of legs, any news on Oscar?"

"The prosthetist at Walter Reed is building Oscar 3.0 as we speak. We should be introduced in a few weeks."

We touch our plastic glasses of Doctor Cola, my proprietary mix of Coca-Cola and Dr. Pepper.

"Lucky for you you've got friends in high places."

"Lucky for me, I've got a friend who knows his way around handguns, even if he isn't supposed to have one."

He exhales. "It was real nice of Marcus to overlook that detail. I owe him one."

"I owe him more than one," I say, taking a bite of the oozy burger.

He crosses himself, his expression turning sad. "I think I better go to confession on Sunday."

I grab his hand. "This was different. You had no choice. We

lawyers call it defense of others, if that helps."

"This was still a killing, kid. I took another man's life. I swore I'd left that life behind."

I see Junior in my mind's eye, red eyes like the lasers in the rifle I used to carry. "Some people deserve a little killing, Vin."

He raises his chin, his expression shifting from remorse to anger in a heartbeat. "I hear ya, sweetheart. There was no way that scum . . ." He stops, his words trailing off on the gentle night breeze. "I'm glad it all worked out like it did."

I take another bite of burger. "Oh my freaking God, I about died a second time when we found out Ozz is alive."

Vinnie puts down his burger and gazes out over the waterway. "I'm happy that father's gonna get a second chance with his boy."

"Eventually," I say. "It could take a while. You know how slowly the wheels of justice turn."

He fixes me with a steely stare. "As long as he gets it before it's too late. That's all that matters."

"Marcus will make sure of it."

He nods. "The pair of you are cut from the same cloth."

I take another bite of burger. "Yeah, and what cloth is that?"

"The honest kind." His eyes reduce down to slits. "And that Sadie, she's goin' away for a long time, right?"

"Abso-freaking-lutely! They found enough dope to anesthetize a small island nation in a shed out back of her house." I tilt my head. "You'd have thought she learned her lesson the first time and found a better hiding place."

"She didn't have to, not when Trey was there to take the fall for her. But I wonder about that."

I put my burger on a paper plate. "You mean how could Trey not have known?"

He nods.

"I've been thinking about that too. But we'll never know now, will we?"

"She's lucky I didn't shoot her too, if you can call that luck."

I take a sip of my drink. "Meaning?"

"Meaning, I'm not sure which is worse—a fast death now, or being locked up until you're too old to make any more trouble, like she'll be."

"That's a choice neither of us is ever going to have to make."

"Amen to that, sweetheart." He raises his glass to mine. "To the good life!"

"Where'd you get that cannon, anyway? You know you can't have—"

He puts two fingers to his lips, then to his eyes, then sticks them in his ears. I have to give it to him. He does play a good innocent.

"Okay, okay, but don't ever let me find out you're in possession of a firearm again. You've used up all your 'get out of jail free' cards."

"Deal." He winks and chomps down on his burger.

For the first time since we brought her home from the vet, Miranda yips like her old self.

30

I'd wager there's no better feeling in the world than cruising along, the warmth of the sun on your face, to a meeting at which you will exact sweet revenge for the royally screwed from the one who did the screwing.

Top down on the Jag, I drive north on A1A from Fort Lauderdale, through Deerfield Beach, a seaside resort that can never seem to shake its seedy side no matter how many dollars developers drop into politicians' pockets. Next up, Boca Raton, a Palm Beach wannabe, a city with some of the cash but with way too much of the flash of the nouveau riche to ever have the class of the real thing—somewhere with actual history and actual class. Beyond Boca, the *per capita* incomes of the residents of oceanfront enclaves like Highland Beach and Manalapan increase exponentially with each mile further north you go until you arrive on Palm Beach island itself. Some see Palm Beach as the winter retreat of the northeastern elite, a secret society of sorts requiring a certain amount of old money or blue blood, or preferably both, to gain entry. I see it as the place I used to call home.

At Southern Boulevard, A1A changes its name to Ocean Boulevard for a few miles, because nothing in Palm Beach can bear so pedestrian a name as one satisfactory to the rest of the plebeian population of the Sunshine State. I pass Mar-a-Lago, the faux Spanish/Moorish garish monstrosity built by cereal heiress Marjorie Merriweather Post in the 1920s and owned subsequently by robber barons and a certain reality TV star who likes gold plating a bit too much. Next, the Breakers Hotel, also built in a faux style, but this one Italian Renaissance, by Henry Flagler, the oil and railroad tycoon who was Florida's king of sorts until his tracks blew away in the Labor Day Hurricane in 1935.

I pull up outside Capital Bistro on Royal Poinciana Way, a boulevard lined with identical royal palms so evenly spaced you'd think even nature must bend to the will of the rich in this rarefied enclave. But having grown up here, I know better. I know that it takes an army of underpaid immigrant gardeners to keep the place looking pristine.

"Nice car," the valet says as I drop the keys in his hand. In exchange, he hands me a claim ticket. For a brief moment, there's a flash of recognition in his eyes. Capital Bistro was my father Percy's favorite restaurant, where he used to bring Faith and me on special occasions in this very car. The Capital staff are "lifers;" given the generosity of the clientele for whom tipping the unwashed assuages their guilt at their good fortune, the valet was likely a beneficiary of Percy's largesse.

In keeping with tradition, I crumple a ten-dollar bill into his palm. "Treat my baby well and I'll double this on the way out." As I walk away, I sense his eyes on me, trying to place me. Or maybe he's wondering why I'm limping, Oscar 3.0 having been with me for only one day.

"Ms. Locke, it's been quite a while," the maître d' says the moment I walk inside.

I smile but offer no explanation for my protracted absence,

since neither being too broke to afford this joint nor being in jail for a spell are appropriate for polite conversation.

"Your guest, Mr. Tremayne, is already here," he says, leading me to Percy's regular table in the back.

Tremayne is on his feet, pulling back my chair for me to sit.

"Enjoy your lunch, Ms. Locke," the maître d' says.

"Great table you got us. Seems as if your reputation precedes you," Tremayne says.

"I sure as hell hope not. They'd never let me back in Palm Beach."

He smiles. "I'd wager there are more than a few scoundrels behind the hedgerows in this town."

I narrow an eye, unsure if he's serious, which would be more than a little hypocritical. Maybe he had me checked out. I'd bet on the latter. Guys like Tremayne play every angle.

He unbuttons his suit jacket before sitting, releasing his not-insubstantial paunch. "You did grow up here, did you not?"

"I see you've done your homework."

Tremayne flashes a brilliant smile replete with what looks to be twenty grand worth of cosmetic dentistry. "Much like you, I imagine."

I pull a thick file from my briefcase. "Which brings me to why I'm here."

He rolls his shoulders back, like a boxer readying for a bout. "You know you could simply have had the signed agreements and releases from your clients messengered to my office. I've already authorized the wire of the settlement monies to your trust account."

"I know," I say, running a finger down the oversized leather menu to see if my favorite, steak tartare, is still on offer.

He opens his menu. "Not that I mind having lunch with such a lovely lady."

I slap the menu shut. "Tremayne, no way you can fool me with your Cuban charm. I was once married to one," I say, but in my mind I'm thinking he is more handsome than I remember.

Or maybe he's simply my type, like Manny. Not tall, dark, and unfathomable.

He raises his hands in surrender. "I shall keep the compliments to myself from now on."

Despite his cultivated smoothness, I find myself smiling along with him until I give myself a mental shake and remind myself that guys like him—suave, charming, persuasive—they are my weakness. Also, I'm here to extort him for a second time, so socializing isn't on the agenda.

A waiter dressed in an old-timey ankle-length black apron over black trousers and a starched white shirt with a black bow tie approaches. "Can I take your order?"

"Steak tartare for me."

Tremayne shrugs. "I'll have what she's having."

"Would you care for wine with your meal?" the waiter asks. "Or a cocktail? We have—"

"No, thank you. Water will be fine," I reply too quickly.

"Coke for me," Tremayne says, although I saw him eyeing the cocktail list. I'd wager he's a Manhattan man. Sweet with a bitter edge.

Once the waiter has retreated, I hand over the file containing my clients' documents. "But this isn't why I'm here."

"Then why are we here?" he says, picking some non-existent lint from his sleeve, something Manny does when he's nervous.

I look him in the eye. "I have come about that information I received that suggests you have been providing the Sugar Bay Panthers' players with performance-enhancing drugs."

He pushes back from the table and crosses his legs. "Ms. Locke, we've already had this discussion, and even though I deny the fantasy you're peddling, it would be harmful to my company if such nonsense were to become public, which is one of the reasons we were able to reach this settlement." He points at the file. "From now on, you and your clients are bound to secrecy regarding anything they or you have knowledge of regarding me or my company." He clears his throat. "Or our agents."

"True, but this particular information"—I pat the file—"has come to my attention not by way of any of my clients."

He emits a pseudo long-suffering sigh. "And how would that be?"

"Ozz Gordon left a suicide note."

Do I detect a slight twitch in his jaw muscle? It's at least enough to tell me I'm on the right track.

"You remember Ozz, don't you? The Panthers' star player? A young man with everything to live for, but who chose to die?"

He bows his head. "His death was indeed a tragedy."

I sit back in my chair, biding my time, enjoying watching him battle the impulse to squirm.

"See, Ozz's note says unequivocally that you arranged for your quack to supply him and his talented teammates with PEDs."

I compose my face into a mask of serenity to disguise my outrage. Any outward expression of emotion, even if bona fide righteous indignation, will be read by Tremayne as weakness, something to be exploited.

"Of course, a sophisticated soul such as yourself knows the authorities call that 'trafficking controlled substances to minors.'" I tilt my head. "That is, were they inclined to take any action against you."

Now the jaw is full-on grinding, turning his smile into a lopsided grimace.

"And there's the ten grand that scout gave Ozz's mother to seal the deal, to make sure Ozz did as he was told."

"I did not know anything about that," he says, his tone one of sincere surprise as opposed to crafted reaction.

"Really? You didn't know that scout, your partner in crime, told her that if she breathed a word about the payoff, he'd make sure the world knew Ozz was on PEDs and that she'd taken a kickback, all of which would make Ozz ineligible to play college ball?"

He rubs the bridge of his nose. "And where is this so-called suicide note? I'd like to see it."

I snort. "Not a chance, pal."

He pulls in close to the table and takes a quick look over his shoulder.

"Don't worry, Mr. Tremayne. This table is private. That's why my father always asked for it. He didn't like people listening in on his conversations either."

I take a bite of bread and chew slowly, watching beads of sweat sprout on his forehead.

"You want to know the kicker?"

He takes a deep breath and holds it in.

"Ozz never took any of the shit you and Spire got him. He flushed it all down the toilet."

He opens his mouth to speak, but thinks the better of it and stuffs a piece of bread in instead.

"Like you, football was Ozz's way to get an education, to get out."

"But he never got the chance." His expression softens.

"He'd been depressed, and depressed people kill themselves," I say, spouting the party line, hoping I sound convincing, conciliatory even, given the crack in Tremayne's shell. Maybe honey will work better than vinegar for what I want from him.

He leans back, appraising me, or more likely my own soft underbelly. "The thing with people like you, you have no clue what it's like to go without. To have nothing, not even enough food," he says, his jaw muscles twitching.

I bite back the urge to answer, to tell him I know more than I care to about having nothing, being nothing, losing everything, having nothing left to lose.

"I know you think I'm a monster, but you're wrong. I care about kids like Ozz. I was forced to come to this country when I was ten years old. I left Cuba with nothing, not even my parents. Lucky for me, good people took me in, but they didn't have much to share, enough for us to get by day to day. The day my adopted mother begged for pennies in the street was the day I swore I would not grow up poor. That I'd help others who were, whatever it took."

I roll my eyes. "You think what you're doing is helping those kids? That crap you're peddling has lifelong side effects."

He smirks. "The other thing that people like you forget is that poverty itself has lifelong side effects—to wit, a short, miserable life."

The waiter appears with our meals but leaves them without a word, as if he can feel a disturbance in the atmosphere.

Tremayne pushes his plate away. "Ozz Gordon was a smart kid. Almost anywhere else he would have made it no matter what. But Ozz was from Sugar Bay, where kids still get scurvy, for Christ's sake, and the average lifespan of an adult is sixty-three. No, Ms. Ivy Leaguer from Palm Beach, kids from Sugar Bay don't make it out alive unless they have an edge."

"And that edge is you?" I ask, feeling my own jaw twitch.

"Damn straight it is!" He pounds his fist on the table, which causes diners to turn and, just as fast, look away, although I have no doubt Tremayne's outburst will provide them enough schadenfreude to make them feel on solid high ground, for now.

Unsure of what to say next, I shovel in a mouthful of the steak tartare, the slimy yet fresh, spicy yet sweet flavors a portal to the past, the one where I did have everything a person could hope for, not just one thing to hang all my hopes on like Ozz. The sad irony is I've been given the grace to work on reversing the effects of my dismal choices, but Ozz will never be able to escape the consequences of the choices others made on his behalf, or the few bad ones he made for himself.

Tremayne takes a sip of Coke, the delicate bubbles dancing on the dark surface like fireflies. "Listen, I'm not saying performance-enhancing drugs are good for you. In fact, I agree they're not. But they do give kids who won't otherwise have it a chance at the big time."

I pull back, surprised at the admission. And also the fact that he may be speaking the truth, no matter how much I despise that reality.

"You grew up in Sugar Bay, right? Tell me what it was like in those days."

He chuckles. "You make it sound like I grew up in prehistoric times."

"I—"

"I'm joking, Grace. Are you always so serious?"

I sigh. "So I'm told."

He sets his glass down. "Since you asked, when I got here from Cuba, the Catholic Church placed me with a family of cane cutters. I studied hard, played football at SBH, and got a scholarship to college at USC with the help of my old coach, who called in a few favors for me. I wasn't good enough to play first string, in the end—too small—but football did get me an education. After I graduated, I came home to Sugar Bay and worked my way up from the bottom at the company. My first job was on the loading dock." He studies the look of shock I can't keep off my face. "Surprised?"

"That sounds like Ozz's story."

"In some ways, yes, but not in others. Things are different now. More competitive, even for stars like Ozz."

"Funny thing is, it also sounds like Manny's story." I feel a blush coming on as soon as the words are out of my mouth.

Tremayne shoots his cuffs, another of Manny's habits. "The ex, I take it?"

"Yep, the ex," I say, but the crack of the "x" has less anger behind it now when I say it, more understanding, nostalgia even for a time with someone who knew me best.

I sit back. I'd come here full of piss and vinegar, ready to excoriate Tremayne, use the information I have against him to help my case, but now? I'm not sure.

I pinch my thigh hard, reminding myself to question how a man like this, one who knows poverty, could steal from the pickers he depends on.

"You're probably wondering how in hell the company could

treat your clients so poorly?"

I'd say that's exactly what I was thinking if I weren't afraid that another Cuban man is able to read my mind.

His cheeks redden.

"Why are you blushing now?"

He looks at his manicured hands. "Because, sitting here, talking to you, I realize how far away from my roots I have gotten." He gives a sad smile. "What my adopted family would have called '*demasiado grande para sus pantalones.*'"

I can't help but laugh. "Too big for your britches, huh? That was something my dad said I should try to never be. Although it seems as if I've broken that rule more than a few times myself."

"You speak Spanish?"

"*Como no?*" I point at my naked ring finger. "The ex, Cubano, remember?"

He covers a smile. "You are a woman of many talents, Ms. Locke."

I'm the one blushing now. Again. Just another habit I need to break.

"Whatever could you have done to Señor Cubano to make him into the ex?"

"A story for another day."

"Kidding aside, Grace—may I call you Grace?"

"I think you did already," I reply, and we both laugh. Vinnie's right. I should get out more.

"All kidding aside, Grace, your lawsuit brought to my attention the fact that my company has been overzealous in its cost-cutting measures. While not knowing what was going on is no excuse, it's the truth. But still, I'm the one at the top of the food chain—the buck stops with me. I should have known, that's what matters. And I will do my best to make sure it doesn't happen again."

"Right," I say, unconvinced, unsure of whether he's playing me, which fortunately doesn't matter any longer, given his ten million dollars is waiting in my trust account.

He straightens his tie. "So, on the other topic, what pound of flesh are you here to extract from me today to not let that so-called suicide note see the light of day? After all, that is the real reason why you are here, isn't it?"

"Yes, it is. But now that we've met, gotten to know each other better, I believe we will be able to find some common ground sooner rather than later this time."

He calls the waiter and orders two Cuban coffees. How did he know? Cuban coffee is my favorite beverage. Right after Jack, that is.

"And perhaps we will reach that place of common ground without any more acrimony," he says with the overconfident tone of someone who knows they're beaten but still needs the last word.

31

There's barely enough room for all of us in Coach Wynne's office—me, Marcus, Coach, and Hachi, complete with both of her legs in casts. And then there's her wheelchair, a device she's yet to master. She swears the thing "drives worse than her piece of shit junker," a statement that tells me she's on the mend.

The ultimate irony is that the day after Junior and Sadie tried to kill me, when they tested taking her off the respirator, Hachi started breathing on her own, a fact that surprised even the most seasoned of her doctors.

Tonight, Marcus is playing chauffeur. I offered, but a woman sporting a new prosthetic leg with a mind of its own does not a safe driver make. Besides, we've all had one too many brushes with danger of late.

Coach pats Marcus on the back. "You were quite the player in your day, son."

Marcus's skin is so dark it doesn't look like he blushes, but he does. He's a gentle soul in the body of an Adonis who hates compliments even more than losing at anything. He's like me that way.

"That's a long time ago, Coach," Marcus says, eyes lowered.

"Any time you feel like comin' out here to help me whip these boys into shape, I'd sure be happy to have you," Coach says, his tone insistent, like one anxious to impart his hard-earned wisdom before it's too late. One shoulder lowered, Coach scoots left and then cuts right, his tree trunk legs more nimble than I expected. "I'm sure you've still got a move or two you could show 'em," he says.

"I'd like that, Coach. I'd like that a lot," Marcus replies, eyes twinkling like they do only when he talks about football or locking up bad guys.

"My boys, they need role models like yourself. Someone who was raised in the school of hard knocks and lived to tell the tale." Coach's hand goes to his mouth. "I am sorry, Miss Hachi, I—"

Hachi shakes her head hard from side to side. "Not at all. You, of all folks, you got nothing to be sorry for. Without you, Ozz wouldn't have had any shot at a better life."

Coach looks up at the ceiling. "I wish to God he'd had that chance."

She reaches out and grabs one of his hands with both of hers. "He's in a better place now, Coach. At least I like to think so."

I cut my eyes sideways to Marcus, who's examining his nails.

Coach places his free hand on top of Hachi's. "I'm sorry about your sister. I read about what she was doin' in the papers. I had no idea."

Hachi's features harden. "We all have to live with the consequences of our actions."

Coach turns to me. "You certainly have brought a lot of excitement to our sleepy town, Miss Locke."

"It seems there's nothing sleepy about Sugar Bay. In fact, I'll be glad to get back to the peace and quiet of the big city," I say.

Marcus gives a slight jerk of his head to signal it's time to go take our seats in the stadium.

I point at the clock on the wall. "Five minutes to kickoff. We should get going." I point at Coach. "And you have a game to coach."

The light in Coach's eyes dims. "The last game of the season. It's always bittersweet. And even more so this year." He bows his head. "This one I'm dedicating to Ozz."

—

We proceed to the VIP area, our seats tagged with our names.

Hachi looks back at Marcus, who is pushing her wheelchair. "Thanks for being my driver, handsome."

Marcus gives a slight bow and parks her in the empty space beside our seats. "It is my pleasure, m'lady."

"Don't get too used to it, H. Doc says you won't need that thing for much longer."

Her gaze goes to my legs. "Now I know something about what you went through. But mine will heal."

I pat Oscar 3.0. "I'm as good as new. Nice thing about being a cripple is that there's one less limb to break."

Marcus slaps at my arm. "Don't use that word!"

"But I *am* a cripple."

Marcus pinches my side. "Right! As if! That's an insult to folks who are *bona fide* disabled."

I pull away. "That's not funny, Marcus. Don't say 'disabled'—that's an insult to us folks who are differently abled."

"Right on," Hachi says, her tone overly upbeat to counter the edge in my comment. "She's Our Grace, a force of nature."

While we wait, I track Hachi's gaze to the center of the field where Ozz had lain.

"I appreciate everything you two have done for me," Hachi says. "And for Ozz. We wouldn't have made it without you."

"That's what friends are for," I say.

Marcus looks away. "I wish there was more we could do. But witness protection was the only option."

Hachi stares into the distance. "Ozz is safe, and that's all that matters."

"Maybe one day things will be different, safer, and you'll be able to see him," Marcus says, in a wistful way that sounds more pipe dream than reality.

"Maybe," she says.

I bump her elbow to focus her attention on the players streaming from the tunnel, each one being named by the announcer. Once both teams are assembled on the field, the announcer says, "Ladies and gentlemen, we have a special surprise for you tonight."

Hachi leans forward in the wheelchair, elbows on her knees.

"As you all know, this stadium and our athletic complex are named after Mr. Alonso Tremayne, the most generous benefactor of the Sugar Bay Panthers," the announcer says as Tremayne strides from the tunnel, a spotlight tracking him to mid-field, where a referee hands him a microphone.

"Ladies and gentlemen, tonight I am thrilled to announce that from this day forward, and for as long as it stands, this wonderful stadium and athletic facility will be called the 'Osceola Gordon Stadium and Sports Complex' in honor of Sugar Bay's favorite son, Osceola Gordon," Tremayne says.

The crowd breaks into cheers, their clapping coalescing within seconds into a single, ear-splitting sound.

I look down at Hachi, tears streaming down her cheeks, a look of utter astonishment in her eyes.

"Ozz's family is here with us," Tremayne continues. The spotlight shifts to where we are seated. "Tonight, I am honored to announce that I have established a scholarship fund that will be known as the Gordon Fund. Every year from now on, the Gordon Fund will award ten scholarships based on academic merit to ten worthy Sugar Bay High students to attend the college of their choice, all expenses paid."

Oohs and *aahs* ripple through the crowd, spectators turning to look at each other wide-eyed, as if Tremayne has just emerged from a spaceship and announced that there is, in fact, intelligent life on another planet.

Tremayne raises a hand for quiet. “And, to that end, I’d like to introduce to you the first executive director of the Gordon Fund.” He extends a hand in our direction. “Ms. Grace Locke, would you please stand?”

“What the—” I hear Marcus say as I get to my feet and give a quick wave, before sitting back down.

“Thank you, Ms. Locke. I look forward to working with you to give our worthy young people a better future.”

I nod as the spotlight shifts back to Tremayne.

Marcus grabs my sleeve. “What was that?”

I keep my eyes down.

“And without further ado, let the game begin,” Tremayne says, handing the microphone back to the referee.

Hachi grabs my sleeve. “How? You?”

“A story for another day,” I say, settling back to watch Whitey lead the Panthers to the win, the same boy without whom none of this would have been possible, the one with whom I need to have a word after the game.

—

“Marcus, can you take Hachi to the car? I’ll meet you there in a few.”

I don’t wait for his answer before disappearing around the side of the stadium.

Outside the players’ exit, surrounded by fresh-faced cheerleaders and players trying to look tough despite the deep-seated feelings of inadequacy suffered by every teenager, I am hit with a soul-crushing sense of déjà vu, the ineffable sense I’ve been here before in some other life. And I have, back when I too believed everything was possible, that all dreams could come true.

I lean up against the wall and try to look as if I belong, although I feel ancient, or maybe prehistoric, as Tremayne said.

After a few seconds, Whitey emerges from inside to shouts

of "great game" and "way to go," a duffel bag slung over his shoulder in that devil-may-care way only the truly gifted can pull off without seeming arrogant.

"Nice work," I say, stepping out of the shadows into his path. "You made it look easy."

Whitey hesitates, his brain processing how he knows me.

"Uh, hi. I didn't recognize—I did, but . . ."

I smile. "I agree. I'm out of context here."

He gives me a confused look. "What are you doing here?"

"Wilson, can I ask you something?"

"Sure thing."

I wave him to follow me to a more private spot, out from under the bright lights illuminating the players' exit.

"Did you happen to find a note in your locker?"

He pulls his shoulders back and raises his chin. "What kind of note?"

"One that might have been written by Ozz."

He shakes his head. "Nah."

"You sure?"

"Sure, I'm sure."

I pick up the duffel and hand it to him. "If you happen to find a note, like maybe one you misplaced or something, would you please call me?"

"Sure, but like I said, there's no note," he says in the indignant way kids do when they're trying to get themselves out of trouble, but when, in fact, they did do whatever it is they're being accused of.

"Look, all I'm saying is nothing in the note can do anyone any good now."

"If there ever was a note," he says, a sly smile creeping onto his lips.

I mirror his sly smile. "Yes, if there ever was a note."

—

Marcus wheels Hachi into her living room.

"You sure you don't want to come home with me for a few days? Vinnie can set you up with your own room on the ground floor and ply you with his Italian specialties."

Hachi squares her shoulders. "Nope. No Pocahontas Suite for me. I have to start getting used to doing things for myself again."

I look at Marcus and shrug. "I guess we're done here."

Hachi rolls over to me. "Grace, I have no idea how you did . . ." She shakes her head. "How you did whatever you did."

I lean down and plant a kiss on the top of her head. "Get some rest. You've got physical therapy in the morning."

"Thank you," she says, her eyes as glassy as mine. I thought I'd lost her, but now I've got a second chance to make things right with her. Like Tremayne, I must be getting soft. I used to think second chances were something for the weak.

"Whatever I did, it's the least I can do for a friend," I say before closing the door.

—

"I'm not going to ask how you did that," Marcus says once we're on the road back to Fort Lauderdale.

I keep my eyes focused straight ahead. "Good, because I'm not going to tell you," I say, which I mean in more ways than one.

The real question is whether or not exposing Tremayne for providing PEDs to the players would be worth it, or if keeping my mouth shut would do more harm than good in the end for the kids who do go into his so-called Program. Maybe they'll get out, go to college, play in the pros, but then what? What if they don't hop on Tremayne's bandwagon? What if they do?

I let out a low, unintended moan.

"You all right?"

"Right enough."

"You want to talk about it?"

"No, I do not."

"I won't ask again."

"Good."

Marcus follows my gaze to Sugar Bay's welcome sign: Her Soil is Her Fortune.

"What the heck does that mean?" he says.

"Nothing. Absolutely nothing. It's a blatant lie," I reply.

Epilogue

In the pre-dawn darkness, I stare up at the start-line arch, behind it the jagged skyline of Miami, a city built on reclaimed land and ill-gotten gains. The "Magic City," some call it, because it grew so fast, like magic, during the go-go days of the Cocaine Cowboys and disco fever. But I prefer what Miami means in the Calusa and Tequesta languages—Big Water—which is what the city will be soon if sea levels keep rising.

The pink neon lights embedded in the arch announce, "The Miami Marathon—Where The World Comes to Run," casting a rosy glow onto the faces of the other runners all around me, all stretching and bouncing on their toes, or sucking on energy gels like ravenous newborns.

I like that, the notion of "other runners." It means I'm a runner, too. That I'm a runner, again. One of them. One of us. That no matter what happens today over the course of twenty-six miles three hundred and eighty-five yards, I have already won. I am a runner, just like everyone else here with the same goal as me—to get to the finish.

I fidget with the safety pins attaching the bib to my singlet, my stomach a jumble of nerves. But the good kind of nerves. The kind that lets you know something amazing lies out there in the unknown. And that's the key to it all, I suppose. It's the unknown that drives us to want to run far. If the outcome were certain, what would the point be? Man no longer has the challenge of the hunt, so we have sports to sate our primitive needs. Is that it? Or is my need more personal? Is mine the need to prove to myself that I still can do whatever I put my mind to?

I look down at Oscar 3.0. "It's just you and me, kid. We run as one." I pan the crowd. "We all run as one."

And I like that too. I like that running is all on you. One you, *the* one. If you want to finish a race, you have to make it happen. You. No one else can do it for you. Not one step. There's no hiding in running, no lack of clarity. There's a clock. And the runner. Succeed or fail, all on your own terms.

"Holy mother of God, parking's about as rare around here as an honest cop," Vinnie shouts as he pulls Miranda through the crowd toward me.

Jake shakes his head, his long blond surfer-dude hair tinted pink under the fairy lights. "Given what he's done in his life, you'd think the prospect of getting a parking ticket wouldn't phase him."

Vinnie pulls himself up to his full height, only to Jake's shoulders. "For your information, I am a decent, law-abiding citizen. I refuse to park anywhere it's prohibited. If everyone did what they pleased, imagine the mess we'd be in."

Jake rolls his eyes.

"You know what they say, don't you, Jake?" I ask.

"No, what do they say, Grace?"

"No one is as zealous as a convert," I say, which sends Jake into a laughing fit.

"And you should know," Jake replies.

Vinnie surveys the huge crowd. "Who knew that this many people could get up this early in Miami? Aren't they supposed to be going home from the clubs about now?" He grabs my hands and looks me in the eye. "You're gonna do great out there, sweetheart. I'm so proud of you."

"This new life requires me to run farther than I ever have," I say, my voice unsteady. "It's been such a long road," I say, meaning the training, but also everything else that's allowed me to be standing here.

He gives me a smile so warm, so full of belief that I have to bite back tears. I don't need to be an emotional wreck before we start.

"We'll be at the finish line," Jake says.

I bend over and ruffle Miranda's ears. "Me too," I say.

"Run like the wind, sweetheart," Vinnie says as I plant a kiss on his cheek.

"Hey, don't I get one of those?" Jake says, and Vinnie yanks him away by the shirt sleeve.

"Let's go, Jakie. You can get all lovey-dovey later."

I glance around me, skyscrapers on one side, the waters of Biscayne Bay on the other. A couple of blocks to the north, I recognize the outline of the Freedom Tower, the golden light from the beacon in its cupola a reminder of how the building, now an art museum, was once Miami's version of Ellis Island, the processing center for Cuban refugees fleeing Castro's revolution. Tremayne would have passed through its terrazzo halls, alone, orphaned by history in a way I could never understand. Manny did too.

I file into the starting corral along with the thousands of other runners to await the boom of the starting gun, the traumatic sound of which I've been preparing myself for as long as I've been training, and which I fear more than the many miles ahead.

"Runners, make your final preparations. Two minutes until the start," the race director announces from his elevated post in a cherry picker adjacent to the start line.

I suck in a last few deep breaths. I'll take my first step, then another, and then thousands more until my two legs will have carried me 26.2 miles. Yes I will.

When the gun goes off, I don't flinch, not even for a moment. I am a runner.

Acknowledgments

Like football, getting a book into the hands of readers is a team sport. While the author may toil in solitude, the final product is not hers alone. Thanks to Susan Brooks for having faith in me, Jennica Dotson for an eye for detail beyond compare, and Pozu Mitsuma for your art and your spirit.

To my rescue pup, Talisker, for your precious head tilts and patience during the many days of my reading this manuscript out loud.

To Grace and all the Graces out there for your service.

And, as always, to Andy for your unending support, your keen eye for a missing comma, and for your love.

CPSIA information can be obtained
at www.ICGtesting.com
Printed in the USA
BVHW051427210622
640289BV00004B/359

About the Author

Mandy Miller is an attorney and author of the Grace Locke mystery series. She lives in Steamboat Springs, Colorado, with her husband and rescue mutt where she also teaches psychology to undergraduates. She has a J.D. and PhD in Psychology. In her spare time she competes in ultramarathons.

You can visit her website www.mandymillerbooks.com and read more of her writing on www.Flash4Words.blogspot.com. Subscribers will receive information regarding new books, giveaways, and contests. Be assured that if you leave your email on either site, it will not be shared with anyone and you may unsubscribe whenever you wish.